P9-CQL-921

Praise for
Elizabeth Peters

"No one else can write the kind of mystery
Ms. Peters is so adept at producing."
Dallas Morning News

"If bestsellerdom were based on merit and
displayed ability, Elizabeth Peters would be
one of the most popular and famous
adventure authors in America."
Baltimore Sun

"Peters really knows how to spin romance
and adventure into a mystery."
Boston Herald

"No one is better at juggling torches while
dancing on a high wire than Elizabeth Peters."
Chicago Tribune

"[Peters] keeps the reader
coming back for more."
San Francisco Chronicle

Books by Elizabeth Peters

ELIZABETH PETERS

THE
JACKAL'S HEAD

AVON BOOKS
An Imprint of HarperCollinsPublishers

This is a work of fiction. Names, characters, places, and incidents are products of the author's imagination or are used fictitiously and are not to be construed as real. Any resemblance to actual events, locales, organizations, or persons, living or dead, is entirely coincidental.

AVON BOOKS
An Imprint of HarperCollins*Publishers*
10 East 53rd Street
New York, New York 10022-5299

Copyright © 1968 by Elizabeth Peters
ISBN: 0-380-73117-7
www.avonmystery.com

First Avon Books paperback printing: June 2002

Avon Trademark Reg. U.S. Pat. Off. and in Other Countries, Marca Registrada, Hecho en U.S.A.
HarperCollins ® is a registered trademark of HarperCollins Publishers Inc.

Printed in the U.S.A.

10 9 8 7 6 5 4 3 2 1

THE
JACKAL'S HEAD

Chapter 1

"Scarab, lady, ten piasters, very cheap, lucky scarab, come from king's tomb, very old, very cheap! Scarab, lady, lucky scarab . . . Six piasters?"

The price always comes down if the customer doesn't respond. I kept right on walking, ignoring the peddler who trotted alongside me, his grubby black-and-white-striped robe flapping around his bare heels. It was hard to ignore the scarab, since this very small businessman was waving it right under my nose. But I managed not to look at it. I didn't have to look at it. I knew it wasn't worth six piasters, or even six cents. It didn't come from a king's tomb, it wasn't lucky (what is?), and it wasn't very old. Probably about twenty-four hours old.

"Wait a minute, Althee-a. You're going too fast again. And I wanna look at this stuff."

That awful whine again! For five long days I had been listening to Dee complain. From Idlewild to Orly, through the salons of half the famous couturiers of Paris, from Orly to Fiumicino, through more salons, from Fiumicino to Cairo, from Cairo to Luxor. From there to eternity, it seemed.

I glanced at the girl, and the sight of her did nothing to relieve my annoyance. She was a spoiled mess, from her bleached hair, now wilting into wisps under the impact of Upper Egyptian heat, to her padded figure crammed into clothing that was too new, too expensive, and too tight. There was a jarring note in the general picture of uncouth youth—the unwieldy plaster cast and the crutches.

I stopped walking, feeling like a heel—and resenting the poor little wretch even more because she made me feel like a heel.

"Sorry, Dee. I was just . . . I'm sorry. Where's your father? Isn't he meeting us?"

Dee shrugged. I gathered that she meant the gesture as a negative reply to my question, but it was hardly necessary. The air-terminal building was emptying rapidly as our fellow passengers from the Cairo-Luxor plane headed for waiting taxis and buses. There was no one present who corresponded to the picture I had formed of Dee's father—a man of middle age, since Dee admitted to seventeen years, a wealthy man, since he could afford to indulge his daughter in Parisian frocks and a companion—me—to nurse the cast and crutches from New York to Egypt. There was nobody there but just us tourists and the horde of insatiable peddlers, swarming like big black-and-white flies over every chunk of human flesh. An unattractive simile, I had to admit. But I was not in an attractive mood. Ever since we touched down on Egyptian soil my insides had been feeling faintly queasy, and the feeling got worse the farther south we came.

I turned back to Dee after my survey of the building to find that her open interest had attracted a particularly insistent crowd of the black-and-white robes.

"Scarab, lady, five piasters! Come from king's tomb, bring much luck . . ."

Our own original peddler had managed to press his wares into Dee's hands. That, as all good peddlers know, is half the battle. Dee grinned, and held the scarab out for my inspection. It was the usual oval, about an inch and a half long. The dull blue-green surface was roughly cut into the stylized beetle shape, and the underside had some crude scratches which were meant to be hieroglyphic writing.

"It's a fake," I said—too loudly, too emphatically. With the word the sensation of queasy discomfort that had haunted me coalesced into a stab of almost physical pain.

Surprised by my near-shout, Dee stared at me.

"What's the matter? You look absolutely green. Sun got you already?"

"I guess so . . . Let's find a taxi before they're all taken. Your father must be meeting us at the hotel."

"Okay, okay." She was good-natured. I had to admit that. She handed the scarab back to its reluctant owner and batted her artificial lashes at him. "Sorry, buster. No sale."

"Yes, yes, you buy!" The peddler's voice rose to a heartrending shriek. "Four piasters only! Lady, you buy, you say you buy—"

I wasn't thinking. I cut him short with one curt Arabic phrase. It was almost worth the blunder to hear his outraged shriek fade into a gurgle of surprise. Almost.

"Hotel Winter Palace," I told the taxi driver, and busied myself easing Dee and her cast into the cab. Mentally I was cursing myself, in both

English and Arabic. I hadn't been in Luxor for five minutes and already I had made my first mistake. After all the effort I had gone through to turn myself into just another tourist . . .

As the taxi bumped off down the road in a cloud of dust, I took out my compact. My nose actually did need powdering, but that wasn't what worried me. I needed to reassure myself that my new face looked as different as I meant it to.

It wasn't a disguise—nothing so crude as that. It was protective coloring, a frightened animal's defense against predatory enemies. Nature helps the hunted animals, but I had to help myself. I had widened my mouth with lipstick, turned my hazel eyes brown through a careful selection of eye makeup. The most effective change of coloration was the one I had applied to my hair. I couldn't do much about the style; my hair is too thick and curly for any but the simplest of short cuts. But I had been a brunette for twenty-five years, and the new ash-blond curls looked startling.

Forty dollars worth of peroxide, a new lipstick, and a kit labeled "Eye Magic"—that was the new Althea Tomlinson. Probably even that small effort had been unnecessary. After all, none of them had seen me for ten years. I was, as they used to say, "slow to develop." At fifteen my figure had been a neat, uncomplicated 30-30-30; Jake used to say I made my dresses by fitting them around a tree trunk. They wouldn't recognize the shapeless, sloppily dressed tomboy in the blond young woman wearing a well-tailored blue linen suit which displayed a well-tailored figure.

Not that I was vain about my figure. It was just my bread and butter—with no jam on the bread. Modeling sounds like a glamorous occupation, but modeling bathing suits and sweaters for a mail-order catalogue has all the giddy fascination of digging potatoes. It doesn't pay all that well, either—especially when every extra cent is popped into a little envelope marked "vacation." Vacation? Rest, relaxation, change of scene . . . Admittedly I had indulged in a bit of irony when I labeled that envelope.

My thoughts were falling back into the old familiar rut. In an effort to distract them I glanced at Dee, but she seemed to have no need of my ministrations. She was staring out the window, apparently fascinated by the view. The airfield lies in the desert, away from the modern village of Luxor, but our driver was pushing his rattling machine to its limit—a mad, breathtaking thirty-five miles an hour. Over that excuse for a road it felt like sixty. With clashing gears and flapping fenders we roared toward the town, which is right on the Nile, in the middle of the fertile regions which border the river on either bank. Ahead I could see the vivid greens of the fields and the graceful shapes of date palms. The colors were almost dazzling in their intensity after the sun-bleached rock of the desert. Above it all stretched the illimitable sky of Upper Egypt, of a blue so pure and intense that it suggests a rare type of Chinese pottery.

I was chagrined to realize that my eyes were blurred, and not by the dust which surrounded our progress. Egypt is not a kindly land. The lush green fields are only thin strips masking the merciless desolation of the desert. But there was something in the clear air and the ruthless sunlight—something that got into one's blood like malaria, a nostalgia no medicine could cure.

". . . fakes?" said Dee.

I jerked as if she had slapped me.

"Were all those things the men were selling fakes?" she repeated, sublimely suppressing syntax.

There was the cure for my relapse into sentimentality. One key word, functional, operative.

"Fakes," I said, trying it out. "Yes. They were all fakes. Most of the fellahin make them. Jolly little home industries. Scarabs, ushabti—those are the statuettes. All fakes, forgeries, imitations . . ."

The taxi swung in a wide exuberant curve, cutting off my list of synonyms and throwing Dee against me. She straightened up with a muttered word that lifted my eyebrows. Modern teenagers really got a liberal education.

At first I didn't recognize the hotel. That was good; too many fond old memories had hit me in the last half hour. Since my time the management had added a handsome new section, and it was at the plate-glass doors of this part of the hotel that the taxi stopped. I paid the driver what he asked, which was stupid; everyone in Luxor expects, and enjoys, a good loud argument over prices. But I was afraid that if I started haggling I might forget myself again. A tourist who speaks fluent gutter Arabic is worth mentioning during the evening gossip session. The grapevine works quickly in small towns all over the world.

I hadn't realized how hot I was until the air conditioning in the lobby hit me; I felt my whole body sag with sheer delight. It evidently affected Dee the same way, for she dropped heavily into the nearest chair and closed her eyes.

"I'm absolutely dead," she announced flatly. "See about things, will you? Dad must be around somewhere."

I looked "around," but since I had never seen a

photograph of my temporary employer, I didn't expect to find him. Almost any of the lounging male tourists in the lobby might have been my middle-aged, rich Mr. Bloch. It takes money to winter in Egypt, and it takes most men half a lifetime to accumulate that much money.

I went to the desk, feeling mildly exasperated with the elusive Mr. Bloch. He was a widower with an only child; one would think he would be hovering, anxious to embrace his darling daughter. However, the desk clerk's response to my question left no doubt that we were expected, and impatiently. There was a flurry of bellboys and buzzers and telephones; and a few minutes later a tall, grizzled man emerged from one of the elevators and came toward me.

"Miss Tomlinson?" His voice was a surprise after Dee's nasal New York twang; it was soft, very deep, and held a suspicion of a drawl. At my nod he extended a large, well-manicured hand and gave me a firm grip. His face was pink and closely shaved; it wore an expression of sleepy affability that was attractive. Decidedly I preferred Mr. Bloch to Miss Bloch. It was only reasonable to assume, however, that he preferred her to me, so I led the way to the chair where Dee had collapsed. She looked as if she had fallen asleep. I poked her, and was rewarded by signs of life.

"Oh," she said, blinking, "Dad. Hi."

Bloch gave her a gingerly peck on the cheek. He had the same look I have seen on the faces of other fathers of adolescent females—wary, alert, and apprehensive, the look of a man defusing a live bomb. I found it quite pathetic.

Unlike certain of her contemporaries, Dee was at least polite. She allowed her father to take her arm and nodded agreeably as he explained that he hadn't been able to get us rooms near his suite in the new section. The hotel was crowded to the roof.

"I'm afraid the old section isn't air-conditioned," he said, eyeing her nervously. "But it gets real cool here at night. And you may find it kind of quaint."

We walked through the doors into the older section—and straight into my past.

Fifty years ago the Winter Palace must have been the last word in elegance. Ten years ago I had fallen in love with its *fin-de-siècle* graciousness, its wide central staircase with the gilt balustrades, its music room with the red plush chairs. We always spent a night or two in the hotel before settling down for the winter in the efficient but dreary quarters at the Institute. We couldn't really afford it, but that was one of the ways in which Jake differed from the usual penny-pinching archaeologist. We did things first and worried about whether we could pay for them later. Actually, Jake never did worry much about saving money. Sometimes, as I got older, I lectured him about it, but it was hard to be stern with Jake; he had a way of dismissing criticism with a quirk of his eyebrows and a hilarious comment. I used to wonder whether my mother could have handled him better, but that was one subject we never discussed—the one subject that drove all traces of humor from Jake's face and voice. It had been hard for him, being left with an infant daughter and a memory—just one of those rare, one-percent casualties in a medical category which is statistically safer than driving a car. I had no memories of loss myself, but I was always conscious, I suppose, of trying to fill a gap. In the minor, superficial aspects, I succeeded. Jake and I had fun together, more in the manner of contemporaries than as father and daughter. Certainly not like this dreary child and her worried dad . . .

The rooms had shrunk and gotten shabbier. But my bed looked just like the one I remembered from my last visit, so high I had to use a chair to climb into it, enveloped in great white clouds of mosquito netting that gathered into a magnificent lace-frilled crown above the pillow.

The first time I climbed into one of those beds I felt like a royal bride.

I offered, in duty bound, to help Dee get settled, but Mr. Bloch said he would take care of that himself. He wanted to have a long chat with his baby. The nice man also told me that he intended to pay for my room—I had been so good to his little girl. Dee and I both came close to choking at that one. I had been barely civil to the child, and she, I knew, considered me the dullest prig since Queen Victoria.

Of course I thanked Mr. Bloch. Then he thanked me; and Dee—nudged—thanked me, and I probably would have thanked Dee, for heaven knows what, if Mr. Bloch hadn't gathered his daughter together and removed her, leaving me alone—with my memories.

I have had better company.

I don't know how long I would have stood there in the middle of the room, as animated as a stone column, if something hadn't happened to jar me out of my trance and remind me of another friendly old Egyptian custom which had slipped my mind.

The door flew open, hitting the wall with a bang that sounded like a pistol shot. It was only the chambermaid, bringing fresh towels, but it might just as well have been a waiter or a bell-boy. Knocking on doors is not a Luxor custom, nor is locking those same doors. When people go out they lock the doors of their rooms, but during the day it is imperative to have the door not only unlocked but ajar, in order to cultivate a cross-breeze. Luxor's climate is that of the desert—cool at night, hot during the day.

I took the towels, and a shower, locking the door before the second operation. Then I called Room Service and ordered tea sent up. I unlocked the door—the waiter would have been terribly hurt if I hadn't—and went out on the balcony, which had a round iron table and two wicker chairs. I hadn't meant to sit down. But it was impossible to glance briefly at that view and leave it.

The hotel is on the east bank of the river, along with the modern village and the ancient temple ruins of Karnak and Luxor. Across the Nile, which now reflected all the colors of the sunset, lies the west bank. Today, as in ancient times, there are several small villages on the west, but it is pre-eminently the land of the dead.

It was strange, I thought, that the west should be the direction of heaven in so many widely separated mythologies. Tir na nOg, the Islands of the Blessed, Amenti . . . And then, as I watched the sun go down in a blaze of glory, I knew that it wasn't strange at all. Like man, the solar orb vanished inexorably into darkness; but it passed in flaming triumph.

The rich golden light made luminous the greens of palms and cotton fields on the west bank, and gilded the rugged heights of the western cliffs. On the placid breadth of the river the triangular sails of the graceful boats called feluccas dipped and swayed with the current. Boats were still the only bridge between east bank and west; and modern tourists crossed the river, as the ancients had done, to visit the houses of the dead—tombs and temples set into and against the rocky heights of the cliffs behind which the sun went down daily in fiery death.

The waiter burst in with my tea. His show of haste was canceled by the tepid state of the tea; he had probably stopped along the way for a chat with the pretty black-eyed maid. The sun dropped below the top of the cliffs, leaving the sky splashed with crimson and gold and streaks of purple. Luxor specializes in gorgeous sunsets. But the cliffs are high; the sun still had some way to go before dropping below the invisible horizon. It was light. Light enough to read.

I took the letter out of my purse. I had read it dozens of times; the cheap paper was frayed along the folds. I smoothed them out with careful fingers and glanced again at the words I already knew by heart.

> *Honorable Miss,*
> *Beg to write this letter hoping that you are enjoying good health and ask the Almighty to keep you in safety.*
> *Beg to ask you, honorable Miss, to come again to Luxor. There is a need to informing you of a matter which is important. It is a matter of your revered father, on whom be peace. It is a matter of importance. Beg to hope that you will come soon.*
> *Longing to your early coming,*
>
> > *Your most obedient*
> > *Reis Abdelal Hassan*

The writing was small and precise, but tremulous with the uncertainty of old age. Abdelal must be nearly eighty. For forty of those years he had been headman of the excavations. I had known him all my life. This was the only letter I had ever received from him, and on the basis of those formal paragraphs it was hard to imagine why he had bothered to write this one. Something about Jake. Something—surely—about that black episode of ten years ago. But why, then, had he waited ten years to tell me that "matter of importance"?

What could he know that was so important? The affair had never concerned him. It was not the main body of the letter that had brought me thousands of miles in such disorganized haste. It was the scrawled Arabic under the signature:

> *Do you remember the day in the Place of Milk when you were the Great Queen Nefertiti, and I your faithful vizier? We played a game then, when you were a child. But now you are a woman, and I am old. The thing I know you too must know, and you must come now to hear of it; for the steps of the Gatherer of Souls sound louder in my ears.*

He had always been half a pagan at heart; I used to accuse him, only partly in jest, of believing in the old gods whose images he helped to discover. He was tall and thin, his mahogany face covered with fine wrinkles like lines drawn in hardened plaster. When he smiled, displaying the brown, broken teeth of his generation and class, the plaster cracked, and he looked quite a lot like the famous painting of St. Francis in Assisi. I used to go and have tea with him in his house. He had two little twin boys—lean brown babies with brilliant white grins. He had taught me most of the Arabic I knew. . . .

The night came with desert swiftness. A curtain of stars dropped into place against a blueblack sky. The western cliffs, retaining the last of the fading light, shone faintly luminous, like rose-gold specters of themselves.

I held the letter between my hands, and all at once it was as if I felt Abdelal's hard leathery palm. There was a desperate urgency beneath the inherent dignity of his written words. I had sensed it earlier. Now, so near the source, the pull of his appeal was strong enough to make me burn with impatience.

"You blasted fool," I said aloud, and rose stiffly from the hard wicker chair. I was becoming entirely too susceptible to moods and premonitions. Abdelal was not the man to waste money on newfangled ideas such as airmail. His letter had taken three months to reach me. Whatever it was he wanted, it could wait one more day.

On my way to dinner I tapped on Dee's door, but got no answer. Evidently she and her father had already gone down.

They were in the lobby of the new section when I arrived, their heads cozily together. Bloch looked up and saw me and immediately beckoned me to join them. I did, and accepted the offer of a cocktail.

Dee was resplendent in a dress which I had *not* helped her select in Paris. In fact, I had tried to talk her out of it. Not that it wasn't gorgeous, but black chiffon, sequins, and black pearls seemed inappropriate for a seventeen-year-old. It looked particularly silly next to the white plaster cast, which had Dee's pink toes sticking out of the end of it.

At any rate, she looked stunning in it; her figure was very well developed. I decided my reaction was at least fifty percent jealousy. With wry amusement I contemplated my own demure, flowered Dacron sheer. It had bare shoulders, with only the narrowest of straps, but it was obviously not Lanvin, or even Lord and Taylor.

"You look mighty pretty," said Mr. Bloch, beaming at me.

"Thanks," I said dryly.

"Feels real fine to sit here with two pretty young ladies," Mr. Bloch went on, in his soft drawl. "Wish I could ask you to have dinner with us, Miss Tomlinson, but I stupidly made a date already—it's sort of a business dinner, you might say . . ."

Mr. Bloch was almost too good to be true, but I didn't find his old-fashioned manners ludicrous or laughable. On the contrary, they were as soothing as soft music.

"I knew a fellow once named Jake Tomlinson,"

Mr. Bloch continued calmly. "You're his little girl, aren't you?"

I couldn't have been more stunned if a friendly old family sheep dog had turned and sunk his fangs into my hand. Trying to articulate a convincing No, I met Bloch's blue eyes and saw knowledge and recognition, and shrewdness that saw through my lie even before I voiced it.

"Yes. I'm Jake's daughter."

"I was terribly sorry to hear of his death. A great loss to his profession. He was one of the finest archaeologists I ever met, and one of the nicest guys."

My breath came out in a gasp, and I ducked my head into my glass of vermouth. He didn't know the whole story—only the tidy lie John had constructed. Thank God for that, I thought.

"Well, now," Bloch's voice flowed on, "here I was going to ask you if you wanted to join us in a little tour tomorrow. I want Dee to see the Valley of the Kings and some of the sights across the river. Old stuff to me, but she hasn't seen them, and to tell you the truth, I never get enough of Egypt. But I guess an expert like you would be bored with tourists."

"Oh, no," I said, recovering myself. Here was the opening I needed—a chance to get across the river to Abdelal without being conspicuous.

Sooner or later John would find out that I was here—oh, yes, he'd find out. But I didn't dare face him without all the ammunition I could collect. "Thank you, Mr. Bloch, I'd love to come."

"Good." Bloch's slow smile spread across his rather plain features. "How about joining us for dinner too? It's John I'm meeting—young Michael too. Be like Old Home Week for you. Have you called the Institute yet?"

I shook my head dumbly.

"Who's John?" Dee asked—and received my sincere, if silent, thanks. The question and answer gave me time to collect my wits.

"Why, now, honey, you've heard me talk about him. John McIntire—Dr. McIntire—he's the head man at Luxor Institute, the place the university maintains down here. You'll like him. And," Mr. Bloch added, with a twinkle, "you'll like his assistant, Mike Cassata. He's more your age. How old is Mike, Miss Tomlinson?"

"Twenty-eight . . . Mr. Bloch?"

"Yes, my dear?"

"I'm . . . I'm traveling sort of incognito . . . I don't mean literally, I had to give my real name, after all, it's on my passport. But I'd rather not meet John and . . . and the others right now. I wanted to have a few days to myself before I called them."

It was the lamest excuse for an excuse I'd ever heard, much less invented. But Mr. Bloch was that rare and vanishing personage, a gentleman. He didn't even blink.

"Why, that's all right. I understand, I won't say a word. Want to surprise them, do you? In that case, my dear, you'd better run along. I'm expecting John any minute."

Unlike her father, Dee didn't bother to conceal her disbelief. Chin propped on her hand, she studied me through narrowed eyes, smiling slightly. Maybe she thought Mike had jilted me, ten years back. That was the type of motive she would think of. I didn't care. It was better than the truth.

I arranged to meet father and daughter next morning for the promised tour, and then I fled. If John was expected any minute, I wanted out. Yet a perverse curiosity made me linger in the doorway, where a big, ugly, potted palm cast enough of a shadow to make me feel safe from casual glances.

I had forgotten that John's glance was never casual.

His appearance was a dreadful shock. He hadn't changed at all.

His hair had always been prematurely white, and it had always contrasted theatrically with his tanned skin and the big black moustache he cultivated with such care. He carried himself with the same arrogance, chin outthrust, body poised and straight as a lance. In his dark suit and tie he looked not so much ill at ease as impatient with such time-consuming frivolities as polished shoes and pressed trousers. The clothes he wore on the dig looked as if they had never been near an iron. When I was fourteen I was madly in love with him. When I was fifteen I knew that I hated him more than anyone in the whole world.

His companion was the one who had changed. I hadn't believed Mike could get any taller; ten years ago he had towered a foot over my sixty inches. Now he was twenty-eight and more than six feet by a good four inches. His hair was almost as light as John's, a silly sun-bleached primrose against his brown face. I knew, from reading the university bulletins, that he was now an associate professor and second in command of the Luxor staff. In my day he had been the infant prodigy of the Egyptology Department, and a pain in the neck. Only three years older than I was, he behaved like a patronizing grandfather. He called me "the infant," and I retaliated with all the silly practical jokes I could think of. Rubber spiders swam in his tea, plastic inkblots appeared on his manuscripts, and whenever he sat down, things blew up or made vulgar noises.

Come to think of it, maybe he had some justification for that "infant."

I forgot my feeble disguise, and my hate, and the potted palm. I felt as if I were caught in one of those nightmares where you stand stark-naked in the middle of Times Square. Then John, who always had an uncanny awareness of things he wasn't supposed to see, turned his head and began to rake the room with his intent gaze.

I was saved by Mr. Bloch, who was beginning to feel like my guardian angel in a somewhat incongruous disguise. He rose, waving, and John saw him. John's face broke into one of his sudden electric smiles—white teeth framed by two deep laughter lines, eyes alight and shooting sparks—and he walked over to Bloch's table. Mike trailed him, looking vague. "Satellite," I thought nastily.

All at once I was as limp as a dishrag, all tension gone. The worst was over. I had seen them, and they weren't demons; they were just men. Men engaged in a particularly humiliating job—buttering up a rich man in the hope, no doubt, of a nice fat contribution. It was an unavoidable part of the profession, since there is never enough money to satisfy the lust of archaeologists for digging things up. My father always hated it, but it was a job often assigned to him because he was so damned charming, as he used to say.

John wasn't charming. He bellowed like a bull when people annoyed him, which they often did, and he had a store of invectives that sounded nastier from him than they did from anyone else. He must like Bloch, or he couldn't have put on that big dental grin. He never was any good at pretending.

Careless of the glances I was attracting, rooted like a statue in the doorway, I contemplated myself and felt my self-confidence increase. They wouldn't know me; not in a million years.

However, I waited till the other party was seated before I sneaked into the big dining room, and I took a table as far away from them as possible. I couldn't help noticing that Dee was finding Mike just as fascinating as her father had promised. His back was turned to me, but I watched her give him the works—pout, fluttering eyelashes, outthrust bosom, and all. And he didn't exactly recoil in horror.

I got out of the dining room while they were lingering over coffee and went straight up to my room. Courage was one thing, and confidence was another thing, but I didn't want to press my luck. I had seen John, and John hadn't seen me, and that was fine with me.

Chapter 2

Mr. Bloch's private tour turned out to be a real mob scene. He had invited everybody he knew—hospitable soul—and he seemed to know a lot of people, most of them well-dressed, middle-aged tourists like himself. But he greeted me with special warmth, I thought. I gravitated over to Dee, who was sleepy and out of sorts. I was able to be pleasant to her, since I felt wonderful. In part it was anticipation, but mostly it was just the morning in Luxor—the cool, crisp air, the sun turning the western cliffs pink, the profound, cloudless sky. I had forgotten that feeling. Poor Dee, the hothouse flower, found it too repulsive for words. I had to admit that the cast would have dimmed my own enthusiasm, and I wondered how her father planned to deal with the problem.

Money. Since I have none myself, I keep forgetting how adequately it deals with most problems. Mr. Bloch had hired two stalwart Egyptians just to carry Dee, which they did by making a seat with their hands, in the traditional worldwide fashion. I must say that all three of them—Dee and her porters—seemed to enjoy it immensely. The men conveyed her down to the waiting boat and deposited her tenderly on one of the long benches that ran along the sides.

After we were all seated, amid a group of Egyptians heading for home or work on the west bank, there was a delay while the skipper argued with two boys who didn't have the fare, supervised the loading of crates of soft drinks for the rest house on the other side, and engaged in incomprehensible but impassioned debate with his crew—three barefoot Egyptians. Finally he spread out a grimy, tattered piece of cloth on which, after much study, I made out the black-white-red stripes and green stars of the Egyptian flag. When this emblem had been hoisted on its pole, one of the barefoot crew made his way aft and took the tiller. The engine chugged. We were off.

When we docked on the other side, Dee's

porters only had to carry her to the car Bloch had ordered. We took the road that leads back into the cliffs, through the pass that ends in the fabled Valley of the Kings.

For most people, I suppose, the word "valley" conjures up pictures of green fields backed by hills, verdured and soft, with a placid river winding between grassy banks. The Valley of the Kings is as much like a river valley as a mummy is like a man. The Valley is a canyon, a dry-as-a-bone cleft in the dry-as-dust desert cliffs. No seed of grass or flower finds sustenance there, and the only relief for eyes wearied by yellow brown rock is the brilliant blue of the sky above.

Bloch had a wheelchair for Dee when we got out of the car. One of her happy bearers took charge of it, and off we went in slow procession down the path that leads through the main part of the Valley. The tourists were out in force, and they did add color to an otherwise drab landscape. Bright orange shirts seemed to be popular that year. Two nuns shepherded a group of giggling schoolgirls, who were far less interested in antiquities than they were in the scarlet ribbons and blue and green beads with which they had brightened their navy-blue uniforms.

The babble of voices was less attractive; shrill French and emphatic German mingled with the guttural Arabic to produce a good imitation of the original Babel. Above the din one anguished Italian voice rose in piercing accents: *"Enrico! Enrico! Vieni qua, vieni a mamma!"* Enrico was about seven years old; I spotted him at once in his purple shirt, perched on a rock about twenty feet above Mamma's head.

On either side of us yawned the square openings of the entrances to the royal tombs which gave the Valley its name. Now empty and despoiled, these holes in the rock had once sheltered Egypt's ancient rulers and the treasures of gold and jewels and precious oils which were to adorn them in the Hereafter.

Mr. Bloch had hired a guide, no less a person than the young, energetic American Express representative of Luxor. Mr. Fakhry was a charming young man about four and a half feet tall. He spoke excellent English, and knew his patter cold. In fact, he rose to poetic heights when we stood in the most famous tomb of all—the only unplundered tomb in the Valley, that of the boy king whose name became a household word three thousand years after his death.

"And still he sleeps here," said Mr. Fakhry, with a magnificent gesture of his hands toward the gilded coffin, made in the shape of a man, which lay deep within the stone sides of the rectangular sarcophagus. The carved boy's face stared sightlessly up at the painted ceiling of the chamber; the sculptured hands were crossed on the gilded breast.

"You mean," said Dee, in a squeaky voice, "the guy's body is still in that thing? I thought all the mummies were in that museum in Cairo."

She hadn't been keen on visiting "that museum in Cairo," which has the finest collection of Egyptian antiquities in the world. I got her there by a careful mixture of threats and cajolery. Once inside the place she had been fascinated, in spite of herself, by some of the exhibits—notably the Jewel Room, which any woman would love, and the royal mummies, which appeal (if that word is appropriate) to the ghoul in all of us. I was pleased that she remembered something about what she had seen.

"Yes, yes, the other royal mummies, they are all in Cairo. But their discovery was different." Fakhry glanced at his watch and then at Bloch. Obviously we were running behind time, but as Bloch's smiling nod indicated, this was too good a story to ignore. Fakhry took a deep breath and plunged in.

"You see, my friends, the men of the village of Gurnah, which we will pass through later today, always they have lived among the tombs and always they have robbed the tombs, even in the days of the Pharaohs themselves. We must not judge them, my friends; the gold in the tombs helped no one, and the men of Gurnah are poor men. I mean to say," Fakhry added hastily, "that they *were* poor men, until our present excellent government brought to the fellahin the modern services and comforts."

There was a slight rustle—nothing more— from the ladies and gentlemen present, who knew what was expected of guests in a foreign country; and Fakhry, slightly red around the ears, went on.

"In the year of 1887 there was a family of Gurnah who found a hole in the cliffs not far from the temple of Deir el Bahri. It was a hard place to reach, but these men knew that gold and valuable antiquities might be found. One entered the hole. And within"—dramatic pause—"within he found the bodies of many kings and queens, where they had been hidden in ancient times to save them from the tomb robbers of that day. For years these men took small objects from this tomb and sold them, but they were found out at last by Maspero, the director of the antiquities. The bodies of the kings and queens were taken to Cairo, where now they stay. But Tutankhamen— King Tut, as he is called—he was found by archaeologists, not by robbers. And when they had carefully taken from the tomb all the treasures you see in the Cairo Museum, they put the young king back in his own place. And here he lies."

The story prompted a torrent of questions, and Fakhry had to do all he could to sweep us out so that the next group of tourists could crowd into the small chamber. We got back into the cars and were driven on to the next stop, the temple of Deir el Bahri.

I love Deir el Bahri; it is one of the most beautiful temples in Egypt. But the time was wearing on and my impatience was growing. I trailed distractedly after Fakhry, half hearing his animated lecture on the temple and its builder, the great queen who ruled as a king and who had a lowborn lover. Fakhry got a lot of smirks and titters out of that story. But my eyes, and my attention, were fixed on a huddle of small houses off to the north. The village of Gurnah.

We got there eventually. The houses of the village are built right in among the tombs—not kings' tombs, but the burial places of the great nobles of the Empire. Painted and carved with bas-relief, some of these are deservedly famous, and when we reached the Ramose tomb, one of the biggest and best, I dropped casually to the

rear of the group. When the rest of Bloch's party
filed through the entrance, I took to my heels.

Gurnah is on a slope. I was out of breath before
I had gone twenty feet, stumbling along the
rocky path lined with houses. Two of the vicious
pariah dogs ran up, snarling; with an automatic
gesture I stooped for a handful of stones and
threw one at the nearest dog. I missed. I always
did. Once long ago I used to carry table scraps
for the poor brutes, who are not pets. Several of
the village children ran along beside me, black
eyes snapping, thin brown hands imperative—
"Baksheesh, mees, baksheesh!"

I went on, more slowly now. I knew the path as
if I had come this way the day before. Abdelal's
house was one of the largest, and highest, in the
village. When I finally stood in the courtyard before the door, my heart was pounding, and not
just with violent exercise.

The door was open, but I could see nothing inside except blackness. These houses are kept as
dark as possible, since sunlight brings unbearable
heat. I stood hesitating, my hand pressed to the
stitch in my side. Then a young man came out.

He was quite young, not more than eighteen,
though he had a carefully clipped moustache
and the sometimes startling beauty one finds
among the fellahin, until hard work and primi-

tive living conditions age them prematurely. His face was that of a young saint cast in copper; his thick black hair shone like a satin cap—and gave off a penetrating aroma of sweet hair oil. Instead of the usual striped robe he wore tight blue jeans and an iridescent magenta shirt which looked like a tip from a California tourist.

"You look for a guide, mees?" He grinned, displaying beautiful white teeth. "I am best guide in Luxor, I take you. But first you have tea, yes, and see the antiquities I have found."

"Thank you. I've come to see Abdelal."

An invisible skin slid down over his face, freezing nerves and muscles into a watchful mask.

"Abdelal?" He spoke very slowly. "He does not live here."

"Yes, he does," I said impatiently. "I know this house well. He wrote to me. Please tell him that I have come."

"Ah." The smile reappeared, but the watchful eyes did not alter. "He wrote to you?"

"Yes."

He stood there, unmoving, smiling pleasantly. I knew the habits of the East, which scorn haste and love slow ceremonial; but this was different. I let my annoyance show.

"Please take me to Abdelal. He is expecting me."

"I regret." He half bowed, spreading his hands.

"Is he here?"

"Alas, no."

"Then can you tell me when he will be here?"

"I cannot do that."

It was fearfully hot; even through my hat the sun's rays beat down on my head like blows from a hammer. The sunlight turned the pale rock and mud brick from which the village is built into a dazzle of colorlessness. I began to think I must be suffering from sunstroke; the conversation sounded like a mad, Arabic version of *Alice in Wonderland*. But I had come too far to be turned back by a rude young man. I was about to try again when someone else came out of the darkened doorway.

It would have taken more than a casual glance to see that the two young men were twins. The newcomer wore the local robe, though its black-and-white stripes were cleaner than usual, but he had the same dark, beautiful face. On his head was one of the skullcaps commonly worn by Egyptian villagers, woven in bright, clashing colors. His had a pattern of green diamonds on amber, with chevrons of blue and red. He glanced sharply from his brother to me.

"Yes, mees. You are lost?"

"Maybe I am," I said helplessly. "I'm looking for Abdelal. I'm an old friend of his. He wanted to see me."

The two pairs of black eyes met for a moment. Then the first boy gave a tiny, almost imperceptible shrug. Lounging back against the wall of the house, he took out a pack of cigarettes and offered me one, with the most candid smile imaginable. I refused.

"Where is Abdelal?" I demanded.

There was a moment of silence. I began to feel slightly hysterical. Then the second boy, the one in the robe, said gravely, "I regret. You are his friend? Then you will be sad to hear that my father is dead."

I had been standing out in the sun for long minutes, getting more and more annoyed. Now the dazzle of sunlight turned, not black, but blinding white. For a moment I could see nothing at all. Then the ground steadied and I found that two pairs of hands were holding me erect.

"I'm all right," I said, brushing ineffectually at one arm which encircled my waist in an unnecessarily tight grasp.

The boy in the robe slapped his brother's arm down.

"It is the sun," he said. "Come into the house, Sitt. My mother will make tea. I will tell you, if you wish, of my father."

His hand remained on my arm; it was a firm, steadying hand, and I was glad to lean on it. The interior of the house seemed pitch-black at first after the glare of light outside; I could dimly make out a narrow walled corridor, then a room with a beaten earth floor. The boy sat me down on a bench covered with tattered cushions. He went out, taking his brother with him, and then I was alone.

I needed the solitude, not only to accustom my eyes to the gloom but to recover my wits. I didn't know why the news had been such a shock. Abdelal was an old man, very old by Egyptian standards. And it had been three months since he had written the letter . . .

When the boys came back with a tray, I caught a glimpse of a black-robed form hovering outside the door, and raised a hand in greeting; but I was not surprised when the black skirts whisked around the corner and vanished. Egyptian women do not hide from foreign females, but neither do they carry on social activities which are the prerogative of the superior sex.

The tea was excellent, as it always is—very dark, almost black, and very sweet. We drank a cup in silence, and then the boy in the robe re-filled my cup, offered me a plate containing chunks of bread, and cleared his throat.

"Excuse us, Sitt, that we did not receive you with politeness. I am Achmed, Abdelal's son. This is my brother Hassan."

I studied the plate of bread, as if deciding which piece to take. I loathe the stuff, actually—it tastes like rancid butter—but I had eaten many a loaf of it before, and the pause gave me time to think. It was now my turn to introduce myself. I preferred anonymity, but it was possible that Abdelal had left some message for me, and in order to receive it I would have to identify myself.

"My name is Tomlinson," I said, taking the smallest piece of bread. "Althea Tomlinson. I remember you. You were very small children when I was last here."

"Tomlinson, yes." Achmed smiled. "I remember you also, Sitt, though you have changed very much."

"Very much," Hassan agreed. I felt myself coloring, and realized how much inflection affects the meanings of words. Achmed's tone and glance had converted a statement into a nicely turned compliment. Coming from Hassan, the same remark became an impertinence.

"If it does not pain you to speak of it," I said

carefully, "will you tell me of your father and how—"

"How he died? It is not sad, Sitt. He was happy, not to live on old and sick. And it has been, you understand, three months."

"Three months . . ." Just after he wrote to me.

"He fell," Hassan added. "He fell and his neck was broken."

I gasped; the tone, even more than the words, was brutally abrupt. Achmed gave his brother a quick, hard stare.

"He walked often at night. This is not a custom here, but the old, he said, do not sleep well. On moonless nights it is very dark. We thought he knew every part of the hills, but perhaps he had a pain, and fell . . . We will never know."

"I am sorry."

"No, but why? He was old; he had lived well."

"That is true." I added, "The peace of God be upon him."

I sipped my tea, glancing around the room. It was all too familiar—the bare earthen floor, the faded chintz cushions on the bench, the rough table and heavy homemade cupboard, which were the only other articles of furniture. Everything the same—except that Abdelal was gone.

"You say our father wrote a letter to you."

Hassan dropped his cigarette on the floor. "What did he say?"

This open discourtesy was too much for his brother. He turned on Hassan with a sharp admonition in Arabic, to which Hassan responded with an insolent shrug.

"I am sorry, Sitt," Achmed said.

"That's all right. Naturally you would want to know." I put my cup down and Achmed at once refilled it. I didn't need time now to think what to say; the lie came out as smoothly as toothpaste from a tube. "He sent greetings, and said he hoped to see me again. I had been planning a vacation anyhow, so . . ." I produced a shrug of my own which was, I felt, fully the equal of Hassan's.

"Yes," Achmed said thoughtfully. "I am sorry you came too late."

Too late . . . too late. The words, surely the saddest words in the language, echoed despondently in my mind. All at once the room and all it conveyed were too much for me. I rose abruptly.

"I must go now. Thank you."

They both accompanied me to the courtyard, Achmed gravely, like a good host, Hassan with the conscious air of a bad little boy who will not be bribed to leave the adults alone. I gave him my hand in parting, feeling that I could not slight him openly, but disliking the bold grasp of his thin fingers.

"How long you stay in Luxor?" he asked.

"I don't know. A few days."

"I am sorry," Achmed said, "that you did not see my father."

I knew then, as I met the glance of his grave dark eyes, that he had not told me all he could tell me. I had been less than candid with him, so he had no reason for confiding in me. Usually, I'm inclined to trust people—or, as Jake used to say, I'm a sucker for an honest-looking face.

All the while, though, I was aware of Hassan lounging against the wall in his pose of studied indolence. He was strikingly handsome; even the ghastly western clothes, which look bad enough on westerners and blasphemous on the descendants of the Pharaohs, could not mar his good looks. His face was beautiful—but it wasn't an honest-looking face. I had no inclination to trust in the mind behind that face, and I suspected that Achmed's reticence must be attributable to the same doubt. There was nothing for it but to go, so I did; but all the way down the path I seemed to feel Hassan's mocking black eyes boring into my back.

I had lost all track of time, and was surprised to find the others just emerging from the Ramose tomb. Mr. Bloch accepted my stumbling apologies without comment; he seemed to find it natural that I should want to wander about on my own.

By the time we got back to the hotel the sun was up to broiling temperature, and the group dispersed in search of cold showers and colder drinks. I spent the rest of the day in my room. I didn't even go down to dinner.

One small, analytical section of my brain wondered at the intensity of the despair that filled the larger, remaining section. I hadn't seen Abdelal for years, yet the news of his death affected me as painfully as if I had seen him die. And above the sense of personal loss was the awareness of failure. In some odd, illogical fashion I had looked forward to my interview with the old man as an ending, a resolution of the neurotic emotions that had been driving me for ten years.

Neurotic? Not a nice thing to admit about oneself; I had managed to push that word down into my subconscious for a long time. Now, pacing restlessly up and down the hot hotel room, I faced part of the truth. Hate is a destructive emotion, but it does not destroy the object of hatred. It destroys the one who hates.

I told myself that I hated John and the others because they had hurt my father. I told myself that I wanted to face them in order to clear his name. That was part of the truth; but it was a very small part. I had come back, not for revenge or justice, but for rescue. I was encysted by my hate, and hypnotized by it. For ten years I had felt no other emotion. I hadn't had a friend, or a husband, or a lover; none of those positive, normal relationships could penetrate the icy shell I had built up around myself. Somehow, soon, that shell had to be broken, before I suffocated inside it. I had counted on Abdelal to help me break it— to supply part of the weapon for the great confrontation which would satisfy hatred, and put an end to it. And Abdelal had failed me. That was the real root of my distress—not grief for a good old man, gone at last to join his beloved pagan gods in Amenti, but selfish regret that he had gone without helping me to break free.

My trip had been a failure. I couldn't face John now; I had no more ammunition than I had had ten years ago, and I never was good at bluffing. Not with John. There was nothing for it now but to pack up and go home—home to the drab efficiency apartment, to the lonely TV dinners and the evening paper for company.

I reached my nadir that afternoon; I had had times of depression before, but nothing so bad as that. I sank so low that there were only two

possible courses of action open to me: I could
cheer up, or cut my throat. The second alternative seemed too drastic; I might be neurotic, but
I wasn't crazy, yet. And when the sun went
down and a cool breeze slid into the room—
well, that was one small thing to be thankful for.
I realized that part of my trouble was hunger; I
hadn't eaten anything since morning. So I called
down and ordered some food, and showered,
and brushed my hair, and put on a new nightgown I had bought just for the trip. Small things,
but they helped; I had learned, through painful
experience, the importance of the small routine
activities.

The routine helped, and so did the food. As I
munched a rather dry chicken sandwich, my
mind kept turning back to the picture of the
apartment and the evening newspaper, but now
the image was colored not by despair but by curiosity. Looking back on it, I realize that I had
reached some sort of turning point. The first faint
crack in the ice wall had come, and for the first
time my obsession was shaken by something like
common sense.

It had been odd, that business of the newspaper.

At the time it had seemed like an answer to
prayer. I didn't even question it—which shows,

I realize now, how badly my neurosis had gripped me.

After Abdelal's letter arrived I was frantic to get to Luxor. I asked for time off, and told everyone about my plans—without the slightest idea of how I was going to accomplish them. I didn't have enough money, that was the simple fact of the matter. There were a few bonds, but I never meant to spend those. They were for an emergency, for one of those unimaginable but inevitable disasters that hits everyone sooner or later. I was alone in the world, with no relatives to fall back on; I didn't dare spend my last cent on such a mad venture. I must have had just barely enough sense to realize that.

That particular night, when I came home from work, I found the evening paper on the mat, where it always lay. My newsboy was prompt and efficient. But this was the first time he had taken the trouble to put the Classified section outside the front page, and to circle an item in the Personal column with a ring of heavy red ink.

There was nothing out of the way about the advertisement itself. People travel to Egypt all the time, and some people are so filthy rich that an extra plane fare means no more to them than an extra tube of toothpaste does to me. And if I had a daughter like Dee, I certainly wouldn't want her roaming the world—especially the salons of Rome and Paris—unchaperoned. Her fractured leg, the result of a skiing accident the week before she was due to join her father, made a companion almost imperative.

No, the request for a respectable young lady (with references) to accompany a seventeen-year-old out to Egypt in return for her plane ticket was normal enough. The real question was, Who cared enough about me and my plans to draw the ad to my attention in such an unusual fashion?

I didn't even ask. I just assumed it was one of my many acquaintances (I had no friends). The next days were busy, what with contacting Dee, establishing my respectability, and making my own arrangements. I didn't have time to call every stray acquaintance.

The hotel room was almost dark. I switched on the lights, but they shed no illumination over the old problem, which had now become newly important. When I stopped to consider the matter sensibly, I realized that none of my acquaintances would have taken such a strange way of drawing my attention to that ad. They would have talked to me personally, or sent me a clipping in an envelope, with a covering note. Someone unknown wanted me to get to Egypt.

Someone had searched the newspapers on my behalf. Someone, then, was a Friend.

I sat down and watched the night breeze ruffle the folds of the mosquito netting. It was nice to know that I had a Friend. Only . . .

Only, if my Friend wanted to help me, why hadn't he or she done so directly? Why the fun and games with the newspapers? The trip had turned out to be a fiasco. Was someone hoping for just such a result?

That theory made even less sense than the other. I might think I had no friends, but I knew I had no enemies. Even John, my chief *bête noir*, probably felt for me no stronger emotion than casual contempt. . . .

The outer door, which I had again forgotten to lock, swung open. John stood in the doorway.

If I had had a weak heart, I would have dropped dead. Coming on the heels of my thought of him, his appearance was as appropriately, abruptly supernatural as that of a jinni out of a bottle.

My brand-new nightgown consisted of several layers of nylon—the poor girl's substitute for genuine glamour. My hands flew up and clutched at my bare shoulders in a silly gesture as old as ancient Greece, and maybe older. My mouth opened, but not with incipient speech; I was speechless.

He stood with one hand on the doorjamb, his brows drawn together in a scowl. I was painfully familiar with that expression; he and I used to have little interviews in his office periodically, especially after Mike had found a spider or an inkblot. He had gotten himself all dressed up for Bloch, but not for me; he wore his working outfit of grubby cotton pants and a wrinkled shirt. The rolled-up sleeves and open collar displayed skin as brown as an Arab's.

Without saying a word or waiting for an invitation, he strode into the room and threw himself into a chair. All his movements were like that, abrupt, explosive. Then I saw that Mike was with him—in body, anyhow; Mike's expression suggested some doubt as to why he had come.

I let my arms fall to my sides and turned to face John, who was stuffing tobacco into a smelly old pipe with an air of insufferable calm.

"Same old John," I said. "Get out of here. This minute."

John's narrowed eyes swept from my head to my bare feet and back up again. It was a leisured survey, impertinent in its very lack of impertinence, if you follow me. I don't enjoy being leered at, but I am not accustomed to being studied with the impersonal enthusiasm with which an archaeologist views a battered old statue.

"You've changed your hair," John said. He lit his pipe, and added, "I don't like it."

"Who asked you?" I took a deep breath, clenched my fists, and counted to ten. "John . . . I am no longer fifteen years old, and I'm damned if I am going to exchange adolescent wisecracks with you. Are you going to leave, or do I call the manager?"

It was a futile threat, and I knew it; the manager was probably one of John's oldest and closest friends. He knew, and terrorized, every soul in Luxor.

"You've turned into a damn good-looking woman," he went on, ignoring my last speech. "I never would have believed it, would you, Mike?"

I looked at Mike, who was standing stiffly against the wall, like a statue of one of the duller Pharaohs—eyes straight ahead, arms rigidly at his sides—and at the sight of him all my fine resolutions about mature conversation went up in smoke.

"Oh, does it talk?" I asked sweetly. "Or do you have to plug it in first?"

Mike turned an odd shade of purple. For a moment he looked just like the maddened eighteen-year-old who had, on a certain memorable occasion, found himself in bed with a scorpion. It was a dead scorpion, but Mike didn't know that right away.

"Tommy!" John's roar brought me around, quivering. It was the nickname as much as the volume of sound that affected me; and he knew it, damn him. I met his eyes directly and saw in them the true image of the man—the cold, complex intelligence that was so effectively masked by his bearish behavior.

"Sit down," he said, in a more moderate bellow. "You don't look fifteen, by a damn sight, but you act as if you were. When are you leaving Luxor?"

"When I'm good and ready. And I'm not ready."

"Tommy, do you know what you're doing? Do you want to dig it all up again?"

"What are you afraid of?" I flared. "Oh, sure— if I dig it up, maybe some of the dirt might get smeared around. Well, that's fine with me. It's taken me ten years, but—"

"I'll get you, Moriarty, if it's the last thing I do," he said out of the side of his mouth. Then his grin faded and he held up one hand; so intense was the force of his personality that the gesture stopped me on the brink of an impassioned retort. "I'm sorry, Tommy, that wasn't in very good taste. But I had hoped you had forgotten."

"How could I?"

"Pardon me. My choice of words was poor. I hoped, rather, that you had chosen to bury your dead decently. Your feelings for Jake were unhealthy enough when he was alive; if you continue to cling to a corpse you are indulging in emotional necrophilia."

The words were brutal enough in themselves. Confirming, as they did, my bout of self-analysis earlier that day, they had the impact of a hard blow in the pit of the stomach.

"You . . . louse," I said, choking. "I can't bury . . . something that isn't dead. It won't die, it festers and crawls with . . ." I hid my face behind my hands and said between taut fingers, "Damn you. You and your repulsive mind . . ."

His hand touched my arm. Before I could pull away, he had lifted me and sat me down on the bed. I perched there with my feet dangling, peering at him through my fingers and struggling for control. It helped to note that his expression was no longer so self-satisfied.

"All right," he said. "If that's how it is, talk. Get it out of your system."

I couldn't. I was still dizzy and sick from that nasty blow below the belt.

"How did you find out I was here?" I said,

stalling. "Don't tell me that nice Mr. Bloch turned me in."

"Bloch? How do you know him?"

"I came out with his daughter. She needed a chaperone."

"I'll bet she did," Mike said unexpectedly. I gave him an outraged stare, to which he responded with a wide grin.

"Bloch," John repeated thoughtfully. "No, he didn't tell me you were here. Achmed did."

"Achmed? But how—"

"You saw him today, didn't you? He came around to the Institute later and gave me a message for you."

He dug into the pocket of his wrinkled shirt and handed me an envelope. I didn't need to open it; the flap was hanging free.

"You read it!"

"Yep."

"Of all the nosy, arrogant—"

"Well, I wanted to know what he had to say," John explained reasonably. "He asks if you could meet him tomorrow morning. Says he has something for you from his father."

The news temporarily canceled my annoyance. My hunch about Achmed had been correct, then. No doubt he had not wanted his inquisitive brother to know about Abdelal's message. So the poor young fool had turned right around and confided in John—straight into the lion's jaws. I groaned silently.

"I've been expecting you for some time," John went on maddeningly. "We knew Abdelal had written to you. How do you think he got your address?"

"From you, of course," I said slowly. "Mr. Omniscience. Why didn't I think of that?"

"From Mike. The old man came to him, not to me."

"So Mike told you. Naturally."

"Yes, naturally. Why shouldn't he?"

"No reason. The well-trained stooge . . . All right, you know everything about everybody. Why don't you tell me what Abdelal's message is, then I won't have to get up early tomorrow?"

"I don't know what it is. I wasn't going to tell you about the message, Tommy. Thought I could talk you into getting the hell out of here. But as long as you're so neurotic—"

"Shut up!"

"I'm going with you tomorrow. We'll take Mike along too. So you'd better fill him in on the background."

"He knows more about it than I do."

"No. I told Jake I'd hush it up, and I did. Mike knows nothing. Go ahead, you tell him. Then you can't accuse me of biasing the case."

The moment had arrived—and I shrank away from it. Odd. I had planned this speech so often, even said it aloud to myself. Now it sounded worn, secondhand.

Mike broke the tension. He ambled over to the other armchair and collapsed into it, his long legs giving him the look of a worried spider.

"I know more than you think, John," he said. "Rumors get around. I know Jake was fired. For faking antiquities."

It was the breach in the dam. The words came pouring out of me.

"Not fired. Blacklisted. You made damn good and sure he couldn't get another job, in the only field he knew. What did you expect him to do with the rest of his life—study plumbing? And all for some stupid old statue—why, it isn't even illegal!"

"Fraud is illegal," John said coldly. "He was trying to sell that statue to a tourist. Ten thousand dollars' worth of fraud. Egyptian jails aren't very comfortable."

"So you let him go. Weren't you noble? You didn't fool me, all you cared about was the university and the scandal. You told him if he resigned quietly you'd hush it up. But you sneaked, and whispered, and saw to it that the word got around. All you did was take away his life!"

"Tommy—"

"A week after we got home," I went on relentlessly, watching John's face, "he rented a car and drove out of New York. He never came back. They found the car at the bottom of a cliff. But you know that, don't you? Sure you do; I can see it in your face . . . You've had a little something on your mind for the last ten years too. You didn't get off scot-free after all. You killed him, and by God, you know it!"

"It was an accident . . ."

"That's what the police report says. But you and I know better, don't we?"

John didn't answer. He didn't have to; his answer was printed on his face. It had taken long nights of sleeplessness to wear those lines into flesh.

Mike stood up. He stalked over to the bed, took me firmly by the shoulders and shook me, methodically, four times.

"I ought to turn you over my knee," he said furiously. "And I would, if you hadn't had such a lousy time. Stop tearing yourself to pieces,

Tommy. Jake didn't kill himself. He wouldn't have done that."

I looked up at him, seeing him for the first time as an individual instead of John's elongated shadow. His blue eyes met mine with steady assurance.

"You sound very sure of yourself," I said shakily.

"I was Jake's pet disciple that last year." Mike sat down on the bed next to me—his legs were long enough to perform the feat without climbing onto a chair—and offered me a cigarette. "He was a very lovable guy. Even the workmen fell for him, and they're fairly cynical about foreigners. One of his most lovable traits was his gaiety. It wasn't a pose. He honestly believed that this is a good world, and that the good old world was his oyster. He was the last person to sneak away from a challenge."

I took the cigarette and let him light it. I felt better. I would have felt fine—if it hadn't been for John, silent and somehow shrunken, in the other chair. The worst was yet to come and he was waiting for it, hunched as if against an expected blow.

"While I'm on the subject of Jake," Mike went on coolly, "let's get one thing straight. We loved him, but what he did was wrong. Sure, lots of people forge antiquities. These poor devils in Luxor turn out fakes by the thousand. But you can't expect honesty from a starving peasant who squats in his mud hovel while the idle rich saunter past his door. Compared to the peasant, Jake was a rich man; and he was trained as a scholar. We are taught—God help us—to respect truth. For Jake to try to chisel some innocent sucker out of his money was illegal. For him to betray his training was worse. It was immoral."

"Very eloquent," I said. "There's just one thing. Jake didn't forge that famous statue."

"Who else could have?" Mike was being patient. "Jake was in charge of the lab—treating fragile objects, testing possible forgeries. When you learn how to detect a fake, you learn how to make one that can't be detected. I'm not talking about junk like the scarabs these peddlers market. They're lousy fakes, a baby could spot them. Jake could turn out forgeries which would pass the most rigid tests. It's been done before; hell, half our museums still contain questionable objects, so well made that they could, and did, fool experts. And a good forgery is worth a lot of money."

"I know all that."

"So what are you trying to prove?"

"I don't have to try. That statue wasn't a fake. It was genuine." The cigarette tasted foul. I stubbed it out, and swung around to face John. "Wasn't it?"

The silence lasted a long time—long enough for Mike's astounded expression to turn to horror, long enough for the sickness churning in my stomach to rise to my throat.

"Wasn't it?" I demanded.

John's clasped hands loosened. His bent knee dropped, and his booted foot hit the floor with a thud.

"Yes. It was genuine."

Chapter 3

I sat on a rock—a hard rock—and looked at a camel. The camel looked back at me, making no attempt to conceal its disapproval. Camels, like Pooh-Bah, were born sneering, and their expressions are accurate indicators of their feelings. Camels hate people—with reason, since people whack them with sticks and load them with burdens like this camel's load, sugarcane which stuck out three feet on either side of the beast's back and filled the narrow road.

The road, dusty and rutted, but full of traffic, ran by the gates of Luxor Institute and along the west bank of the Nile. It was not quite eight o'clock, but the villagers were already astir: women robed and veiled in black, bearing earth-

enware pots on their heads, camels loaded with
sugarcane; donkeys loaded with wood; men in
striped robes and bright woven caps.

The camels stared at me as I sat on my rock,
but the people did not. I knew that was indica-
tive. Like the inhabitants of small towns everywhere, the villagers of the west bank were
frankly curious about strangers, and ordinarily I
would have been greeted by smiles and nods
and the softly spoken *saida* of greeting. Obviously the word had gotten around; these people
knew who I was. They might not know why I
had come—how could they, when I wasn't sure
myself?—but they sensed that my coming meant
Trouble.

I sat with my back to the river, looking past the
walls of the Institute toward a view which ought
to have stirred the dullest senses. A vista of
green fields, golden rock, and pinky-yellow cliffs
stretched out under the deepening blue vault of
the sky. In the distance, dim and delicate, was the
miniature shape of columned terraces, framed
by the rocky backdrop of the cliffs—the terraces
of my favorite temple, Deir el Bahri.

I had no eyes for the temple. I was trying to remember—and wondering why I didn't want to
remember—the incredible events of the previous
night.

I had challenged John in the heat of anger; I never expected him to admit the charge. His flat confession left me disarmed and mute. And it was typical of him to have managed the affair so that my victory melted into air before I could grasp it. While I sat gaping he got to his feet and walked out the door, pausing only long enough to toss a sentence over his shoulder:

"Eight o'clock tomorrow, Tommy, at the Institute."

Mike hesitated. If my reeling brain had been capable of compassion, I would have felt sorry for him as his wide eyes moved from my face to John's stiff, rejecting back. It is not pleasant to watch your idols crack right across their clay faces. I ought to know.

Loyalty—or maybe it was just habit—won out. Mike straightened his shoulders and closed his mouth and followed his leader. The door shut—very quietly—and I sat with my feet dangling helplessly and tried to think.

I was still trying to think, without appreciable results. I had to keep that arrogantly given appointment; there was no other way for me to reach Achmed, and I wanted, very badly, to talk with him. I wanted to talk with John too—or perhaps that wasn't the right verb. I didn't want to cross swords with him again, he was far too expert for me. But I had to try. He couldn't get away with an exit like that one. He couldn't leave me with an admission that had nothing to back it up, a confirmation that rested on thin air.

The statue was genuine. I had known that all along, but it was not the testimony of experts that had convinced me. Experts, as Mike said, can be wrong, and many experts had goofed on the touchy question of forged antiquities. I knew Jake hadn't faked that statue because I knew Jake. Jake didn't like substitutes. The spurious, the sham, the copy roused his amused contempt. His insistence on the genuine article had cleaned out our bank account many times. Not that Jake was a plaster saint. Even when I was fifteen I knew that there were occasional days, and nights, in his life that he didn't want the university to know about. Some things he was capable of, things that a narrow mind might regard as immoral or sinful. But that particular sin he would not have committed.

It is possible to argue against knowledge based on evidence and reason. The knowledge based on faith is not shaken by denial. If John had denied my accusation I wouldn't have been surprised, but neither would I have been shaken in my belief. To have him confirm what I knew to be true stunned me as no denial could have done.

"Yes, it was genuine." I clenched my fists with impotent fury. How did he dare walk out after a statement like that? How could he admit so calmly that he had deliberately framed my father? What motive could explain, let alone excuse, such a vicious act? He and Jake had never been close friends, though they had both kept a polite gloss of professional courtesy over an antipathy that arose from personality differences rather than from specific acts. It had been rather a blow to Jake when John was made director; Jake was a few years older, had been in the field longer. But Jake never held grudges over things like that. And it certainly gave John no excuse for resenting Jake.

A movement behind the closed gates of the Institute attracted my attention. The house stood in its own compound, walled and isolated. It had a gatekeeper who granted admission to the grounds. I recognized the brown face peering through the bars as that of Abdul, who had been gatekeeper ever since my day. He had once taught me an interminable local game played with pebbles and bits of stick; I played it with him one whole summer. Now he stared out at me, blank-faced, as if at a total stranger.

I heard the sound of voices within, and Abdul's face vanished. I stood up; instinct told me that it would be bad strategy to greet John from a squatting position.

He wore the same outfit he had worn the night before, or another one equally grubby. I wondered if anyone ever pressed his shirts. Trailing him was Mike, looking, by contrast, like some movie director's version of a gallant archaeologist, in a sun helmet and neatly pressed tan slacks. John was bareheaded. I used to wonder why he never got sunstroke.

"What are you doing out here?" John demanded. "Why didn't you come in?"

I opened my mouth, but as usual he didn't wait for an answer. I had to follow, ignominiously, to a car which was parked beside the road—a Land Rover, one of the staff vehicles. He had the motor running by the time I got there, and he barely waited until Mike and I had jammed ourselves into the front seat with him before starting off. After all those years in Egypt John drove like an Egyptian, and the roads were just slightly smoothed strips of desert; I had to save my breath for breathing, and concentrate on keeping my hat from flying off. At home I never wore hats, except when it rained; I had bought this one, a cheap, broad-brimmed straw, in Rome. Only mad dogs and John go out in the noonday Luxor sun without some head covering.

The small shape of the Deir el Bahri temple swelled and took on detail. John brought the car to a crashing halt below the first ramp of the temple. He jumped out without so much as a sideward glance, and started walking.

"What the Hades does he think he's doing?" I demanded, brushing aside the gentlemanly hand Mike had extended to help me out of the car. "I can understand why he doesn't want to talk to me, but he can't get away with this indefinitely."

"You don't know John."

"Oh, yes, I do! Would you mind moving back a couple of feet?" I added irritably. "Looking up at you from close quarters gives me a crick in the neck. Mike, what did he say last night, after you left?"

"Nothing."

"And you asked nothing? I know John well enough, but I'll be . . . I'll be darned if I can understand you! What are you, a robot or something? A computer, programmed by John? Haven't you the slightest curiosity, not to say alarm, about what he admitted?"

"I'm not a robot," Mike said, with a glint in his eye that made me step back a pace. "And if you don't stop baiting me, Tommy, I'll prove it. But I hadn't had time—"

"Come on!" The roar, only slightly dimmed by the ten yards between my ears and John's vocal cords, made me jump.

Mike's stirring of chivalry had been destroyed by my remarks about robots. He stamped off without waiting for me.

Deir el Bahri, the site after which the temple is named, is a shallow bay in the façade of the western cliffs, which curve out toward the river on either side of the ruins. I followed Mike along a line which ran obliquely from the temple ramp to the right-hand horn of the bay. John was waiting for us at the foot of the cliffs. In the dazzling sunlight of high noon the rock loses most of its color, but at this hour it was still a striking yellow-brown. Against this tawny shade a white line, formed by crushed rock, looped in and out across the steep face of the cliffs—the path over the plateau to the Valley of the Kings. Only the hardiest of tourists take this path; most go by car via the road, which penetrates the cliffs some distance from Deir el Bahri.

John was standing in a characteristic pose, fists on his hips, head tilted back to glower at the sky. He whirled around as I plodded up.

"Keep quiet, Tommy, and don't interrupt. We'll talk after we meet Achmed. I have a notion of what he'll tell you, and it will confirm my long interesting story—which you have no doubt made up your mind not to believe."

"But I—"

"I said we'll talk later. We're late now. Save your breath for the climb. After all these years you're undoubtedly out of shape."

From Mike came an imperfectly suppressed chuckle, and I gave him an outraged glance.

"All right, I won't say it," he said grinning. "But you will admit those slacks are a little—"

"These days," I said coldly, starting up the slope, "it is impossible to buy slacks that aren't."

"Couldn't you have gotten 'em a couple of sizes too big?" Mike sounded as if he really wanted to know.

"If I had, they would fall off," I said shortly, and then saved my breath. John was right about my wind, but I was prepared to die of asphyxiation before admitting it.

Unlike most objects, which shrink in size as you get older, those cliffs had gotten taller. The path is erratic; in the steepest spots it makes switchbacks, but in some places the slope is sharp enough to require four-footed progress. I preferred not to bend over, since Mike was right behind me. I thought I was going to collapse before John stopped for the first rest.

He wasn't even puffing, damn him. I sank

down on a rock—handy things, rocks—and tried not to whoop for air. At my right the cliffs dropped straight down, and the view was unique; the whole temple area was laid out, like a model of itself, with colonnades and ramps outlined by sharp black shadows. On the far side of the queen's temple were the ruins of the earlier Eleventh Dynasty building; the outline of the pyramid which had once crowned it was as clear as if it had been drawn with a pen and straight edge.

Then it happened again—it was always happening, happening too darned often—that dizzying attack of *déjà vu*, of having been here once before. Only I knew when I had been here. I could have counted off the times on my fingers and toes. It had been one of my favorite walks when I was young and spry. I used to bound up this same path like a goat—often alone, sometimes with Jake (he preferred cars to feet, he always said). Sometimes with Abdelal.

"Where are we meeting Achmed?" I asked, squelching the voice of nostalgia.

"Near the Valley."

"Oh, Lord—all the way."

"It's easy going once we reach the plateau."

"I know."

When John got up, I followed him without

protest, though my lungs still ached. After about ten feet I felt a large, hard hand in the middle of my back. I never could have made the last twenty feet without it, so when we reached the top and Mike came up to walk beside me, I let him take my arm. I even said "thanks."

There was plenty of room up there in which to walk two or three abreast. We were on the plateau and would not descend until we reached the canyon which is the Valley of the Kings.

As we plodded on across the rough, barren surface, I realized that my mood had changed. The plateau isn't spectacularly high, but it is so barren, so featureless, that it seems closer to the sky than higher mountains. I felt suspended between heaven and earth; and suspended, as well, between one emotional crisis and another. The sun raked at my shoulders through the cotton blouse, and sharp stones made themselves felt even through the thick rubber soles of my shoes; but I could have gone on in that queer calm forever.

By the time we reached the Valley, the tourist rush had begun. We were as high above the royal tombs as we had been high above the temple; a precipitous path led down the cliff into the Valley, amid boulders and patches of gravel, empty beer cans, and orange peels. I could see the black holes of the tomb entrances against the paling buff of the canyon walls. Almost directly below was the low stone balustrade which marked the tomb of Tutankhamen. The bright blouses and shirts of the early-bird tourists made splotches of color—primrose, crimson, fuchsia—against the drab brown of the valley floor. And from the terrace of the new rest house rose a faint, familiar cry:

"Enrico! Vieni qua, vieni a mamma!"

John paid no attention to the scene below except for a quick, sweeping survey which apparently betrayed nothing of interest to him. He glanced at his wristwatch and then walked back, away from the path and the Valley. There was nothing in that direction except tumbled rock, rough and unformed as chunks of modeling clay flung from the hand of an impatient child god and left to harden.

Some distance from the edge of the Valley cliff John stopped, in the shade of a boulder. Anyone who has been in Upper Egypt for more than a day automatically seeks shade. Again he looked at his watch.

"He isn't here yet," Mike said, voicing the obvious; in that vast emptiness any human figure would have been easy to see.

"We're late."

"Maybe he's lurking. Want me to give him a hail?"

"If he's lurking it's because he shuns publicity. We'll wait; he'll be looking for us."

We waited. Five minutes. Ten.

John never sat still easily; now he was as tense as an amateur actor waiting to go on stage. After fifteen minutes he stood up with a profane murmur and climbed on top of the boulder in whose shadow we had been standing. I turned to watch him, sensing his growing anxiety, so I caught the movement when his straight, lean body stiffened and his intent gaze focused on an object.

It was nothing near at hand, on the level of the plateau. He was looking up, squinting against the sunlight till his eyes were slitted. High under the azure sky something hovered and dipped on wide, motionless wings.

Mike was looking too, hands funneled to shield his eyes. Then, even before I recognized the object consciously, even in the blistering heat of the advancing sun, a prickle of cold ran down my back. The hovering object had to be a bird. But now I knew what bird it must be.

"Where's it heading?" Mike spoke softly, as if the creature could hear him.

John's eyes were fixed on the black outline,

now low enough to be identifiable, as it sank in narrowing circles.

"Not far . . ."

"Maybe a goat."

"No."

He left the rock in a long jump, knees bent, and began moving, in quick, swinging strides. Almost at once he stopped and bent to pick up some object which had been hidden behind another of the omnipresent rocks. Mike followed, his long legs covering the ground with a speed I couldn't hope to equal. By the time I reached Mike, John was on the move again, walking more slowly now, eyes fixed on the ground. Mike held the object John had found—one of the gay woven skullcaps that Egyptian men wear. This one had a pattern of green diamonds on amber, with chevrons of blue and red.

My eyes met Mike's, and saw mirrored in them my own recognition. Involuntarily we both looked up at the graceful, deadly shape of the vulture swinging on the clear blue air.

"You go that way," Mike said, pointing.

I went. He went loping off at right angles. But it was John who found what we were all looking for, and were hoping not to find.

His wordless, summoning shout brought us

both running, to join him where he stood on the edge of a narrow cleft in the floor of the plateau. The sides were jagged but almost perpendicular, ending in a narrow space ten feet below us.

At first the object looked like a bundle of laundry, soiled and tumbled by its fall down onto the rocks at the bottom of the cleft. White dust stained the black stripes of the cloth. But there was a brown foot visible at one end of the bundle—and at the other end a dark head. Its short crisp hair seemed to move, as if stirred by a breeze. But there was no breeze down in that hole. There were, however, flies.

The broken ground under my feet heaved and then sank. Somebody grabbed my arm. It wasn't Mike; he was on his way down, swinging recklessly hand below hand, his feet barely touching the rocks.

John dropped to one knee and stared down, as if trying to memorize the scene. I looked at his bent head, and a new wave of sickness washed over me.

"Your witness?" I asked.

The moment before he answered seemed as long as a year.

"My witness. Mike!"

The last word sounded like a shout in contrast to the uninflected whisper of the first two. Mike looked up. He was perspiring, and no wonder; the temperature and the tension were both high.

"He's still breathing," he called.

"Get up here, fast."

"He needs a doctor," Mike said, bending over the still form. "I can't tell how badly he's hurt."

"Go get one then." John swung himself into the hole. "There may be a doctor in that mob of tourists down below. If not, you'll have to telephone."

"Telephone?" I repeated idiotically, as Mike's head came up into the open air.

"There's one in the guard's office in the Valley." Mike was off, his long legs eating up the distance.

I looked down. John was kneeling; his back hid the movements of his hands. Without premeditation I flopped down on my stomach and let my legs drop into the hole, groping for a foothold.

It was a short descent but a nasty one; the rocks were sharp enough to cut my palms.

"What the hell do you think you're doing?" John's hands caught me by the waist and swung me down the rest of the way. There was barely room for three of us in that narrow space. I stood with my back pressed against the rock side. I needed the support, since my knees had gone oddly weak; but at the same time I wished I had a little more space behind me. I was close enough to John to see every detail of his features—the stubble of dark beard, the twitching of a small muscle at the corner of his mouth. His face was a livid hue, the effect of pallor under a deep tan.

"What do you think you're doing?" he demanded again.

If I had had my wits about me, I would have made some innocuous reply; but fear and distress took away what little sense I ordinarily possess.

"He's still alive. I intend to see that he stays alive."

He moved so quickly that I had no time to retreat, even if there had been room for a retreat. His hands caught me by the shoulders, the thumbs digging painfully into the hollow at the base of my throat. I expected to be shaken, to feel my head smash agonizingly against the wall of rock immediately behind me; but he controlled himself, though the effort brought out rigid, corded muscles under the tanned skin of his forearms.

"Watch it," I said, in a voice that shook with strain. "Mike will be back any minute."

"You keep asking for it, don't you?"

"All I'm asking for is the truth."

The pressure of his fingers relaxed, but not much.

"A defendant doesn't murder his own witness."

"You don't act much like a man on the defensive," I blazed. "And who said he was your witness?"

"I told you—"

"You said he might confirm a story which was basically unbelievable. You said it after he—not you—had asked for a meeting. One thing I must admire," I said, from a dry throat, "is your candor. You admitted you didn't intend to give me Achmed's message. When you found out you couldn't scare me into leaving town, you invited yourself along this morning. A certain skepticism as to motives is, I think, justified, by—"

His fingers tightened till the air darkened, and dull reddish spots swam in front of my eyes. I clutched at his wrists, tugging and scratching, but my hands were too weak. I felt my arms drop, like dead branches. Then the sunlight came back, and my eyes focused on a patch of wrinkled tan cloth. John's shirt. His arms were around me, but they were rigid as iron and purely functional; as soon as he felt me tense, he stood me up and shook me, more gently than I had expected.

"If somebody else doesn't murder you, I probably will," he said grimly. "Wallow in your evil thoughts, Tommy, and be damned to you. Now make yourself useful, as long as you're here. See if you can't keep the flies off him."

He handed me my own hat, which had fallen off my agitated head. After a few tries my shaking fingers found the wide brim. I knelt beside Achmed and tried to fan the bloodthirsty insects away from the sticky wet patch on the back of his head.

I've never seen a fly since without experiencing a vicious desire to smash it. The little horrors swarmed so thickly they bumped into one another in midair, and I swung my hat at the buzzing black clouds in hysterical swipes. I was just as glad not to pursue that conversation any further. I had come terrifyingly close to danger then; I hadn't realized that John had such a capacity for violence. I had better be careful not to challenge him openly again . . . But I knew I would. He brought out my worst qualities—as I seemed to bring out his.

So I watched him without trying to conceal my suspicion as his big brown hands moved over Achmed's body, feeling for a pulse, testing for broken bones. In his earlier days he had been something of an amateur doctor—as many archaeologists of that era had been, forced into an unwilling practice by pity and the grim knowledge that nothing better was available. Even fifteen years ago there were people in Luxor who preferred John's ministrations to those of the local doctor.

Still, I didn't expect spectacular results from this particular ministration. When John shook the boy's shoulder gently and repeated his name, I almost remonstrated. I let out a bleat of pure amazement when the boy groaned and sat up.

He fell back at once, his eyes closing, but John's arm supported him. Gradually his eyes focused and came alive.

"*Wa'allah*," he groaned, and added another Arabic phrase which was just as predictable as its English equivalent: "What happened?"

"Somebody hit you on the head," John said, glancing at me; the switch into English was obviously for my benefit, his Arabic was of native fluency, far better than mine ever had been.

Achmed's foggy eyes saw me.

"Mees . . . Tommy," he said; and the old name, and his gallant effort, softened me so thoroughly that I didn't correct him. I was getting tired of that name, though. I never did like "Althea," but at least it had no dead memories connected with it.

"Don't try to talk," I said, smiling at him. "Wait till the doctor comes."

"Who hit you?" John demanded, less sentimentally.

"Don't know. Saw . . . no one."

Dizzy as he must have been, his face had hardened into the mask Egyptians wear before strangers. I couldn't tell whether he was lying or not.

Chapter 4

An hour later we were all holding a conference in a tomb.

As Mike pointed out, it was the only place in which we could get any privacy. By the time Achmed's head had been patched up by an elderly doctor who had been extracted from the tomb of Tutankhamen, we were the center of a gaping crowd of tourists, guides, and donkeys. We had to wait—preferably somewhere out of the sun—for the car Mike had ordered, and a long, informative discussion seemed to be called for. The air was seething with unspoken questions—many of them mine.

Some of the tombs in the Valley are only opened upon request, so we were able to find an unpopular sepulcher whose guard unlocked the grilled-iron gate and then, at John's request, locked it again behind us. When we reached the burial chamber, at the far end of the corridor, John lowered Achmed to a semi-reclining position against the wall and then sat cross-legged on the floor. There wasn't anywhere else to sit. The only object in the room was the enormous stone box that occupied the center of the floor— the sarcophagus, now empty, which had once held the coffins of a king.

Yet the room did not feel empty. All around the walls, in stately procession, marched the gods and demons of ancient Egypt, brought to illusory life by the bare electric light bulbs of the modern world. The mummiform stiffness of Osiris, Lord of the Westerners, was swathed in snowy white; his face and hands had the dead black shade which signifies divinity. Behind him, one hand resting on his shoulder, stood the slim form of his sister-wife Isis, wearing the golden horned crown. Thoth, god of wisdom, attended them; his broad shoulders were topped by the long-beaked head of an ibis. The scene was the Judgment of the Soul, where the heart of the dead man is weighed on the scales against the image of Truth, to determine whether he is fit for eternal life. And into the Hall of the Judgment came

Death—Anubis, patron deity of cemeteries and the rite of mummification, with the body of a man and the jackal's head. It must have been the relative coolness of the underground room after the heat of a sunny day that sent a long, uncontrolled shiver running through me.

By that time our little group included Mr. Bloch and daughter. They had been among the tourists, and Bloch, his big blue eyes wide with innocent curiosity, had attached himself to John like a polite leech. John, for reasons which then eluded me, had not objected. Mike, who was still annoyed with me for doubting his hero, welcomed Dee with exaggerated shouts of joy.

Now I watched with a poorly concealed grin while the perfect gentleman tried to find a place where Dee could sit. She ended up on the floor, like all the rest of us, but since her cast was completely unbendable, Mike had to lower her like a derrick dealing with a piano. He also had to try to keep his eyes away from the hem of her dress, an impractical but gorgeous raspberry-pink shift, which went zooming up as Dee went down. He was not particularly successful.

"Maybe we'd better go back to the guesthouse," said Mr. Bloch, viewing his daughter's contortions with alarm.

"No," John said briefly. "I want you here."

"Why me?"

"Because you were the tourist Jake tried to sell that statue to, ten years ago."

Mr. Bloch glanced guiltily at me.

"Well, now . . . I'm sorry, Miss Tomlinson. I always felt like I got Jake into trouble somehow . . ."

"You had no intention of getting him into trouble," John said sharply. "If I hadn't caught him in the act, you'd have bought the statue and broken half a dozen laws smuggling it out."

"It's a disease," Mr. Bloch mumbled guiltily. "Collecting, I mean. And the statue sure looked genuine to me."

"It was."

If I'd had a pin handy, I would have dropped it. I think I could have heard it hit the floor. I did hear John's wristwatch ticking through the thick silence, and counted five ticks before Bloch exploded.

"Why, you old—you low-down, chiseling . . ."

With a sheepish glance at me, he swallowed the noun; it almost choked him. Then he began to chuckle.

"Okay, John. I guess it is kind of funny, at that. You fooled me good and proper."

John wasn't amused. He fumbled for his pipe and made a big production out of filling and lighting it; and as I watched the deliberation of his movements, a formless apprehension invaded my brain.

"You're a fool, Sam," John said finally. "So are the rest of you. None of you seem to have thought of the big question. If that statue is genuine . . . *Where did it come from?*"

So there it was, blunt and explicit, the question I had never allowed myself to ask. The answer was as glaringly obvious as Dee's pink dress against the gray-buff floor.

I suppose Dee was the only one in the room who didn't know the answer. Achmed's trained brown mask never changed, but his eyes betrayed him. Bloch caught his breath audibly, and a spot of color appeared in each plump cheek. There was an answering flush on Mike's thin face. He must have known since the night before, when the significant admission had been made. But he didn't believe it. He couldn't believe it.

"The statue could have been an isolated find," he said, his voice higher than usual. "From temple ruins . . ."

"Possible," John said calmly. "All right, Tommy, let me have it."

He held out his hand. My own hand went, betrayingly, to the clasp of my shoulder bag.

"How did you know?" I gasped.

"You wouldn't leave it lying around in the hotel. Let me have it."

I opened my purse and removed the concealing wad of tissues. The thing was heavy, despite its small size, only eight inches high. But they were eight inches of solid metal.

I handed it to John, avoiding his eyes as he avoided mine. He held it up, balanced on the palm of his hand, where it caught and held six pairs of eyes.

My eyes too. I had seen it a hundred times, but each time it worked the same magic.

The statue was that of a woman. At first glance she seemed to be naked, her small breasts and gently rounded limbs those of a girl still young. Then you noticed the delicately incised lines of pleated material along her thighs, and the hem of the sheer dress at her ankles. But first of all you saw the face, poised atop a long curving neck—the full, gently smiling lips and tilted eyes, the beautiful miniature modeling of the facial bones, unsoftened by falling hair; for the lady's tresses were concealed under a tall headdress or cap which continued the upsweep of throat and head.

After a full minute, Mike said hoarsely, "It's her."

"Who?" Dee demanded, glancing nervously over her shoulder.

For once Mike was unaware of living females. His gaze, focused on the tiny perfection of the gilded face, had the ardor of a lover.

"It could be an isolated find," he repeated.

John, carefully refilling his pipe, did not answer for a moment. When he did speak, his remark seemed irrelevant.

"I suppose they got it, Achmed?"

Achmed sat up a little straighter. The corners of his thin, well-formed mouth twitched. In an American boy the expression would have been a wide, delighted grin.

"No, Director."

"But surely that was why—"

"Yes, I am thinking it was the reason for the attack on me. But I am the son of my father."

From somewhere in the folds of his sweeping robe he produced a small packet wrapped in paper, which he unswathed to display his lunch—a thick slab of the repulsive bread and a chunk of odoriferous cheese. We all stared in fascinated silence while Achmed, enjoying his moment of triumph, inserted slim fingers into the bread, pulled out a plug of dough, and from the hollowed interior brought out a tiny wooden box, almost covered by blobs of reddish wax.

Achmed rose and walked over to me, wobbling a little. He extended his hand, palm flat, with the package resting on it as on a salver.

"It is for you," he said solemnly. "From my father."

"Thank you," I said, with equal solemnity. I was thanking him, not only for the box, but for what he had endured in order to carry out his trust. He was indeed the son of his father—clever, farsighted, and honorable.

The wax had hardened into cementlike consistency. John had to toss me his pocketknife before I could get the box open. The object inside was swathed in shredded paper. I poked my fingers into the padding, and held the contents up between my thumb and forefinger.

It was a scarab, of roughly the same size and shape as the fake I had seen at the airport. But there the resemblance stopped. Carved of opaque, dark-green stone, this scarab was cut with exquisite precision. Around its circumference ran a band of shining yellow metal.

"Turn it over," said a voice which sounded a long way off. I obeyed, half mesmerized. Little birds and flowers and animals, and the other less obvious symbols of the picture writing of ancient Egypt, ran in rows down the long axis of the beetle's body.

"Do you remember enough of your Egyptian to read it?" asked the same voice—John's.

"No," I said dully. "I suppose it's the usual spell, from the Book of the Dead."

"No names or titles?"

"No . . . Wait. On the gold band . . ."

I turned the scarab so that the fragile incised signs in the gold caught the light. Now I could read them. They included the one name, the one set of titles, that I had learned to read almost as soon as I read English. The silence in the small chamber was so profound that I could hear people breathing; and into the silence my whisper fell like a chanted chorus:

"The king's great wife, whom he loves, lady of the two lands . . . Nefertiti."

"Yahoo!"

The shout startled me so that I nearly dropped the scarab. I looked up to see a rare and splendid sight—a dignified, middle-aged American gentleman jumping up and down like a jack-in-the-box.

"Wow!" shouted Mr. Bloch, following this remark by other, less articulate, cries of delight. He bounded over to John and smacked him heavily on the back. "You old son of a gun! My God, this will be the greatest thing in the history of archaeology! Greater than Pompeii, Mycenae,

Tut—I've got to be in on it. John, I'll finance the whole thing . . . Look, son, if I ever did anything for you—"

"I don't get it!" Dee said, in the familiar whine. "What's everybody grinning about?"

Everybody answered at once. Everybody except Tommy Tomlinson, who sat with her hands folded in her lap, staring at them as if she had never seen fingers before. How much longer were they going to avoid the question? They all knew now, all but Dee, and she didn't count.

"Let me tell her," Mike's voice rose over that of Dee's hysterical parent. "Let me spell it out. I still don't believe it, there's got to be a flaw somewhere . . ."

"Spell it out, then," John said impatiently. "We'll find the flaws. If there are flaws."

Mike dropped back down to the floor—he had joined Bloch in the last measures of his wild dance—and took Dee's hand.

"Start with the statue," he said, pointing to it. "It's a queen's statue, Dee, see her crown? The material is gilded bronze, maybe even gold—"

"Gold?" Dee said.

One word. And with it something entered the stifling air of the tomb chamber, some emotion that made the air seem staler, heavier.

"The gold—the gold isn't important," Mike

said more soberly. "Pay attention, Dee. The point is, this statue is about three thousand years old. Where has it been all that time?"

"Buried in the ground?" Dee said brightly.

"Well. Yeah, sort of . . . Let's take the weakest possibility first. Jake could have found this in an antiquities shop."

He glanced involuntarily at my set face, and then looked quickly away.

"That only takes the problem of its ultimate origin back one stage," he went on, "but I don't believe it anyhow. Something so unique as this statue wouldn't be on a dealer's shelf. I think we can assume Jake found the statue himself."

There was a general murmur of agreement, in which I did not join.

"Some objects of this type have been found in digs, in excavations of temples, houses, and palaces," Mike continued, warming to his subject now that the painful part of it had been passed. "If we had only the statue we wouldn't know where it came from. There are a hell of a lot of ruins around Luxor.

"But now we have this." He put out his hand, and I gave him the scarab, without looking at him or it. He studied it, his eyes running up and down the rows of figures.

"Fantastic," he muttered. "It isn't the standard

text, but we might have expected that. Nefertiti was a follower of her husband's new religion, which denied the old gods. This is a prayer to his god Aton. But the scarab itself is of a type we know well, Dee. These things occur by the hundreds. They are called heart scarabs, and they were made for one purpose, and one purpose only. They were buried with the dead, right on the mummy."

Dee was frowning, and very prettily, too.

"But the old guy, what was his name, had the scarab, and Tommy had the statue. What's the connection?"

"I was just coming to that," Mike said, beaming at her. "Very important point. Look here."

He held up the statue, his fingers caressing the golden curves.

"In the Berlin Museum there is a world-famous head of an Egyptian queen. Gosh, Dee, you must have seen a copy of it. It's been reproduced on postcards and jewelry—I even saw one of the tourists last summer wearing a dress with Nefertiti's head stamped all over it, and it looked like hell, I might add. Well, damn it—this statue of ours is Nefertiti, there's no mistaking her. The face is the same as the one in the Berlin head. And the scarab was hers too, it has her name right on it, also the name of her husband, who was a famous character himself—Akhenaton, the king who tried to destroy the old pantheon of Egypt and substitute the sun-god, Aton. He was the older brother of King Tutankhamen—"

"Father," said John, around the stem of his pipe.

"Brother! The lock of hair in the tomb—"

Dee looked utterly baffled by this weird dialogue, and Bloch said impatiently,

"For Pete's sake, boys, let's not drag that old argument out now. How can you waste time—"

"Any two Egyptologists will argue about trivia any old time," I said nastily. "In a burning house, with the flames charring their socks, in a shipwreck, while the water rises—"

"Anyhow," Mike shouted drowning me out, "the point is, the heart scarab could only have come from one place. And that place wasn't a temple, or a house, or—"

"For God's sake," John interrupted, "say it! That place was a tomb. One particular tomb. The tomb of Nefertiti."

The conclusion came as no surprise to any of the enthusiasts, but just hearing the words spoken almost set them off again. Bloch was making soft noises like a teakettle about to boil. Mike's face was bright pink.

94   Elizabeth Peters

"I get it," Dee said calmly. "But I thought all the kings' tombs had been discovered. Right here."

"True, true," Mike babbled. "Most of the kings' tombs are here in the Valley, all but the tomb of Nefertiti's husband, as a matter of fact. He was buried in the city of Amarna, which he founded. That's about two hundred miles north of here. Actually . . ."

He broke off, frowning, as a new idea came to him; and John took up the tale with the assurance of a man who had already considered and solved the objection.

"Actually, we always assumed that Nefertiti was also buried at Amarna. But we don't know when she died, and if she outlived her husband and survived into the reign of Tutankhamen . . . He moved back to Thebes shortly after he came to the throne, and she could have come back with him, died, and been buried here. As, apparently, she did and was."

"Mmmm," Mike said, still cogitating. "I guess so . . . Jake was here, in Thebes, all that year, wasn't he?"

John carefully did not look at me.

"There is no doubt in my mind," he said, "that these objects were found here."

"Holy mackerel," Mike said dreamily. "I can't believe it. Nefertiti's tomb . . . It ought to make

Tutankhamen look like a pauper. Gold coffins, jewelry, maybe even texts . . ."

He looked like a young saint getting his first glimpse of the Pearly Gates. I couldn't stand it. I said sharply,

"It's a lovely dream. And maybe it's only a dream. How do you know the tomb, if there is a tomb, hasn't been robbed? All the rest of them were."

Almost my heart smote me, seeing the change in Mike's face. Almost, but not quite. And John, who was still avoiding my eyes, said remotely,

"You know better than that, Tommy. If the tomb had been robbed in antiquity, objects like the scarab and the statue would have been among the first to go. They're small, portable, valuable. The fact that they didn't turn up till ten years ago suggests strongly that the tomb was intact, or nearly so, up to that time. If the tomb had been cleared since then, objects would have turned up on the international antiquities market. Word of such finds gets around, no matter how secret the negotiations are. No such objects have appeared. I know."

"Right," Mike said, with a gusty gasp of relief.

"Therefore, friends," John went on, "reason and logic support what is admittedly a fantastic fact. We seem to have the ultimate object of every

Egyptologist's secret dreams. The kind of thing we fantasize about, but never really expect to see. A lost, unrobbed, royal tomb."

"John . . ." Bloch's voice was a groan.

"Sam, you know I can't promise. If I have any voice in the decision—sure. But we aren't exactly popular in Egypt these days. If the Antiquities Department gets wind of this, they'll have us out and local archaeologists in so fast it'll make your heads swim."

"Oh, no," Mike said, losing some of the pretty pink color in his cheeks.

"Oh, yes. I thought you sympathized with nationalist aspirations?"

"I do, I do. Only . . ."

"Only not when they interfere with your aspirations? Don't get indignant with me, I'm on your side. As far as I'm concerned, the only thing that gives a man a legitimate aspiration to do a professional job is his skill."

"They have good archaeologists," Mike said, unwillingly.

"Yes, they do. But not enough for a job like this. And—let's be honest, for once, gentlemen—politics will rear its ugly head, as it often does here. Hell's bells, why not admit it? I want to be in on this. I'd give twenty years of my life to be in charge of it."

Bloch, who had seated himself on the floor next to his daughter, placed his plump pink hands on his knees and studied John intently.

"So what do you plan to do?"

"Blackmail everybody I can," John said bluntly. "I know where a few bodies are buried. That's why our little group has been here as long as it has, through the periodic antiforeign unrest. I also have, odd as it may seem, a few honest friends who'll support me. But for this I'll need something more. A lever. An ace in the hole. A big fat prize that I can offer in exchange for control of the project. An item," his voice was bland, "such as the precise location of the tomb."

He glanced around the circle of suddenly blank faces and then exploded.

"You blockheads! I've been sitting here listening to all of you counting your gold coffins, and wondering how the hell you expect to find them. Your deductions are fine. They may even be correct. What you seem to forget is that nobody knows where the tomb is!"

"But I thought you . . ." Mike said feebly.

"Do you think I'd have sat around biting my thumbs for ten years if I knew? Of course I realized the statue was genuine, I realized that the instant I set eyes on it. But Jake outfoxed me. He swore he'd forged the statue and begged me to let him resign without a scandal. I had to go to Aswan next day, and by the time I got back, Jake had skipped the country."

He stopped, ostensibly for breath. I knew the real reason for his hesitation, and I sat with head bowed and fists clenched, wondering why he was trying to be tactful about a subject which had gone far beyond any need for tact.

"It wasn't until much later," John said, finally, "that I began to suspect Abdelal's involvement. He must have been in on the discovery from the first; the scarab was his souvenir from the tomb, as the statue was Jake's. But by the time I caught on to that, Abdelal was also beyond questioning. So far as I am aware, only the two of them knew the location of the tomb. And both of them—may I remind you—are dead."

The last word fell like a stone into a dismayed silence, which was broken only by the shuffling footsteps of a wizened little Egyptian who had come to tell us that the Director's car had arrived. Obvious though it should have been, John's statement had come as a shock to minds which had been too muffled in dreams of glory to be sensible. I knew the discussion wasn't finished; neither John nor Mike would abandon the problem with a shrug, and Bloch's firm lips and abstracted gaze indicated that he was already considering possible lines of attack. But at the moment everyone needed time to calm down; and Achmed needed rest and more medical attention. John had to half carry the boy down the corridor and lift him into the waiting car. Mike, grimly silent, climbed into the back seat.

"I've got to put this boy to bed," John said, turning to Bloch. "See you later."

"You're damn right," Bloch said, with a lazy smile.

"Sorry I can't offer you a lift, but we're full up. Get in the front, Tommy."

"No, thanks," I said calmly. "I'll thumb a ride. Maybe with Mr. Bloch."

"Sure," said that gentleman agreeably.

"You are not going back to the hotel," John told me. "I'll send one of the men over for your bags."

"Yes, I am, and no, you will not, and don't bother yelling. I've got trouble enough right now without moving into the Institute."

John opened his mouth for one of the roars that undoubtedly did a lot to relieve his blood pressure; then he glanced at the thronging tourists and thought better of it.

"You can't go back to the hotel. It isn't safe."

"That's pretty feeble, even for you," I said, with a halfhearted sneer. "Do you really take me for a fool, John? I know exactly what you're thinking. Five minutes after I arrived at the dear old Institute you'd have me strapped into a chair with bright lights glaring and rubber hoses swinging. Maybe drugs, for God's sake; I wouldn't put it past you."

John's moustache was vibrating the way it did when he was really beside himself. I had always assumed the motion came from a furious mastication of his upper lip, but I never got close enough to pursue the theory. I think he would have grabbed me and crammed me into the car forcibly if Bloch hadn't intervened.

"John, you're a no-good rascal, if that's what you're thinking. This young lady doesn't know where that—er—that item is, any more than you do. It's as you said. Would she have waited ten years if she had known?"

John paid no attention to him.

"Tommy, I don't believe Jake told you anything. But I'm damned sure you know something you haven't told me. That in itself is not so important as the fact that other parties may be thinking along the same lines. Remember what happened to Achmed this morning. I don't want some chambermaid to find you in the same condition tomorrow morning."

"No!" I stepped back from the ingratiating hand he had extended to help me into the car. "You're just trying to scare me. I don't know a blasted thing, and I don't have—Hey! Give me back my statue!"

"No, no, and again, no," said John, in a loud voice. "That's one temptation I can remove from your immediate vicinity. Last chance, Tommy. Are you coming?"

"No!"

"God damn it all to hell!" That blast, delivered in his most carrying voice, drew a staring crowd. He withered them with a collective glare and flung himself into the car. Then he stuck his head out the window and delivered his final comment. "You're still wallowing in your past, aren't you? If Jake weren't dead, I'd like to kill him myself, for what he did to you!"

I held myself together till we got back to the hotel. I might have managed, even then, if Mr. Bloch hadn't precipitated the deluge. Instead of accompanying Dee into her room, he followed me into mine, and closed the door.

"Tommy—is it all right if I call you that?"

"Sure," I said dully, throwing my purse onto the bed.

"Tommy, don't pay any attention to John. You know how he is."

"If you tell me about his heart of gold I'll—I'll scream. He hasn't got a heart. Maybe a block of granite—covered with Egyptian hieroglyphs."

"He loves you," Bloch said, and grinned at my expression. "He's known you since you were a baby, my dear. He just hasn't had much experience at expressing his paternal feelings. I know just how he feels, myself."

"Would you mind?" I put my hand to my head; it was splitting. "I don't want to be rude, but I can't stand much more. Not today."

"Just one thing. The same thing John has been trying to say. Forget Jake, Tommy. Stop agonizing over what he did."

"I didn't care," I said, half to myself, "when he was accused of forging antiquities. I wonder why? Because it seemed exotic, unusual, romantic? Then I decided he was innocent. That was even more romantic."

"He didn't tell you the truth?"

"He didn't have . . . he didn't have time to tell me anything. I'll never know, now, what he would have said, or what he would have done. It was so sudden," I said, and giggled, abruptly, shockingly. "That afternoon, when he left, he was all dressed up in his best gray suit. He was so handsome. He looked about twenty-two. He grinned at me, and pulled my hair. He said, 'You know that bank I've been meaning to rob, baby? Today's the day.' Then he left. I heard him whistling as he went down the stairs. They found the car almost at once. It wasn't very late that night when they came and told me."

"I would guess," said Mr. Bloch grimly, "that they didn't tell you very tactfully."

"They tried. News like that can't be told tactfully."

"No . . . It was just the end of the world," said Mr. Bloch, and his voice had all the gentleness the distressed, embarrassed policeman's had lacked. "I think I understand. Not only how you felt, but why you reacted as you did. Impersonal disasters are the hardest kind to accept. People want to blame somebody, anybody. Cursing God," said Mr. Bloch, "isn't much satisfaction."

"So I cursed John. Oh, you're so right, I had to have someone to hate. But that wasn't the worst of it. I could only blame John if I believed Jake was innocent. I hung that word, *innocent*, up like a billboard right across the front of my mind, so that it hid everything else. I couldn't let myself think logically, because then I'd have to face the truth. That Jake—my father—wasn't a figure of romance. That he was a cheap, ordinary thief."

"Not cheap . . ."

"No, not cheap. Most thieves don't stumble on such incredible riches. And the victim already dead. There's a word for people who rob the dead, isn't there? Ghouls."

"Tommy, child . . ."

"Child is right. It's time I grew up, don't you think? What Jake did was worse than robbery. He wasn't only stealing from a dead woman, or from the Egyptian government. He was robbing living millions who have the past as their rightful heritage. He was betraying the creed he pretended to live by. Selling out knowledge for money. He . . ."

It wasn't till my voice gave way that I realized the tears were raining down my face. I tried to stop crying and couldn't.

Mr. Bloch found the aspirin in my purse. He made me lie down on the bed. He took my shoes off. He got a wet cloth to put on my head. It dripped a regular flood all over my hair and the pillow, but it was a beautiful thought. Then he went away, having done his job and done it well.

I went to sleep.

I didn't wake up until someone knocked on the door, and my first hazy thought was indignation that I should have been able to sleep. My hair was sodden from Mr. Bloch's dripping cloth, and my head ached all the way back to my ears.

By the time I finished counting my aches and pains, the waiter was already in the room, wishing me a cheery good evening. I hadn't ordered dinner, but I knew who had; and as I sat down and contemplated the lamb kebabs and kale, I wondered if Mr. Bloch would let me adopt him. Or maybe he would adopt me. Lucky Dee—she probably didn't appreciate how lucky she was.

The food tasted better than I had expected, but it didn't make me feel like dancing. Or even thinking. Not the kind of thoughts I'd been enjoying lately. I went back to bed.

And woke, in the dead dark hours after midnight, with the knowledge that someone was in my room.

The sounds were small ones—a scuffle, a scrape, a catch of breath as some portion of human anatomy painfully encountered a hard object. I had locked my door; but I hadn't locked the French doors onto the balcony.

I lay rigid in the darkness, my muscles aching with the shock of abrupt awakening, and tried to think what to do. None of my poor possessions were worth fighting about. Few possessions are. But I knew that the intruder wasn't looking for diamonds, or portable radios, or money. The thing he was after was in the pocket of my small suitcase. When I put it there, just to get it out of my overloaded purse, I didn't know what it meant. I still didn't know; but now I realized, after the day's disclosures, that it did have a meaning.

Could the intruder, whoever he was, interpret the hint in Abdelal's postscript, the hint that still eluded me? Probably not; it was a reference to something so personal that I had forgotten it myself. Yet I couldn't be sure that the lost memory was not known to others. Not until I had retrieved it myself.

All this went through my mind in the usual flash, not so coherently reasoned as it sounds when I write it out, but wholly convincing for all that. I didn't even need the advice of logic to tell me what to do. My sound coward's instincts told me that. Lie still. Pretend to be asleep. Leave him, whoever he is, alone.

I could see him now, but only as a dim, formless blob of darker darkness. So I got up out of the bed, flinging back the covers in the same movement, and threw myself at my visitor.

I must have been crazy. I did have a plan, of sorts; I wasn't stupid enough to believe I could overwhelm a burglar singlehanded. I planned to scream. It seemed to me that I ought to be able to detain the man, after catching him by surprise, until help could arrive.

One little point had slipped my mind—the fact that the door was locked and bolted. It didn't matter. I had miscalculated on a more important matter. I hadn't realized how quick he would be, how instinctive his reactions were.

He went reeling back when I landed on him, but even as his breath went out in a ragged gasp of surprise, his hands were moving, finding my arms and running up them, quick as scuttling rats, to my throat. The breath for my carefully planned scream was already in my lungs. It never got out. But the worst was not the agony of my laboring lungs, nor the pain in my throat; the worst was the way the fingers moved, without ever relaxing their throttling pressure, exploring the curve of my jaw, sliding into the hollow at the base of my throat. Just before the mottled darkness swallowed me up, I heard a soft, breathy sound that might have been a laugh.

A long time later there was light—odd, streaked light that ran in narrow bright lines across a dusky gloom. My throat hurt like an abscessed tooth, except that the pain covered a broader area. It took me a long time to figure out what the light streaks must be—sunlight coming through the cracks in the shutters onto the balcony. My visitor had thoughtfully drawn the doors closed when he left.

The gaping emptiness of my suitcases told me what I already knew. Abdelal's letter was gone. The intruder had had plenty of time in which to look for it.

I thought about sitting up and decided against it. I did manage to roll over, lifting myself onto my elbows; and then I realized why the rough nap of the rug had felt so harsh against my back. My back was bare and so was my front; looking down, I could see a sizeable expanse of skin. So dim was the light and so odd the mingled effect of sunlight and shadow that it took me several incredulous moments to realize that what looked like bruises were bruises, and not shadows.

I made it to the bathroom before being sick. I'd like to think that what affected me was outraged modesty, but I suspect it was just rage. A blouse with elbow-length sleeves concealed all the marks except those on my face, which makeup covered fairly well, and the handsome set of bruises on my throat. I was contemplating those in the mirror, and seething, when there was a knock on the door and Dee's voice requested entry.

I had about thirty seconds in which to decide what to do. But as my hands automatically caught up a thin scarf and wound it around my throat, I realized that I had already made up my mind. Nothing was missing except a dirty old letter, and my dignity. The man had not intended murder; he had had half the night in which to finish me off, and he hadn't done so. As for the other bruises—well, I had no desire to destroy what was left of my self-respect by advertising those. In a way, I had brought them on myself, and I was lucky to have gotten off as easily as I had.

Dee called again, more peremptorily. I stuffed the ends of the scarf into the *V* of my blouse and staggered to the door.

I guess I looked worse than I realized. After one startled glance Dee stepped back, nearly losing her crutches.

"What happened to you?"

"I ran into a door," I said unimaginatively, and then stopped, appalled at the sound of my voice. It was cracked and hoarse, as if I had a sore throat. Which I certainly did.

"Come on in," I went on, inspired by my croaks. "Sounds funny, doesn't it? Must have had a nightmare. I woke up all of a sudden, jumped out of bed, and crashed into the edge of the bathroom door. Cut my lip, and knocked myself out. I was lying there in the draft from the window half the night. Now I've caught a terrible cold."

Dee's skeptical grin faded as I developed my extemporaneous drama, which sounded, I must say, fairly convincing. I almost believed it myself.

"Geeze, Tommy, I'm sorry. I came in to ask you if you wanted to go to Karnak with us, but you look like you ought to be in bed. Maybe you oughta see a doctor."

"That's okay. But I think I'll skip Karnak."

"Had any breakfast?"

I repressed a shudder.

"No."

"Listen, I'm not kidding, you need to eat, especially with a cold. Get back in bed and I'll have them send something up. Want me to help you undress?"

That I definitely did not want. But the incident left me feeling more kindly toward Dee. Unlike some people I could mention she did seem to have a heart under her rough exterior.

By evening my hatred of that hotel room verged on the maniacal. I had fought too many battles in the shabby room—and lost every damned one of them. The latest conflict, being purely physical, was less annihilating than the successive shocks which had destroyed the memories I lived on, but it was the last straw that was going to break this camel's back. Morbidly contemplating my black-and-blue neck and my swollen lower lip in the mirror over the dresser, I said aloud,

"Tomorrow. Tomorrow I'm leaving."

I hadn't locked the door. The corridor outside was filled with people—waiters, guests, chambermaids. I wanted them to be able to get in, fast, if I needed them. But I didn't want the one who now appeared, without so much as a knock.

"Walked into a door, eh?" said John.

I backed up, clutching the collar of my blouse.

"What is this, a delegation?" I demanded. "Damn you, Dee—you told him."

"Don't blame her," Bloch said, closing the door behind himself. He was the last of the crowd, which, naturally, included Mike. "Dee told me and I told John. I didn't like the sound of it, after yesterday."

John's hand swept across the light switches, flicking on the whole lot—overhead, bedside table, dressing table. Ordinarily he moved like a lumbering bear. I forgot that he could, if necessary, cover ground with the smooth speed of a cat. He was beside me before I could retreat, hands on my wrists, pulling them away from my throat. The loosened collar fell back.

"Jee-sus," said Dee, impressed.

"You shut up," I told her.

John's hands continued to move with a firm efficiency that foiled my feeble attempts to brush them off. His face hadn't changed an iota; it still didn't change as he folded my blouse back from my shoulders like a doctor examining a patient.

"Take a look at that," he said calmly, addressing Mike over his shoulder.

His hands and his face were as impersonal as his voice. It was Mike's face—reddening, horrified—that shook me out of my momentary stupor. Mike's face, and the memory of those other bruises, as explicit as a paragraph out of a book. I struck out at John's hands and turned my back on the circle of gaping faces.

"Pack her stuff," said John, behind me. He was close, but he didn't touch me. If he had, I would have bitten him.

For once Mike didn't move to obey the boss's lightest request.

"Good God," he said. "Tommy . . . Who was it?"

"Don't know," I said.

"Did he—did he attack you?"

John's snort blew the hair away from my neck.

"Obviously," he said dryly. "What you mean is, did he rape her? That I wouldn't know. Tommy?"

"You skunk," I said, wishing I could use a

more emphatic word, but fearing I might shock Mr. Bloch. "No, as a matter of fact, he didn't! Too bad, isn't it?"

"You young devil," Bloch said coldly. My jaw dropped with a thud when I realized he was addressing John. "Stop harassing the girl. Tommy, honey, sit down and tell us what happened."

"What happened is only too obvious." John's narrowed eyes took in the suitcases, which I had not repacked. "What was he after, Tommy? Did he get it? He must have; he had plenty of time, after choking you—"

"Cut it out, John." This time, incredibly, it was Mike who stopped the inquisition. "I don't give a damn what Tommy has, or had, or whether she still has it. I want to know who this guy was. I suppose it was dark, Tommy? Did you get any impression at all? His height, for instance?"

He knelt down by the chair and took my hand. His hand was big and hard and warm; I found its clasp very pleasant. Even more pleasant was the bulk of his body between me and John, whose glare now included his erstwhile stooge as well as me.

"I don't know," I said. "Size is deceptive, especially in the dark and under those conditions. When you're being strangled, I mean."

"How about the other senses? Smell, for instance. Did you smell tobacco, hair oil, tooth-paste—anything?"

"No," I said, trying to remember.

"Touch, then," Mike said patiently. "Did you feel his hands? His hair? His clothes?"

"Clothes . . . Mike, you ought to be a cop. He wasn't wearing native clothing."

"He must have been. Some local thief—"

"No, I'd have felt the folds of a robe, especially on his arms. They were bare, at least to the elbow. And, Mike—Mike, I must have marked his wrists. I clawed at his hands, with my nails."

John chose that precise moment to let his arms drop to his sides. Mike's body concealed the right half of John's, but the latter's left forearm was in full view, close to my eyes. His hand was balled into a tight fist; the scratches on his wrist made a lacy network of red lines.

"No," I said, in spite of myself. "Oh, no."

"No, what?" John stared at me. "Quit stalling, Tommy. Pack your stuff."

"No."

"Would you rather stay here next to that handy balcony and have your boyfriend come back tonight to finish his business?"

The thought had occurred to me, but it sounded worse when he said it.

"But he got the letter," I said, and bit my lip in annoyance as I realized I had slipped.

"Abdelal's letter? That's what I thought." John scowled. "But that wasn't the business to which I was referring. Burglars don't strangle. Mostly they run like hell when disturbed, being timid souls. At least," he added reflectively, "all the burglars I know here in Luxor do. I'm surprised he— What did you do, jump him?"

"You have a pretty low opinion of my intelligence, don't you?"

"Well, yes. Come now, Tommy, he came to burgle, it's unlikely that he'd bother you unless you provoked him. The trouble is, once he's gotten a taste he may come back for more."

Bloch made a protesting sound, and John turned on him.

"For Christ's sake, let's not be so mealy-mouthed. Maybe I've got a low, vulgar mind, but it's apparent that our unknown friend has too. If Tommy wants to stay here and take a chance . . . she can damn well forget it. She's coming with me."

He put out a peremptory hand; and then, at long last, he saw what I had been staring at. I guess everyone else saw it too. He jerked, literally, as if someone had hit him.

"You don't think . . . Tommy, you remember when that happened . . ."

I began to laugh, and it wasn't just over-wrought nerves.

"I remember," I gurgled. "But maybe you'd better not explain. It might—it might create an unfavorable impression."

"He's right," Dee said suddenly. "Tommy, you can't stay here—and I won't, either! No, Daddy, I won't! If that—that creature comes back tonight and Tommy isn't here . . . I'm right next door, you could get from Tommy's balcony to mine . . . oh, my God! Daddy . . ."

"Now, baby," Bloch said feebly, patting her. "Now, baby."

"I don't blame her," Mike remarked. "How about it, John?"

"Oh, what the hell!" John's eyes rolled heaven-ward. "The more the merrier. Tommy, if what's-her-name comes along, will you feel safer? You, too, Sam, you can protect all the girls, I don't give a damn who comes, but let's go! Mike, shut Tommy up and get her out of here; that silly giggling is going to turn to hysterics any minute!"

Chapter 5

There were no ghosts in the Institute. Not even Jake's. I had been sure I would feel his presence, slim and elegant even in his khaki work clothes, one eyebrow raised in the quizzical expression I remembered too well. But he was gone, as if he had never been—as if he had been exorcised by the silent condemnation of his peers.

I didn't know whether to be relieved or sorry.

Trouble started almost at once. As usual, it was all John's fault.

I had anticipated his purpose: to concentrate every possible facility on an all-out search for the tomb. It was his way of going about it that caused the difficulty. Instead of taking the rest of the staff into his confidence, or, alternatively, finding some plausible excuse for interrupting the planned season's work, he dropped his arbitrary announcement like a bomb, into the middle of breakfast the morning after I arrived: He was taking most of the workmen, and hiring new ones, for a detailed survey of the western mountains. Only one project would continue, the clearing of a noble's tomb at Gurnah, but the two junior members of the staff would have to manage it without Mike, who had been supervising them.

The junior members were graduate students who were getting their first field experience. One of them, Al Schneider, was a placid redhead who read excavation reports even at the breakfast table; he tore himself away from a fascinating study of pottery types just long enough to nod vaguely. Mark Rosen, the other boy, was a horse of a different color. A short, stocky youngster with an engaging grin, he wore enormous horn-rimmed glasses which magnified bright brown eyes. He reminded me of a squirrel: brisk, bouncy, and curious; and the flash of speculation in those big brown eyes, when John made his announcement, gave me a qualm.

I'm sure it was Mark who started the rumors. By evening the place was buzzing with them, and even the staff photographer, a dreamy man who spent the winter reading seed catalogs and planning the garden he would plant when he got home, got Dee off in a corner and tried to pump her. He got nowhere, but only because her interest in the tomb was purely perfunctory.

We had guests for dinner, members of an archaeological commission from Europe, who had been invited weeks before and couldn't be put off. John greeted them with less than his usual charm, which means not much charm; he was completely preoccupied by his private thoughts, and his behavior, as much as anything else, fed Mark's growing suspicions.

So maybe it was extrasensory perception instead of accident which prompted Mark to start that memorable discussion.

"Have you seen the latest autopsy report on Akhenaton?" he asked one of the visitors, a bearded professor from Heidelberg.

From Dee's expression I could tell that she thought Akhenaton was a recent murder victim—an Ay-rab, maybe, or a Chinaman. The rest of us, who knew that Akhenaton was, among other things, the husband of Nefertiti, jumped like nervous panthers. Mike, who had been staring blankly into his bean soup, poured a steaming spoonful into his lap and had to pretend that a mosquito had stung him. When that sensation quieted down, Mark repeated his question. Unfortunately, he did not receive a polite, disinterested reply. He had flushed a fanatic.

I don't know why it is, but Akhenaton starts more arguments than any other person or thing in Egyptology. Kindly scholars who would never fight about religion or politics or personal matters get purple in the face over the activities of a man who has been dead for three thousand years. Was Akhenaton's new religion really monotheism, an idea which is usually credited to the Hebrews? Why do his statues and painted portraits show him with such a peculiar shape? Did he actually marry his own daughter and beget a child on her? Was he queer for his son-in-law? And—the question Mark had now raised— was the skeleton found in the strange little tomb in the Valley of the Kings that of the "heretic Pharaoh," or of somebody else?

As far as the professor from Heidelberg was concerned, those bones were Akhenaton's, and nobody, not even a surgeon, was going to tell him they weren't. He produced a lot of learned arguments, most of them unintelligible because his mounting passion wrecked his feeble English, but that's what it came down to in the end—a matter of faith.

Then he appealed to the distinguished *Herr Direktor*; and the expression on John's face almost made me lose control of myself. I knew his opinions; he had never believed that the bones were those of Nefertiti's husband, and the most recent postmortem (very post indeed) had confirmed his belief. But he didn't want to enflame his visitor by disagreeing with him, because if the argument got out of hand, someone might blurt out something about Nefertiti. He wanted to change the subject, but he didn't know how; so he just sat there nodding like a mandarin, with a ghastly smile on his face and his eyes darting rapidly from me to Dee to Mike.

"Surely," I said, moved by pure mischief, "you must agree, *Herr Professor*, that the doctor who examined the bones couldn't be mistaken about the age of the individual. If the man was only twenty-three when he died, he couldn't have been Akhenaton, unless he fathered a child when he was eight years old."

Five minutes later half the people at the table were yelling back and forth at each other.

"How can you call it monotheism?" Mike demanded, ignoring John's piercing glare. "He made the people worship *him*, not his god Aton."

"There is no way to the Father but through Me," I misquoted, loud and clear. I hadn't in-

tended to be irreverent, but Mike gave me the
sort of look Luther must have bestowed on the
Pope, or vice versa, if they ever did meet. From
one of the visiting firemen, a Jesuit priest who was
one of the world's leading authorities on biblical
archaeology, came a quickly subdued chuckle.

Luckily the service was fast that night, and we
got through dessert before John had an apoplec-
tic fit. He got us out of the dining room so fast we
made a perceptible breeze.

Later, when the conspirators met in John's
study for a discussion on Ways and Means, John
suggested that we avoid Akhenaton as a topic of
conversation for a while. His stare indicated that
he held me solely responsible for the argument,
so I countered by accusing him of unnecessary
mystification.

"That boy Mark is already suspicious," I
warned him. "And I'll bet the village grapevine
is vibrating like fury. The men of Gurnah have a
positive instinct for secrets, especially for hidden
tombs."

John poured himself a drink from the bottle of
Scotch which sat in splendid isolation on a corner of his desk—his sole concession to the "cock-
tails with the Director" routine.

"So what?" he said inelegantly. "Granting that
you're probably correct, there isn't a damn thing

we can do about it—except find the tomb ourselves before one of the local geniuses beats us
to it."

I reached for the bottle. John absently slid it
out from under my hand and put it down on the
far side of the desk.

"Get me drunk," I suggested. "Maybe I'll start
to babble."

"What was in Abdelal's letter?" John waved
the bottle in front of me like a carrot before a
balky mule.

"Good wishes, reminiscences about the good
old days. I don't care all that much for Scotch.
Try me with gin."

"God damn it!" John slammed the bottle
down so hard that a wave of amber liquid
sloshed out the top. Mike, with a reproving look,
snatched the precious thing out of John's hand.

"If you do have any bright ideas, Tommy, I
wish you'd speak up," he said mildly. "We're sitting here bright-eyed and bushy-tailed and rar-
ing to go. The only trouble is we don't know
where to go."

"Why not?" asked Dee.

"The territory is too big, Dee. We don't even
know the general location."

"I should think that would be obvious," said
Dee.

Four heads turned to stare.

"Obvious?" said Mike weakly.

"Sure." Dee batted her eyelashes at him and smiled. "This is a queen's tomb, right? Well, on the map there's a place called the Valley of the Queens. So what's the problem?"

Four heads drooped.

"Gee," Mike muttered. "For a minute there, I thought maybe . . . Look, baby. There are queens' tombs in the Valley of the Queens. Very bright of you to figure it out. But this one won't be there."

"Why not?"

"It's the wrong period," John answered, his eyes oddly intent on her pouting face. "The tombs in the Valley of the Queens are later."

"Then how about the Valley of the Kings?" said Dee brightly.

I didn't know whether to laugh or swear. It was John who laughed, and not at Dee; I was the source of his innocent merriment.

"Tommy, if you could see your face . . . Tell the girl how about the Valley of the Kings."

"In the first place, every stone in the darned Valley has been turned over a hundred times. In the second place the burials there are mostly of kings, not queens."

"Well, now," Mike said, absentmindedly embracing the bottle of Scotch and rocking slightly in his absorption, "it's possible that some queens of that dynasty were buried in their husbands' tombs. Amenhotep III—"

"Oh, let's not start another of those interminable archaeological arguments about nothing! This queen certainly wasn't buried in her husband's tomb, because his tomb is two hundred miles away from here. She can't be buried in the Valley of the Queens because it wasn't used for tombs until—when, Nineteenth Dynasty?—later, in any case. We can't extrapolate from other Eighteenth Dynasty queens' tombs, because the few that have been found are scattered all over the cliffs. There was one up on—"

I stopped, realizing that John was staring at me. The ends of his moustache were vibrating madly. So he thought I'd get carried away and divulge my supposed secret, did he? I clamped my lips shut and stared back at him.

"That's right, Tommy," Mike said obliviously. "The damn thing could be anywhere, anywhere in ten square miles. John, where do you plan to start looking?"

"Hmph," said John. He took the bottle away from Mike and planted it on the desk to pin down one corner of the map he had unrolled. A heavy book pinned down another corner, and there were plenty of eager hands to do the rest of the job. We all gathered around the desk. My eyes were intent on the map, but they had a more precise focus than the others. I was looking at the names. The result, as I had expected, was negative. There was no "Place of Milk."

"Somewhere in this area," said John, and his pen drew a bold black curve across the upper left corner of the map. "Between the Valley of the Queens and the end of the main Valley of the Kings. Even that's just a guess, but we've got to start somewhere. It doesn't look like a great amount of territory, and, in fact, the distance as the crow flies is less than a mile. But the thing we're looking for is only a few feet square. And, don't forget, it is concealed so well that it escaped discovery for thousands of years. One small opening, two feet, maybe, by three . . . and how many hundreds of thousands of square feet of rock to search? If we had a clue to the general area—one particular valley, one section of cliff—then we would have a fighting chance."

Mike glanced up at him.

"Where were Jake's haunts?"

"In the hotels on the other side of the river," John said briefly. "That won't work, Mike. I remember quite well what Jake was doing that year. I had him copying texts at the Ramesseum, and he hated it like hell."

I stared at the map in a silence that smoldered, and there was an awkward pause. After a moment John went on, "Jake's movements are irrelevant. I don't believe for a minute that he was the original discoverer of the tomb."

"You're right," Bloch drawled. "I thought of that one myself."

"Jake wasn't a hiker," John explained. "Whereas Abdelal knew every foot of the region. He came from Gurnah, where the instinct for buried treasure is almost a sixth sense. Did you know he claimed to be related to the Abderrassul family?"

"The boys that found the royal mummies back in the last century?" Bloch's eyes were alight with interest.

"And the mass burial of the High Priests of Amon a few years later. These Gurnah families have something, they've made too many discoveries for coincidence. I don't believe in ancestral memory, so I suppose their success is based on family tradition and detailed knowledge of the terrain. In any case, I'm sure Abdelal was the finder of the tomb."

"Funny," Mike mused. "Abdelal's behavior, I mean. You would expect him either to peddle the stuff himself or report it to us officially. Instead he went privately to Jake. Why?"

"Jake's famous charm," John suggested, with an unpleasant curl of the lip.

"Oh, you're all so complacent and logical," I said, glowering at John. "None of you understand how Egyptians think."

"And you do?" Mike asked, a little too respectfully.

"Well, I was still a child when I knew Abdelal. A child's mind is more flexible than an adult's; it can comprehend different points of view more readily. I understood the old village traditions—suspicion of strangers, loyalty to the family and the community, and an amused contempt for crazy archaeologists who think antiquities belong in museums. That was Abdelal's background, and it was strong. But on top of his old habits he had forty years of archaeological training, which denied the village values."

"Go on," John said.

"Okay, so in this one man we find two equally powerful but contradictory viewpoints. Under ordinary circumstances there was no real conflict. But when a treasure trove did turn up, the poor guy's old instincts rose up, screaming. By the village tradition a find like the one he made was loot, wealth beyond the wildest dreams, wealth that belonged, by their standards, to the men of Gurnah. By Abdelal's new mores, the tomb was an archaeological discovery, the possession of all the people of Egypt. I wonder how many years ago he found the tomb? How many years did he hesitate and argue with himself?"

"Poor devil," Bloch muttered. "So finally he went to Jake—as a compromise?"

"I think that was it. A compromise. He liked and trusted Jake; what Jake said, he would do. And when Jake . . . when Jake voted in favor of the old village tradition, Abdelal wouldn't fight it. After Jake died, the conflict was again unresolved. So Abdelal, not knowing what to do, did . . . nothing. I don't think it's at all surprising."

"Cogent," said John, "but not particularly helpful."

"I wouldn't say that," Bloch objected. "You talk about family and village loyalties. Surely, if a clue exists, it must be in the minds of the old man's relatives and friends."

"If that's the only place where it exists, we'll never find it," John said. "The other villagers don't suffer from any conflicts."

"How about Achmed?"

"Well—he might tell us. He's a chip off the old block; has his father's intelligence and interest in excavation . . ."

"He might make a good headman one day," Bloch suggested.

John gave him an odd look.

"He might make a good archaeologist one day. I'm trying to talk him into going to the university next year."

"I thought you had convinced him," Mike said.

"I thought so too. Lately he's been behaving peculiarly." John chewed meditatively on the stem of his pipe. "I wish I knew what's on his mind . . . No, Sam, I don't think it's the tomb, not in the way you're thinking. That box Abdelal left for Tommy hadn't been opened. Which suggests that Achmed is not only unwitting, he's honest as well. The further conclusion is that if Abdelal didn't confide in his own trusted son, he didn't tell anybody."

This time I was expecting it. When the glare, and the question, came, I had my answer ready.

"Damn it, Tommy, what was in that letter?"

"Good wishes and reminiscences," I said sweetly, "of the good old days."

Out in the courtyard the shadows were like black velvet laced with silver strips of moonlight. The jasmine on the inner walls was in bloom; the sweet, heavy scent filled the night and the white blossoms were pale blurs in the darkness.

I should have been up in my room with the door locked and bolted, but I couldn't endure the confinement just then. The conference in John's office had ended in a discussion of where to start work next morning. It had been a long discussion. Dee dropped off to sleep in the middle of it. She snored. Mike seemed to think it was cute, and I guess she did have an appeal of sorts, curled up in the big leather chair with her mouth hanging open and her blond hair tumbled.

I produced a few yawns myself as the argument waxed hotter and, to a nonexpert, fairly unintelligible. Between them John and Mike discussed every square meter of a ten-mile stretch of cliffs, suggesting possibilities and disagreeing with each other's suggestions. Bloch had quite a bit to contribute too. He hadn't the figure for exploring, but he had evidently read voluminously, and he kept quoting obscure travel books of the past century which mentioned caves and tombs. Every time he said something, Mike or John or both would counter with, "That was the Amenhotep II tomb," or "That's in the Valley of the Kings, no use looking there," or some other discouraging remark. Finally, though, they all agreed on a general area in which to start looking, and the conference broke up.

I don't know why I stayed. Though John's attention was ostensibly focused on the map, I knew he was studying me the whole time. I don't know what he expected—that I would suddenly leap to my feet and shriek, "I confess! I'll tell you where to look!"

I didn't. Partly because I didn't know. But I realized that John sensed the reservations that lay beneath my rude wisecracks, and as I walked slowly around the deserted court, raising a hanging cluster of flowers to my nostrils from time to time, I was genuinely troubled as to what to do.

The mention of Nefertiti in Abdelal's letter had not been accidental. Feeling his years, and realizing the uncertainty of fate, the old man had tried to tell me something that would give me the vital hint and yet be meaningless to anyone else.

He had succeeded in half his purpose—which is about average as human intentions work out. The hint was meaningless to a third party. I was pretty certain of that, because it was meaningless to me as well.

The day I pretended I was the great Queen Nefertiti . . . Did that refer to a specific day and a specific place, or was it just a way of introducing that vitally significant name? I rather thought the first alternative was the correct one. The mention of the oddly named "Place of Milk" confirmed my hunch.

The name wasn't on any of the maps; I had checked several. So it must not be a proper name at all. It must be a name Abdelal and I had given to a particular spot, but it couldn't be one of our permanent nicknames or I would remember it. No, it had to be a passing reference, maybe a joke, made once and then forgotten—by me. Abdelal had good reason for remembering it. Near or on the same spot he had found his tomb—the "ultimate object of every Egyptologist's secret dreams," as John called it.

Good for me, I thought. I reason like a logician. But it didn't bring me any closer to an answer.

All it brought me to was another question: Did I really want an answer?

Consciously I didn't give a damn—I told myself—whether anyone ever found the lost tomb. I was no archaeologist; in fact, I had a number of good reasons for hating the profession and everyone in it, even better reasons for wiping the whole business out of my mind—tombs, treasures, tomb-robbing, Egypt.

Subconsciously? I didn't like exploring that boggy terrain, but I was honest enough to admit one of the less attractive motives that moved me.

John wanted to find the tomb. I hated John, hated him all the more because he had been right and I had been insanely wrong, because I had done him a grave injustice and he had tried, in his clumsy way, to help me. So I was doing all I could, not to actively prevent him from finding his precious tomb, but to avoid contributing to his success.

It was possible that my little scrap of information was as useless to the rest of them as it was to me. But there was a remote chance that the allusion, now lost to me, might mean something to an old acquaintance whose memory was not fogged by unpleasant obsessions. It was also time to start fighting those obsessions, not only because I owed John fair play, at least, but because my treatment of him diminished me as a human being. I didn't have to crawl to him, as if in tacit apology. I could tell Mike. Mike had turned out to be rather a nice guy. Mike didn't—

"How sweet the moonlight sleeps on yonder bank," said his voice, right behind me; a spray of jasmine tickled my nose.

"What bank?" I said, recovering myself, and removing the flowers from my right nostril. "If that's the sort of thing you tell all the girls, they must be pretty dim."

"It's not what I say, it's how I say it."

I turned with deliberate casualness, to find him looming. His teeth made a dim gleam in the shadow of his face. Then the gleam faded, and he said gravely,

"I got worried when I couldn't find you. You shouldn't be out alone, Tommy."

"The gates are locked at night. At least they used to be."

"They still are. But they won't protect you from . . ."

I peered up at his face, wishing it weren't so shadowed and so high up. I would like to have seen his expression.

"From somebody who is already inside?" I said, completing his statement; and he confirmed my guess by his silence.

"Mike, do you think . . ."

"No," he said, too quickly. "Tommy. Those marks on John's wrists . . . you don't really believe . . ."

"You're contradicting yourself. If John is your big hero, you ought not need to ask questions."

"I'm not. Only . . . You surely can't suspect him of being the thief last night."

"No," I said, thinking aloud. "Not because he wouldn't be a thief if he felt it expedient, but because sneaking isn't his style. To begin with, he'd be too damned efficient to wake me up scuffling around in the dark. And if he had, he wouldn't be distracted by anything so trivial as my femaleness. And finally, if that trivial detail *had* interested him . . ."

Mike grinned reluctantly.

"You wouldn't have just a few bruises as souvenirs. I agree with all your remarks. Then why don't you—"

"Trust John? Darned if I know. But there's something . . . just the way he looks at me, sometimes . . . I don't trust you, either," I added. "If that's any consolation."

"I don't blame you," he said morosely. "Just try to believe one thing, Tommy. I admire John; he's probably the finest excavator alive, one of the best of all time. But if he were involved in any dirty work, I'd be the first to turn him in. Especially if the dirty work threatened you."

"Thanks."

"You don't believe me?"

"I wish I could . . ."

"You're shivering," he said, and took a step toward me.

"Who wouldn't?" I said, and took a step back. "With all the horrors you keep suggesting . . ."

He took another step, but I couldn't retreat any farther. My back was literally up against the wall; the stems of the jasmine prickled through my thin blouse, and the smell of the darned stuff was as dizzying as (they tell me) airplane glue. Mike put out his arms and gathered me in.

I had been kissed before, but this was on an entirely different plane. This wasn't just expertise, it was fine art. He knew exactly what to do—the small movements of his lips, the skilled fingers exploring that certain area between my shoulder blades that I hadn't even been aware of myself, the precise degree of pressure of arms and mouth. When he lifted his head, I would have dribbled down between his feet like a strand of wet spaghetti if he hadn't continued to hold me.

"Bench," I said, after a while.

"Shame on you."

"I just want to sit down."

He dragged me over to the nearest bench, which happened to be in a particularly dark corner of the courtyard.

"Now," he said, his lips against my hair, "I start insinuating sly, leading questions."

"Like that old chestnut: What was in the letter?"

"Right."

"You're too expert, Mike," I said, trying to hide the fact that I had to breathe between almost every word. "I thought archaeologists were sober souls, dedicated to dead bones."

The arm around my ribs tightened so suddenly that my breath came out in a squawk.

"I can understand why John wants to throttle you periodically."

"Everybody else does, why not you?"

"I'll tell you why not. Because you're so damned pathetic. Oh, no, you don't, you stay right here where I can keep my hands on you. I'm not insulting you, in fact I find you rather admirable, in your own crude way. At least you don't whine and whimper about what happened to you. You try to fight back. If you feel sorry for yourself, you don't expect other people to feel sorry for you. But, my dear girl, you can't fight this problem with smart remarks. And, while I am at present suffering from an insane urge to defend you against all comers, I'm too old and self-conscious to go galloping around the desert like Rudolph Valentino. You've got to protect yourself. Secrets are only dangerous while they are secret."

"But the letter's gone. Whoever took it knows what's in it."

"You know what's in it too. Look, Tommy, you aren't the only one who claims to understand the Arab mind. Abdelal would never have told you anything directly. He'd try to be clever—he'd hint, maybe through some personal reference

that only the two of you would understand . . .
Ha—hit the bull's-eye, didn't I?"

"Let go of me! You've got a nerve, hugging me
so you can feel my reactions. I refuse to be my
own lie detector."

"Quit wriggling and shut up." He kissed me
again, just enough to stun me, and continued
calmly.

"If the old man did leave one of those enig-
matic clues, you're in worse trouble than I
thought. For God's sake, Tommy, do you want to
be dragged off into some cave in the hills and in-
terrogated? If you're not scared, I am!"

"But it didn't mean anything," I muttered. "I
didn't understand it myself."

He didn't argue anymore—at least, not ver-
bally. The evening's entertainment produced
two results. One was my realization, at a particular point in the proceedings, that whoever the
Midnight Intruder had been, he certainly was
not Mike. The second result was probably inevitable. Actually, I had almost made up my
mind to tell him anyhow.

"This is the hottest goddamn country I've ever
been in," said Dee with her usual elegance.

I hated to agree with her, but the perspiration
flowing down my chin was agreement enough.

The sun was almost directly overhead, and the bare rock, bleached bone-white by sunlight, seemed to give off heat like a grill. I knew just how a broiling pork chop must feel.

"At least we're in the shade," I said.

The shade came, as might be expected, from a rock. There was nothing else around except more rocks, and no color except that of the brilliant blue sky above and the little bouquets of red and yellow and green made by the skullcaps of the workers.

They were scattered out over a wide area, much of it perpendicular—checking crevices and rock surfaces on the sides of a little canyon, or wadi, near the Valley of the Queens. There is a road of sorts leading to this valley, which was why Dee was with me, cast and all. Once the crew moved back into wilder country, she would have to stay home, and I wished to heaven she had stayed at home today.

"I'm gonna die," she groaned.

"Why the Hades did you come? You didn't have to."

"I was bored. There isn't a thing to do around that place. I thought this would be exciting."

"Here comes Mike," I said. "Maybe you'll find him more exciting."

I was chagrined to find myself craning forward as eagerly as she to follow the progress of the long lanky figure that had detached itself from a cluster of white-robed workmen and was loping up the slope toward our rock. Thanks to Mr. Bloch, we had an ample supply of cold drinks and an insulated chest to keep them in. I suspected, though, that rest and refreshment were not all Mike had in mind.

He flopped down, with his long legs stretched out for yards, and grinned impartially at both of us.

"Hot," he said.

"You poor boy, out in that broiling sun!" I hope I need not explain that this remark came from Dee. She fussed over him, pouring him a glass of water, and mopping his brow with her lace-edged handkerchief. I pretended great interest in the activities below while all this was going on; but I was absurdly aware of every small movement of his body—the rise and fall of his chest with his quick breathing, the beat of the pulse at the base of his tanned throat, the contraction of minor muscles on the back of his hand. It was the first time I had really seen him—except for a casual and public good-morning—since our impromptu rendezvous in the courtyard.

Dee showered him with idiotic questions, which he answered patiently, and I wondered whether he had passed on to John the tidbit I had given him the night before. He had been as baffled by it as I, but I felt sure he would trot off to his boss with it all the same, like a good dog with a bone. I also wondered whether he would tell John how he had extracted the information. Probably. Men loved to brag about their conquests, and that had been a conspicuous triumph, after my consistent refusals to talk. I thought he hadn't kissed me only to get me to talk, I suspected he had enjoyed it. That would have boosted my ego more if I hadn't felt sure he enjoyed kissing all women.

I didn't regret the incident, nor my pliability. I had been on the verge of telling the truth anyway and Mike's arguments had been singularly persuasive—and I don't mean the indirect argument, I mean the blunt statement that candor might save my life. The only thing I regretted was that I hadn't spoken up before he kissed me.

I sneaked a side glance at him. His profile was admirable. I have a weakness for long, straight noses and prominent chins. He had a pleasant voice too.

"That group in the northern section?" he was saying, in response to Dee's last question. "Yes, they are digging. That's loose rock and gravel, possibly from the big tomb entrance above. We thought maybe the rock might cover another entrance. Probably not, but we've got to check."

I followed his pointing finger, and felt myself stiffen. Amid the dull, omnipresent black-and-white stripes, one patch of color stood out like a shout. As if the focus of my gaze had been audible, the bright shirt and the man who wore it moved away from the other workers and came toward us.

"That's Hassan—Abdelal's son." I clutched at Mike's arm.

"Hey." Dee squinted, shading her eyes with her hand. "He's good-looking. How come he isn't dressed like the others?"

"He appreciates our fine American costumes," said Mike dryly, brushing sand off his sand-colored shirt.

"What's he doing here?" I demanded. "Don't tell me he's trained for this sort of work."

"He's not trained, nor inclined, for any sort of work," Mike said. "But we need all the help we can get, and he picked up a certain amount of technique helping his father when he was a kid."

"But, Mike—I think he—"

"Are you sure?" Mike caught my meaning at once, with an insight which made me think he had been speculating along the same lines.

"No, not to swear to. But . . ."

But I was pretty sure. The possibility had occurred to me earlier, but it wasn't until the previous night, when I realized that I could never mistake the touch of Mike's hands for that of any other man, that I remembered where I had felt a touch like that of the hands that had gripped my throat in the darkness. Hassan was now my favorite candidate for the Midnight Intruder, and, as he came up the slope toward us, smiling ingenuously, I shrank back against Mike's shoulder.

"It's all right, Tommy," Mike said softly.

"I still don't understand why you hired him."

"I wasn't keen on the idea. But John insisted."

His eyes met mine; they were grave and troubled.

"Don't let him upset you," he said.

"It's okay. He affects me the way snakes affect some people. But I could be wrong about—the other thing."

As Hassan came swinging up the slope toward us, his young body as supple as a cat's, I began to think that I was wrong. His amiable smile was no sign of innocence, for duplicity can feign charm; but at that moment he had no eyes for me. He came to a stop in front of Dee and gave her the full effect of his wide-eyed, candidly admiring stare. She stared back. You could almost hear the click.

"What is it, Hassan?" Mike demanded.

The boy started theatrically.

"There is a problem," he said in liquid accents. "If you will come, Master Director of the work—if you are now rested from your heavy labor . . ."

Sarcasm is a weapon these people use well; it is below a boss's dignity to notice the insult in an ostensible compliment. Mike was young enough to redden under his tan, but he said nothing, only unwound his legs and stood up. Hassan was in no hurry to leave.

"If the ladies would honor a poor workman . . . It is hot in the sun, and dusty . . ."

Knowing Hassan, I imagined that he had spent most of the time leaning on a shovel, but he looked very pathetic. Dee almost fell over her crutches getting him a drink of water. He made sure that his fingers brushed hers, in taking the glass and returning it; and when the two men went down the slope together, it was not the taller figure whom Dee's eyes followed. I sighed. My premonition was so strong it amounted to a notarized statement.

The premonition was slow in materializing. For a week nothing happened, except that it got hotter and hotter. I sat under a series of different rocks, whose shade did not prevent me from getting as brown as a plowed field, and I cursed John and the sun and Mike and the rocks, and wished I were back in my nice quiet room in the Institute. When I broached the idea to John, he didn't even bother to argue; he just handed me my broad-brimmed hat.

Neither man had again referred to Abdelal's letter, so I concluded that they had dismissed it as useless. And none of my efforts to recall the lost memory were successful.

One morning there was a brief flurry of excitement when a crew found a tomb entrance that was not recorded on any of the plans. It turned out to be one of a common type—a petty nobleman's tomb which had been robbed in ancient times and then reused by several generations of poorer folk. Ordinarily the staff would have been moderately interested, for after the secondary burials the tomb had not been rediscovered, and it contained a dozen coffins and collections of cheap funeral goods. The men muttered and rolled their eyes when John ordered it closed again, made a mark on his map, and moved on.

Six days after I arrived at the Institute the men were working several miles from the Valley of the Queens in a desolate wadi that looked promising—in a professional sense. Otherwise it was desolation personified, wilder and more abandoned than any spot I had ever seen. I didn't know what had prompted John to concentrate on the place, and what was more, I didn't care.

It was past noon, and near quitting time, when a shout arose from the group working across the canyon from where I sat. The quality of the sound, shrill with excitement, roused me from my heat-sodden lethargy, and I raised my head.

At this end of the wadi, where it narrowed, I was no more than thirty or forty feet from the workers, and I could see quite clearly. I spotted Hassan at once by his magenta shirt; he hadn't been working the past few days, and I wondered why he had decided to appear this morning. He was standing on the rim of the canyon, almost directly opposite my rock, and he was waving his arms and pointing down.

Whatever he saw was hidden from me; I saw only the usual rough rock face, pocked and split by darker regions of shadow. These natural irregularities made a search difficult, almost impossible; any opening might conceal a tomb entrance.

Mike was the first of the group to reach Hassan; after a prolonged stare he smacked the boy on the shoulder and turned to John. An animated conversation ensued. I could hear the voices, but I could not distinguish words; in a way it was like watching a pantomime, and my interest grew. Finally John, his silver head gleaming in the sunlight, dropped flat, with his head and shoulders precariously projecting from the crumbling rock rim of the cliff, and peered down. When he got to his feet, he seemed excited too. Another discussion followed, even more animated than the first. Mike started waving his arms, as if in protest, and John kept shaking his head.

By this time I was genuinely intrigued. They must have found something that looked promising—a hole, no doubt, which was concealed from almost all angles by outcroppings of rock. I considered going over to have a look, but it was a long hot walk around the end of the wadi. Crossing the cleft was out of the question; it was almost three hundred feet deep.

I leaned back, smiling, as the group opposite broke up into flurried activity. It always amused and touched me to see the enthusiasm which fired the workers when a hopeful find was made. They might be poor and illiterate and cheerfully crooked, but their excitement was genuine and their interest intense. A cluster of robes gathered at the cliff edge; Hassan, conspicuous in the center, was telling them all about it. I was glad I had stayed where I was; it was as good as a box seat at a play.

The only practical way of reaching the hole was from above. Someone would have to be lowered by rope. A big debate arose over the question of who was to be lowered. Personally I wouldn't have cared for the honor, especially with a bunch of volatile, enthusiastic Egyptians substituting for a sturdy tree trunk, but John and Mike almost came to blows over which of them was to be bumped and banged down the cliff.

Then Hassan, looking like a male tropical bird among the hens, strutted up to the arguing pair and interrupted them. I watched, amazed at how much of the activity I could interpret without hearing what was said. Mike turned to glare at the Egyptian boy. For once I was on Hassan's side, and I almost said so, before I realized they couldn't hear me. He was small and agile, a much better person to writhe around on the end of a rope than either of the taller, heavier, and older Americans.

Apparently nobody across the way agreed with me. In a few minutes everyone had gotten into the act; John's bare bright head and Mike's sun helmet rose up out of the middle of a cluster of agitated robes and gesticulating brown hands like towers under siege. Finally John's arms moved in a frantic gesture, like someone swatting flies, and the group scattered, still talking. Two figures remained with the Americans. One was Hassan, now radiating outraged dignity from every muscle of his stiff body. The other, wearing the usual striped robe, was his twin.

So the candidates had been narrowed down to two. It seemed to me, in my role of observer, that Hassan was better dressed for the job. The flapping skirts of the native robe should have been a handicap in rock climbing. But I had seen those robes and their wearers in action too often to be misled about that, and when John tossed the end of the rope the other men were holding to Achmed, I could see his point. If the hole did contain the long-sought tomb, Hassan could scoop up a lot of loot in a few unsupervised minutes.

Hassan may have been thinking the same thing; his first reaction to John's decision was a shrill outburst which hurt my ears even at a distance. Then, accepting the fact with better grace than I would have anticipated, he shrugged and helped his brother knot the rope around his waist.

Achmed wriggled to the edge of the cliff and let himself down. His bare toes felt for holds as deftly as fingers. Mike knelt down, his face near

Achmed's, giving the rope a last precautionary adjustment.

I leaned back, clasping my knees. John had retired to supervise the rope gang and Mike, leaning over the face of the cliff, relayed instructions. Though Achmed had, so far, been able to find support for his hands and feet, the rope had to be taut in case the soft rock gave way; even a short fall might dash the climber dangerously against the rock.

Looking like a big striped beetle with an iridescent head, Achmed crept down. He was fifty feet below the cliff edge now, and still moving. Once a rock broke away from under his left foot and went bouncing down into the valley. I caught my breath, but the grip of his hands held, and Mike's shout to the rope crew was unnecessary.

Then it happened, so fast that it was over before I could take it in. Achmed's right hand lost its grip as another rotted fragment broke away, and he threw himself sideways, out of the path of the rock that skimmed his face. The movement threw him off balance. I thanked God for the rope; and then I was on my feet, my voice echoing the scream that rang out from across the wadi. Achmed's body flailed and jerked, amid a wild fluttering of white folds; rocks roared and tumbled and raised clouds of pale dust. When the dust cleared I saw that he was still flattened against the cliff face; but the position had changed. The rope was invisible to me, but I knew where it was—and where it ended. It ended just below the boy's right hand. His right arm was stretched to its full length, his body dangled free, his left arm moved frantically over the rock searching for a handhold that wasn't there. Either the rope had broken or the knot had failed. The only thing that kept Achmed from a fall that would smash half the bones in his body was the grip of his right fist on a rope that had no knot, nor loop, to keep it from slipping through his fingers.

I took three running steps before I caught myself, knowing there was nothing I could do—nothing but watch, in the ultimate agony of helplessness. Achmed was now motionless; he knew that every movement dragged him down toward the end of the slender strand of rope. John was running toward the cliff, but he was too late. Mike hadn't waited for instructions or advice; and, as I watched him, the perspiration that soaked my body seemed to turn to ice.

He had to use the same rope, and he had to move with the delicacy of a spider on a web lest he jar the dangling figure from its finger-touch on life.

I couldn't even scream. It seemed to me that the slightest vibration might fracture the strained air and shake both figures off the invisible strand of rope. I stared at Achmed as if the intensity of a glance could hold him fast. One hand was at my throat, and then I understood the meaning of that seemingly foolish, theatrical gesture, because I couldn't get air into my lungs, I felt as if every breath sucked in some heavy liquid instead of air.

Mike's booted feet were just above Achmed's head, and the most dangerous part of the job was upon him—how to get low enough to grab Achmed without losing his own grasp on the rope. I didn't see how on earth he was going to manage it. Achmed was now completely motionless; even his left arm dangled like an empty sack.

For what seemed an eternity the two figures hung, still as paintings against the rock wall of a tomb. A voice which was almost unrecognizable as my own was pouring out a low unpunctuated stream of words which were meant to be prayers, though they probably sounded more like imprecations. My teeth sank into my lower lip; and at that same moment Mike made his move. He folded at the waist like a hinged doll, his long arm stretching down till his fingers could close over the boy's wrist. As he bent, the sun helmet fell off his head and bounced down two hundred feet in a ghastly series of bumps and thuds.

Achmed, still limp as a dead man, was saved for the moment, but their position was fearfully precarious. Mike's grip on the rope was secure enough, but he was bent over at an acute angle, his arm dragged down by Achmed's weight. From that position it would take a Hercules to straighten up, pulling the boy with the muscles of only one arm.

I closed my eyes so I wouldn't see them fall. But it was impossible not to look. When I opened them again the sun dazzled so that I was temporarily blind.

I saw John first, standing on the edge of the cliff, hands on his hips, peering down. His pose looked relaxed and nonchalant, despite the fact that his toes must have protruded over the rim, and it infuriated me so much that I let out the scream I had been suppressing.

He looked in my direction; and then, with a sort of shrug, he dropped down and slid carelessly over the rim.

I yelled again, this time with outrage and protest. His arrogance had never been more apparent; obviously he felt that he could cope with the situation barehanded and single-handed. All he would accomplish, in fact, was to send three bodies crashing down onto the rocks instead of two.

He moved too quickly, too carelessly for a man with no visible means of support. Chunks of rock snapped under his sliding hands and feet, narrowly missing Mike's head down below. John's course was parallel to the rope but ten feet or more away from it. Mike hadn't moved. I don't suppose he could have moved without losing his grip. The angle between his torso and his twined legs seemed sharper, as if he were being pulled down.

Within seconds John had reached a point on the same level as Achmed, but he was too far away to reach him. He put the sole of one boot against the cliff face and shoved himself out into space.

That was how it looked from where I stood. I saw his arms and legs straighten out and go stiff, his body twist, in midair, so that it fell almost parallel to the edge of the cliff. I tried to close my eyes again. The lids were glued open. My legs folded and I sat down, jarringly, on a jagged piece of rock. I didn't feel it. Everything went slow, slower than a movie film run at half speed. It reminded me of a movie, one of those old silent films of Harold Lloyd, or Chaplin, or somebody, caught in a hilarious, impossible position on top of a skyscraper, dangling by his toes.

Then the sequence of time speeded up, and I saw, too late for satisfaction, what the maniac was trying to do. He did it, too. His body swung back at the end of its arc and smacked into the cliff at a spot right below Achmed. As the boy's right arm fell loose, torn from Mike's numbed clasp, John's arms closed around his body. The jar sent them both swinging madly for a few seconds, but they were safe.

I got up. I started walking toward the end of the wadi. I was staggering like a drunk. By the time I reached the other side they were all back on top, sitting on the ground and grinning feebly at each other, the way people do when a crisis has passed, beyond reasonable hope, without disaster. Achmed was green in the face. As I came up, he tumbled over and lay flat. However, his eyes were open, and I guess he just wanted to feel solid ground under as much of him as possible. John, still attached to a long strand of rope, leaned over and started moving the boy's arms up and down.

"Feel anything?"

"Yes. All right," Achmed said faintly.

"It's a miracle you didn't tear a muscle," John said, prodding the boy's chest and shoulders. "God, it must be great to be eighteen. You're intact, Achmed. In the name of God, the Merciful, the Compassionate."

There was a pious murmur of agreement from the men gathered around, a murmur in which I joined.

John abandoned his patient with an encouraging grin and a light jab in the ribs, and turned to Mike.

"Anything broken?"

"Just my nerve." Mike mopped sweat and dust off his face with the tattered remains of his right sleeve. "And my shirt. The shoulder seam let loose, when I grabbed for Achmed."

"John's is in worse condition," I said slowly. "The front is all . . ."

John turned his back and began working at the rope which still dangled from his waist.

"Cut it off, for Pete's sake," I said, beginning to shake. "Let's get away from this ghastly place."

"In a minute." John called out a set of directions in Arabic to Feisal Reis, the headman, and walked back toward the cliff.

I opened my mouth. Then I closed it. I sat

down on another hard rock and put my hands over my eyes.

"Let me know if he gets back up," I said to Mike, from under my clenched fingers. "Just as a matter of curiosity."

There wasn't anything in the hole. It was just a hole.

Chapter 6

"Where's John?" I asked.

Mark looked vaguely up at the hall ceiling and, not surprisingly, failed to find what he was looking for.

"Isn't he in the lounge?"

"No. I was just there."

"He was out with Achmed a while ago," Mark said. "Come on, Tommy, and have a drink. It's Happy Hour time."

"Happy is right," I said, as a burst of hilarity billowed out of the lounge doors. "They're having a real blast in there. Mr. Bloch has broken out his private stock."

"A celebration is in order after what happened this morning." Mark's brown eyes sobered. "It's a miracle nobody was killed. You look kind of groggy yourself, Tommy. Let's join the merry throng and get some of Bloch's best before it vanishes down Mike's throat."

"Go ahead. I haven't even had time to change clothes. I'll join you later."

I glanced in the lounge as I passed and saw Mike in the middle of an admiring crowd, waving a glass and discoursing. I went on up the stairs. The corridor was empty; everyone was downstairs celebrating. The door wasn't locked. I opened it and walked in.

John glanced over his shoulder but didn't turn around. He finished taking off his shirt before saying mildly, "What the hell do you want?"

"Thought you might need some help." I sat down on the bed and lit a cigarette. "It's a little difficult taping up broken ribs by yourself. How many did you break?"

"None. Thanks just the same."

"Suit yourself." I stood up, casually putting out my cigarette; and then I made a quick dash. Caught off guard, he didn't have time to turn away; and although I had been expecting something of the sort, the sight made my breath suck in sharply.

"It looks worse than it is," he said defensively.

"It looks as if somebody had tried to skin you." My voice was unsteady, and I tried to conceal my squeamishness by a burst of anger. "Who do you think you are, Superman, flying around like a bird? Couldn't you have just quietly crawled across the rock?"

"There was no way of reaching the boy except by jumping. The rock face was dead flat in that area."

I had to accept that; after all, I hadn't been there.

"Sit down," I said, emphasizing the suggestion by a push which dropped him into the nearest chair. "Where do you keep your medical supplies? Oh, you already have them out. Why didn't you get Mike or Mark up here to give you a hand? Talk about my neuroses—you're the biggest egomaniac I ever saw. I'll have to clean this mess up before I can tell what the damage is. Why don't you say something?"

"Can't get a word in edgewise," said John, with a faint grin that vanished abruptly as the damp cloth in my hand touched a raw spot. "What brought you haring up here? Ouch. On your errand of mercy?"

"I had an excellent view of your gymnastics, remember? When you hit that cliff I thought you were going to split the rock. All that T.L.C for

Achmed—you were the one who took the jolt. And you aren't eighteen, either."

That made him wince—or maybe it was the alcohol-soaked cloth touching an inch-wide strip of raw flesh.

"My Lord, that goes all the way around," I said sickly. "The rope must have done it. Did you have to go back down afterward, for God's sake?"

"Twenty of the most talented thieves of Gurnah knew where that hole was. If it had proved to be our tomb, half the contents would have been gone tomorrow morning."

I sat back on my heels, my sponge dripping, and stared at him.

"Archaeology is a fascinating subject, I agree. But I can't imagine letting myself be flayed alive for a set of coffins, even gold ones."

"No?"

"Jake wasn't that obsessed."

"No."

His face was set like rock, which was understandable; he didn't want any sympathy from me. But his even, controlled voice scared me. I would have preferred one of the familiar, reassuring roars of rage.

"Something must be broken," I said, poking wildly at a darkening bruise the size of a salad plate. "You hit hard enough. And Lord knows you don't have any spare fat to cushion a blow. Where—"

"I don't know which is worse," said John, recovering his breath, "your impertinent remarks or your clumsy hands. Yes, I think that one is cracked. If it wasn't before, it is now."

"You ought to see a doctor!" I beamed at him.

"At the risk of inspiring more insults about my egomania, I prefer my treatment to that of the so-called doctors at the reputed hospital. Or yours, if it comes to that. Quit sloshing that stuff around, the place smells like a still. Get the tape; it's in that box."

"You can't put tape on top of those bruises."

"Kindly do what I tell you."

I knew that voice. Rarely used, it always produced instant obedience.

The next five minutes weren't much fun for either of us. I sat on the chair next to him so that I could wind things around his chest; he sat bolt upright, breathing through his nose and swearing, while perspiration poured down his face and throat.

"How much could you see from where you were sitting?" he asked suddenly.

"Quite a bit." I paused, cheek up against his chest, in the act of knotting two ends of gauze together on his far side; and one memory came back with a vividness that made my hands go weak. "I couldn't see the ropes, though. I thought—even when you jumped—I thought you didn't have one."

I finished tying the knot and sat back.

"Will you quit harping on that?" said John, apparently unaware of my twitching face. "I tell you I had to jump. He fell. I didn't pull him loose. Mike let go just before I caught him. Half a second later and he'd have been gone."

"Mike let go?"

"His grip gave way. The position was impossible."

"Oh."

"Pull that tighter. All right. So you couldn't see the ropes?"

"No." I relaxed, drying my palms surreptitiously on the hem of my skirt. My sadistic impulses are limited to the verbal kind; I don't like torturing people physically.

John stood up, and then nearly sat down again; he had to grab the back of the chair to keep on his feet, and his face, which had been gray, went ashen. I sat perfectly still, staring out the window. I knew he would evict me from the room if I so much as spoke.

"I want to show you something," he said, after a moment.

I didn't dare look at him, so I jumped when the "something" suddenly dropped into my lap. It was a thick coil of rope. I knew what rope it was, and what I would find when I lifted the loose end.

"It was cut," said John's voice, now under reasonably good control. "Not all the way through, just enough so that it would snap when the inevitable strain fell on it."

"But who—why—"

"I don't know. Achmed has something on his mind, but he won't talk about it."

"He couldn't know the tomb's location."

"He could, but murdering him would be a poor way of finding out anything. Unless he's already talked to someone, and that someone doesn't need him any longer."

"John, I can't believe Achmed is involved."

"I find it hard to believe myself. If it had been his brother . . ."

He was stalking up and down the room, the pain of his cracked rib and bruises apparently forgotten. I joined him. Pacing was some relief to the nerves, and my nerves were badly shaken by the silent accusation of the slashed rope.

"You don't trust Hassan either," I said. "Why did you hire him?"

"I'd rather have him under my eye, that's why. Of course I don't trust him. He was the one who mauled you and stole Abdelal's letter. Haven't you realized that, or am I still number-one suspect for that attractive part?"

"No! I mean, I thought of Hassan too. Can't we tell the police?"

"Tell them what? You can't identify him, not with any certainty. And there's another reason why we can't bring the police into this. You may have wondered why I haven't done so. A troop of guards patrolling the west desert would relieve my mind considerably. The point is that we can't trust the police."

"Yes, I realized that."

"You did?" He eyed me quizzically.

"Of course. Most of them are local men, just as poor as the other villagers."

"Correct." John stopped at the window and stood looking out. His back was toward me; the strips of bandage stood out white against the tanned skin and taut muscles of his shoulders.

"Tommy, this is the third violent episode since you arrived. We must assume that they are connected with the thing we're searching for."

"You mean—someone else is after the tomb?"

"Someone else is after the tomb. Abdelal's letter was the only thing stolen from you; Achmed was attacked while on his way to deliver the scarab to you. We agree that Hassan was probably your assailant. He could have attacked his brother; it wouldn't be out of character. Today's episode was the worst of the three; it was a definite attempt at murder. Did you see anything, from your vantage point, which would indicate who cut that rope?"

"It could have been Hassan." I frowned, trying to recall the picture: the throng of milling black-and-white robes, the bright fuchsia splash of color that was Hassan's shirt, the khaki-brown forms of the two archaeologists. "It could have been almost anybody."

"Not quite. The rope wasn't fixed till the last minute. We didn't know ahead of time that Achmed would be using it."

"Then I think Hassan is the best suspect. Especially in view of the other episodes."

"That's reasonable, as far as it goes. But do you believe that Hassan is solely responsible for what has happened?"

"I see that you don't," I said, after a moment of shock.

"There are two arguments against such an assumption. Hassan hasn't the character to tackle such a complicated enterprise. He also lacks the necessary information. I can't see Abdelal letting him in on the secret."

"A conspiracy of the villagers?" I said, guessing wildly.

"The methodology is wrong. I tell you, these people don't resort to violence if they can help it. And I think I could tell from their behavior if they were concealing something. They are puzzled, excited, suspicious, but not threatening."

"Then who, for heaven's sake?"

I joined him at the window.

"I'm not sure," he said, making room for me but not looking at me. "But I've got an idea, and I don't like it. Do you know anything about the international black market in art objects and antiquities? Most people don't realize that it's a big business, and a damned lucrative one. Not as big as dope or diamonds, maybe, but well worth a murder or two in the eyes of the people who run it.

"Every year paintings and antiquities vanish into this underground. Some purchasers are willing to buy even on the condition that their acquisitions can never be displayed. We keep forgetting, in our fine scholarly fervor, that the plain cash value of a tomb like this one is absolutely enormous, almost incalculable. Tutankhamen's one coffin was solid twenty-two-carat gold, six feet long and three millimeters thick, and that's not considering the workmanship and the historical value. Tommy. Where did Jake go that day—the last day of his life?"

He turned, one quick quarter turn on his heel, and looked down at me. His face was completely calm; there wasn't the slightest quiver of his eloquent moustache. And I thought I had never seen an expression so inimical, so unalterable in purpose.

"I don't know," I said, stupidly.

"But you're beginning to wonder, aren't you? I don't know either, and God knows I've tried hard enough to find out. He was coming back from Connecticut; that's all the police could say. But he had to have a plan, Tommy; he couldn't deal with a find of that magnitude single-handed. I made a lot of inquiries about his comings and goings in New York, and I think I know what his plan was. It would have scared the devil out of me if I hadn't believed that the knowledge of the tomb's location died with Jake. Now I suspect that that assumption may not have been entirely correct and, what is more important, someone else seems to have the same suspicion. I can deal with crooked cops and dishonest villagers and adolescent psychopathic inferior types like Hassan. I cannot cope with an anonymous, professional criminal organization. If you know anything at all, Tommy, you must tell me."

"I told Mike—"

"I know what you told him."

"Then why do you keep nagging me?"

"Because once the location of the tomb is made public, the violence will stop. The one virtue of a professional thief is that he kills only for profit. He must anticipate our discovery or lose altogether; and as long as he thinks you know anything that will help him, you will be in danger."

"I see . . ."

"You always did see. You aren't that stupid." John turned away, staring down into the garden. "You'll have to make your own decision, but I suggest you do it without delay."

He spoke in the same terrifying, calm voice he had used throughout the conversation. Obviously he didn't believe the story I had passed on to him through Mike. It is particularly maddening to triumph over your baser motives and then find that no one believes the truth when you tell it.

There was nothing more to be said. I stood in silence, looking, as he looked, over the massed

greenery of the palms and vines in the courtyard,
toward the stark heights of the western cliffs,
now flooded by the rich light of sunset. Emerald
palms, golden sands, topaz stone—symbols of
the riches that had drawn so many adventurers.

Symbols as well of the consuming passion
that ruled the man who stood beside me. I used
to wonder, in my younger days, why John had
never married. He was attractive to women;
some of our lady visitors obviously found his
rugged looks and striking coloring more exciting than Jake's dark charm. It wasn't easy for
an archaeologist to find a wife who would
gladly bury herself in the dull, uncomfortable
backwater of Luxor; but love conquers all, including common sense, and heaven knows
John didn't lack that good old animal magne-
tism. I had felt it myself, even though I disliked
him personally.

Now I thought I knew why he had never
concentrated his demands on a woman. They
were too concentrated on his real love, his profession, and on the strange country of con-
trasts—desert and town, stark poverty and
fabulous riches, bare rock and verdant fields—
in which most of his life had been spent. Standing beside him, with his arm brushing mine, I
could feel the intensity of his emotion like the

heat of fever; and I wondered what he would do, to what lengths he would go, to serve that unusual and powerful passion.

John was back on the job next morning, carrying himself warily, but silencing me with a hard look when I inquired after his health. It didn't seem to occur to anyone else that he might have hurt himself in his crazy but effective rescue attempt, not even when he disappeared after the morning's work and was not available the rest of the day. I considered going to his room and offering to soothe his fevered brow, or chest; but the first interview hadn't been so pleasant that I yearned for a repetition. Besides, I assumed he was lying flat on his back itching and cursing, and he didn't need my help with that.

I tried to read, and tried to take a nap, and failed at both. By late afternoon I was prowling restlessly around the place looking for amusement and finding none. Everyone who wasn't hard at work writing up notes on the morning's activities was asleep. I peered into Mike's office and found it deserted. I knocked on Dee's door and got no answer. Finally I ended up in the hot but shady courtyard, staring disconsolately at the big barred iron gates.

I wanted to go for a walk. I would have enjoyed a stroll through Deir el Bahri, or a visit to the temple of Medinet Habu, where the archaeologists from the Oriental Institute were working. I had known some of them in the old days, and liked them. But I knew that wouldn't be very smart. There had always been a friendly rivalry between our group and the staff at Chicago House, across the river; like everyone else in Luxor, they would be buzzing with curiosity at our recent peculiar activities, and I might say the wrong thing.

Besides, I wasn't too keen on leaving the protection of the thick mud walls and iron gates. True, nobody had tried to murder me recently; but a lot of people had earnestly assured me that I was in danger of being murdered, or worse, and repetition was convincing. Nobody seemed to believe my protestations of ignorance. The frustrating part of it was that I was ready to share my memories if I could only get hold of them. John suspected me of withholding information out of spite. It wouldn't be a lasting blight on my young life if he never found his damned tomb, but I certainly didn't want anyone to suffer as a result of my silence. I liked Achmed. I didn't want to see him killed—or Mike, or even John. Or—especially—me.

Hands clasped between my knees, head

bowed, I sat in the drowsy heat of the courtyard, with the buzz of insects the only sound, and tried once more to pin down that elusive tantalizing clue of Abdelal's. It was no use; vagrant memories are not to be captured so easily. It would come back to me, if it ever came back, without prompting and at an entirely unexpected stimulus.

I looked up, startled, as the sound of footsteps broke into my reverie. Only one person walked like that, with a thump-halt-shuffle. But Dee was the last person I'd have expected to go walking in the heat of the afternoon.

She was surprised to see me, too; but she came toward me after only a moment's hesitation, using her crutches quite adeptly. I made room for her on the bench, and asked, idly, where she had been.

"Just out for a little exercise. This place is driving me nuts."

"It seems to have done you good," I said, studying her flushed cheeks and bright eyes. "Oh—look what you've done to that pretty dress!"

Dee stopped in the middle of the awkward process of sitting down, with her shapely bottom sticking out, and tried to look over her shoulder.

"What's the matter?"

"There's a tear at the hem, and the material is stained." I plucked at the green-streaked pink lace with a cautious fingernail. "The cleaners in these parts are far from expert, especially with material like silk and lace. You shouldn't wear such fancy dresses when you're roughing it."

Dee lowered her shape onto the bench and gave my own attire a glance which spoke louder than words.

"I know," I said, smiling. "You wouldn't be caught dead in a white shirt and a full print skirt. But full skirts are handy when you ride camels or climb, unless you like showing a lot of leg. They don't approve of trousers for women down here. And if you could understand some of the remarks the Egyptians make about lady tourists in miniskirts, you wouldn't risk it. They have a low opinion of women anyhow."

"I wouldn't say that," Dee murmured.

"Dee—my advice would be, 'Don't.' "

"Don't what?"

"Flirt, if I may use a euphemism, with any of the workmen."

"Some of them are pretty cute," said Dee, giving me a glance designed to provoke. "That Hassan, for instance . . ."

"Hassan is a . . . well, there are several good words, but I prefer to think you don't know any of them."

Dee stretched out her encased leg and wriggled dusty toes.

"I thought you were a big jolly liberal," she said scornfully. "Are you telling me not to lower myself with the natives?"

"Natives, hell; I'm telling you not to do anything with anybody—brown, pink, or spotted. Your father would murder you if he caught you fooling around with Hassan."

Dee went suddenly utterly white.

"Good heavens, child," I said, "I'm only joking. I have no intention of tattling to your father, if that's what you're afraid of. But Hassan really is dangerous. He's a vicious little rat. Stay away from him."

"Maybe I'd be safer with Mike?"

"Maybe is right."

"When are you going home, Althea?"

"Call me Tommy," I said glumly. "I don't know when I'm going home. Maybe now. Are you hinting?"

"No. I was just wondering . . . Are you in love with Mike?"

"Everybody loves Mike. Why don't you grab

him? Your father would approve of your marrying an archaeologist."

"Are you kidding? Oh, I could go for Mike. He's cute. But—bury myself in this rathole six months a year? I'd go out of my mind. You can have Mike."

"What makes you think I wouldn't go out of my mind in this rathole?" I demanded, insulted.

"You love it," Dee said, with a calm certainty that shook me down to my rubber-soled sneakers. "I could tell the minute you got off that plane."

I stared down at a little pool of sunshine, like a puddle of amber wine, between my feet.

"Why don't *you* go home?" I said. "You hate the place, and it can't be much fun for you in that cast."

"Maybe I will." Dee's voice was so strange that I looked up at her; but she was staring at the sprays of white jasmine on the wall, and her face was blank. "I don't know what to do," she added, as if to herself.

"Maybe your father doesn't realize how tedious this is for you. He's so excited about this tomb . . ."

"What gives with the tomb, anyhow?"

"I don't think they'll ever find it." I stirred the

little pool of sunlight with my toe and watched it shiver and break, almost like water, across my foot.

"It would mean a lot of money, wouldn't it?"

"It's not the money, it's the fame," I said absently. "Or something. I can't explain it to you; only another crazy archaeologist would understand."

"Would it be like that kid's tomb—King What's-'is-name?"

"Tutankhamen? Even richer, they think."

"And there are people who pay money for that stuff?"

"Yes, there are people who pay money for that stuff," I said, glowering at her. She was more interested in archaeology than she let on, and I wondered if the sudden desire for knowledge had any connection with Mike's "cuteness." "Lots and lots of money. Thieves don't peddle antiquities through ordinary fences, but there are always buyers, if you know the market."

"I get it." Dee adjusted her crutches and stood up. "Well. I think I'll grab a nap before dinner."

I watched the pink-and-green-lace sway off between the trees with a wry foreboding. My low mind was pretty well convinced as to the source of those grass stains. I only hoped her father never caught her. Under his placid exterior Bloch probably packed an explosive temper.

My new theory was shaken almost immediately. The gates slammed, and down the walk came Mike, so preoccupied that he didn't even glance in my direction. Mike had also been out for a walk. Quite a coincidence. So maybe it wasn't Hassan after all.

The succeeding days should have had the flatness of anticlimax, after the great fiasco which almost had become a tragedy. They were dull in incident, for blazing noon succeeded hot morning with no discoveries. But instead of relaxing, the atmosphere around the Institute grew increasingly taut. Dee was bothered about something; I suspected part of the cause, but an affair, even with Hassan, didn't seem sufficient to put her into such a state of nerves. Every time anyone spoke to her she started, and much of the time she sat wrapped in sullen silence, brooding.

Bloch's public face was as normal as ever, but occasionally I caught an expression, when he looked at Dee, that made me wonder. If he did have any suspicions about his daughter I could understand her nerves. For all his kindliness he had the look of a bad man to cross.

Mark sat around like a spider on his web, staring, and waiting for someone to slip. John and Mike stalked around like robots, utterly absorbed in the one, the only, problem. Achmed made himself scarce; on the rare occasions when I did see him he slid past me with the slightest of muttered greetings. Hassan was impossible. I encountered him once, on the sole occasion when I ventured outside the grounds, and met him loitering by the gate. His taunting grin and thinly veiled insolence sent me scuttling back into the courtyard. I began to feel as if all these people had private problems whose subject was unknown to me, but which somehow threatened me in ways I couldn't even imagine. The only person whose company I found soothing was young Al Schneider; he was ploughing methodically through all of Petrie's old excavation reports, and I used to go and sit in his office. It was so relaxing to be with someone who wasn't thinking about anything except potsherds. Sometimes he would look up at me with a shy grin and read me a particular fascinating bit on red-polished ware. He never expected an answer, and that was the most relaxing thing of all.

By Tuesday, however, I was getting a little bored with pottery, and suffering intensely from cabin fever. As I stood staring out the windows of the lounge after dinner it seemed to me that I could feel the pressure of other people's worries like weights pressing on my shoulders.

"Full moon tonight," said Mike, materializing behind me. "How about taking a walk?"

"Mike, I'd adore it. But John said—"

"I'll be with you," Mike said magnificently.

"True." I studied him speculatively, and after a minute he began to twitch.

"It's not what you're thinking," he assured me earnestly.

"I may not be thinking what you think I'm thinking. Okay, Mike. If I don't get out of here, I'll start babbling."

But it wasn't until we left the lights of the Institute behind us that I realized how much I had missed all this. The moon was up. Its cold light gave the landscape unbelievable clarity, and made the cliffs glitter as if they had been silver-plated. Every detail was almost as distinct as by day, and yet the light was odd and unearthly. The stars were not the isolated dots seen through a city's muggy air; they were flung lavishly across the sky in clusters and trails of blazing diamond light. I took a deep breath of the cool, pure air, and felt as if I were breathing straight oxygen.

We walked in silence; words would have been

inadequate. The temple of Deir el Bahri was a marvel of silver columns and sweeping ramps. By moonlight it seemed unmarred by time, perfect as a model in the embrace of the enclosing cliffs. When we reached the front of it, Mike spoke for the first time.

"Tired?"

"No."

"Feel like a climb? It's light enough."

"I'd like that."

This time the climb didn't bother me; caught in the spell of the night, my body was unaware of fatigue and my feet were lifted by invisible hands. When we reached the top, Mike took my hand and we strolled on, still in silence. With every step, days seemed to fall away. I was walking back into the past, back into the time when this was my world, a world which legitimately belonged to me and to which I belonged. When we reached the end of the path we stood looking down into the Valley of the Kings; the mystery of its shadowed secrets was framed in pale light and guarded by the towering natural pyramid of the Qurn. The landscape was wine-washed, not by the purple red which is usually considered wine color, but by the silver-gold shade of a pale Moselle. Caught in a lost dream and surrounded by ghosts, I stood in a kind of trance and when Mike pulled me down beside him and put his arm around me, I settled back against his shoulder with no emotion stronger than content.

"How far away are you?" he asked softly.

"Ten years . . . fifteen. Did you do this on purpose?"

"This was one of the views you used to rave about. 'Moonlight on the Biban el Melek.' In your squeaky little voice and your terrible Arabic pronunciation . . ."

"It's not just the view," I said, smiling at his imitation. "It's the history of the place as well."

"Mmm . . . gold and jewels and hidden treasure . . . Funny how words like that can fire the imagination. And the crowds of the strengthless dead . . ."

"I didn't know you read Houseman."

"People who read poetry shouldn't admit it. The phrase isn't really apposite; these dead had plenty of strength, not only power while they lived, but a malignant ability to damn the living even after death."

"The Pharaoh's curse? Come on, now."

"We both know there weren't any curses, not as the newspapers had the story. Buried treasure carries a built-in curse. Think how many poor devils were tortured and impaled in ancient

times for yielding to the temptation of the useless gold buried in these tombs. Not to mention
the more recent victims who have been tor-
mented by desire . . ."

I shivered. His arm tightened, but in an abstracted way. He was thinking, hard, about
something else.

"Mike, are you going to find the tomb?"

"No."

"But—"

"It's absolutely hopeless, Tommy. If we could
narrow the search down to a particular area,
we'd have a chance. As things stand, it could be
anywhere. Anywhere at all."

I leaned forward, jamming my clenched fists
against my forehead.

"Mike, I've tried to remember. Honestly I
have."

"I know." His voice broke into a chuckle.
"I've seen you go into a trance at the most
unlikely times—with a forkful of food halfway
to your mouth, for instance. You're trying too
hard."

"I thought at first I didn't care," I said, staring
at the magnificent vista of creamy white stone
and black shadow. "But the violence frightens
me. Mike, is there any chance that it isn't connected with the tomb?"

"I'm afraid it must be. Unless you brought along some private vendetta?"

"Nobody knows me well enough to hate me," I said forlornly. "Except you and John."

"I don't hate you," Mike said unimaginatively. "And you ought to know John better than to think that of him. Forget it, Tommy, and let's get practical. If you really want to help . . ."

"Yes," I said, drawing a deep breath. "Yes, I do."

"Then think of Abdelal's letter. Damn it, it's the only clue we've got."

"I've looked at all the maps," I said, straightening my shoulders and dismissing private miseries. "There is no such name anywhere in the Theban area."

"I know. I looked too. I also checked the Dictionary."

I knew he didn't mean Webster's *Collegiate*. When an Egyptologist refers to "the Dictionary," he means the huge five-volume *Wörterbuch* of ancient Egyptian.

"I never thought of that," I exclaimed. "You mean one of the ancient names?"

"Precisely. And I think we may be on the right track." He stretched out one long arm and scooped me in. I stiffened, being not in that particular mood at the moment, and Mike said, "Relax, I'm just trying to imitate a psychiatrist's couch. Let your mind go blank."

"Okay," I said, noting, without intending to, that his shoulder was just the right height and shape for my head. "Proceed."

"Do you remember the ancient name for the Valley of the Kings?"

"How would I remember a thing like that?"

"You seem to have picked up quite a bit of information, one way or another. It was called The Place of Truth. Does that come back to you?"

"Vaguely, yes."

"The Valley of the Queens used to be named The Place of Beauty. Hear any bells ringing?"

"Faint and far away . . . Yes, I knew that, once upon a time. How about the West Valley of the Kings?"

"That's another of those interminable archaeological arguments you get so mad about." I couldn't see Mike's face, but I knew from his voice that he was smiling. "Nobody knows for sure. Stop digressing. The Place of Truth, The Place of Beauty. There is no Place of Milk in the dictionary. It must be something you made up, a schoolgirl's imitation of an ancient name. When did you invent it, Tommy?"

"I don't remember!"

"Don't try to remember. Just relax. You used to

do a lot of walking in the old days, with Jake, with Abdelal, even with me once or twice. You never mentioned it to me. It must have happened when you were with Abdelal. He remembered it because his discovery pounded the incident home to him. Once when you were with Abdelal. Think about that . . ."

"I'm thinking," I said dreamily.

It was a lie; I wasn't doing anything so difficult as thinking. For the first time in days I was just relaxing. As a mesmerist, Mike was almost too good.

"You and Abdelal," Mike went on in a droning voice. "Over the path, across the hills . . . One day you played a game. The great Queen Nefertiti . . ."

"Mmmm," I said cooperatively.

He gave me a little shake.

"Hey, wake up."

"It's no use, Mike," I mumbled. "Nefertiti was my favorite heroine. Goodness, any skinny schoolgirl would take her as a model. I talked about her constantly. And I went everywhere with Abdelal—Deir el Medineh, Medinet Habut, the Biban el Melek, Gurnah . . ."

This time I hypnotized myself with my drowsy flow of words. Mike's sudden start jolted me wide awake. Absorbed in our unproductive experiment, neither of us had heard him coming until he spoke.

"Mike."

It was his second voice, the one that went with his calmer, nastier personality. It almost sent Mike into a convulsion.

"John—for God's sake! Don't sneak up on a guy like that!"

He scrambled awkwardly to his feet, spilling me out across the rock.

"If you want to neck—that was the word for it in my remote youth—there are safer places," John said. His voice was quite calm, and scathing enough to take the skin off a dinosaur. I didn't blame Mike for flushing.

"I'm aware of that," he said, trying to match John's sarcasm and succeeding only in sounding very young. "I was trying to conduct an experiment, as a matter of fact."

"Indeed. Was it a success?"

"It might have been, if you hadn't interrupted it."

"Too bad. Want to try again? I can wait."

"It's too late now," Mike muttered.

"Then let's go back, shall we?"

He stepped back, with a mock bow. It was apparent by then that nobody was going to be a gentleman, so I picked myself up. We walked all the way back to the Institute in a silence that would have made a tomb sound noisy. When we got upstairs, Mike went off with a muttered sound that might have been a good-night; the back of his neck was still red.

John opened my door and waved me in. He looked paler than usual, and my annoyance faded a bit. He still must be far from fit, and tearing around the cliffs by moonlight couldn't have been much fun for him after a day in the broiling sun. Maybe he really had been worried.

"I'm sorry, John," I said. "Blame me, not Mike. He was trying to help."

"I blame both of you. But since I credit him with more common sense, I blame him more."

My recent noble determination to start acting like an adult began to crumble.

"You don't have to be so nasty," I said sharply.

"Yes, I do. I'm far too old and infirm to change my personality." He added calmly, "Good night. Sleep well."

It was a good night, and I slept very well. It wasn't until the next night that my Midnight Intruder came back.

After a long hot day on the plateau, where John was driving the grumbling workers long past their usual quitting time, I slept like the dead. The explosion of sound outside my door sent me sprawling dizzily out of bed, half awake but wholly alarmed; and I stumbled to the door and threw it open without bothering with robe or slippers.

The corridor was bright as day. Someone had switched on the overhead lights, which were usually dimmed at night. As I stood yawning and blinking, the other doors up and down the corridor began to pop open and feet began to pound along the adjoining corridor which led to the staff rooms. For a moment I was distracted from the central tableau by a fascinated contemplation of the sleeping attire of my acquaintances. Dee, peering nervously around the edge of her door, was wearing the most vulgar and most gorgeous negligee I had ever seen. The colors, shifting in layers of sheer chiffon from pale-blue to turquoise to green, were all wrong for her, but the style did wonders for her figure. Bloch, blinking from the doorway beyond, was wearing red-and-white-striped silk pajamas.

Mark and Mike were the first of the staff to arrive on the scene, Mark because his room was closest, Mike probably because his legs were longest. The sight of them confirmed what I had always suspected—that most of the men didn't bother with effete things such as pajamas. Probably they kept their trousers by their beds as firemen do, all ready to step into. That was all they were wearing, and Mike displayed a very impressive set of muscles.

John, holding a writhing, twisting Hassan at arm's length, was fully dressed. He stood the boy on his feet, cuffed him lightly to stop the flow of invective, and said,

"Think up an excuse, Hassan. It had better be a good one."

Bloch came padding up, his bare feet soundless on the carpet.

"There isn't any excuse," he said, his drawl flat and ominous. "He's got no business in the house, has he?"

"No."

Hassan straightened up, seeing that resistance was useless and escape out of the question. He drew one hand ostentatiously across his mouth and spat. I couldn't help admiring his nerve, for if ever a man was surrounded, he was; and he was slighter and shorter than anyone else except Mark. That night he had abandoned his California shirt in favor of the customary robe—a wise precaution, because if he had been seen but not apprehended, it would have been hard to prove who he was.

"I have come," he said insolently, "because I was invited. I am a guest."

Bloch made a wild movement, as if to get at him, but John's arm held the older man back.

"Who invited you?" he asked.

Hassan's sleek, black head turned. He didn't say a word. He simply smiled, blindingly, beautifully, straight at me.

Somebody gasped. I think it was Al Schneider. My blank stare caught Mark's eyes and saw them slide away; and then the blood ran up over my cheeks into my hair. What had seemed like a preposterous excuse suddenly didn't look so stupid. John and Mike, Bloch—they might doubt the little devil. But what did the others know about me and my tastes? Even the episode at the hotel—it wouldn't be the first time an invited visitor got carried away, by boyish exuberance or even a lovers' quarrel. I almost gagged at the thought.

Hassan's grin broadened, and then disappeared behind Mike's fist, as it smacked into his jaw.

He went down with a thud, and Mike, purple in the face, bent over to lift him up for further remonstration. John shoved him back.

"That's enough of that, Mike," he said coldly. "If you can restrain your adolescent impulses, take him downstairs to my office. The rest of you go back to bed."

He hadn't looked at me directly, not once. I caught at his arm as he prepared to follow the prisoner and his guard down the stairs.

"John . . ."

He turned a bleakly impersonal gaze on my face, and I blurted out something I hadn't meant to say.

"Why are you still dressed? You haven't been—"

"I have been working late." His eyes wavered, and then steadied. "I heard him on the stairs and caught up with him here."

"How did he get in?" Bloch asked, running a distracted hand through his rumpled gray hair. "I thought this place was locked up at night."

"It wouldn't be hard to get over the wall. Our so-called night watchman spends most of the time sleeping."

"But the house itself . . ."

It was Mark who supplied the answer to that question. With his usual inquisitiveness, he had already considered and investigated the probabilities. Now he came bounding back up the stairs.

"One of the lounge windows is unlocked," he announced.

That did it. I turned blindly back into my room, unable to face any of them—Mark's bright-brown-eyed and squirrelly curiosity, Dee's grin, Bloch's doubtful stare. Those windows could only be opened from the inside. I knew I hadn't opened it, but the others didn't—except for the one who had done the job. Dee, looking for excitement? Perhaps. And perhaps it had been someone else—someone admitting a hired assassin so that his own hands wouldn't be dirtied by murder.

Next morning when my alarm went off, I let it ring itself out. I had decided I wasn't going out on the dig. It was bad enough to have Mark and Al staring at me in fascinated speculation, but I was darned if I wanted to be the center of all the workmen's knowing eyes. Everybody and his uncle Feisal would know of Hassan's latest conquest by now, and they would find it terribly amusing.

Ten minutes later John came banging on my door, and when I said, "Stay out," he came in.

"I'm not going today," I said.

"Oh, yes, you are," he said. "Get dressed, or I'll dress you myself."

I spent the morning in my favorite position, sitting under a rock.

Once I was there, I discovered I didn't mind it

as much as I had expected. The air, which was hot enough to fry most people's brains, didn't bother me, because of my early acclimatization—or possibly because I had no brains to be affected. Yet it seemed to me that I could detect a difference in the way the men were working. None of them had paid any attention to me, except for a casual *saida*. In fact, they seemed to be avoiding one another. Groups had a tendency to disperse, with men scattering out on odd little side strolls. There was a surreptitious air about them that hadn't been present before. No doubt about it, the word was out. None of the Gurnah men were looking very hard any longer. Not officially.

I had plenty of leisure in which to consider the nocturnal visit of Hassan, who was conspicuously not present among the workers. Of course it had been Dee whom he had come to visit; that gorgeous negligee had not been flung on after an unexpected alarm. How she had gotten herself and her cast down the stairs to unfasten the window I couldn't imagine, until I realized that she must have done it before going upstairs. At first I was annoyed with her for not coming to my defense, and then I knew that was naïve. In her place I probably wouldn't have spoken up either. Not with Daddy standing there breathing fire. I had no such guardian dragon to beat me if I misbehaved.

Still, I didn't feel too kindly toward Dee, and when she knocked on my door late that afternoon, I let her in without bothering to look delighted.

"You should be asleep," I said. "You must be tired after waiting up last night."

"I am," she said, and sat down.

Surprised at her candor, I peered more closely at her face. She looked haggard, ten years older than the age she claimed.

"What's the matter?" I asked.

"I'm sorry about last night. I didn't mean for you—"

"Oh, forget it," I said uncomfortably. "I guess I'd have done the same thing. But honestly, Dee—that loathsome little twerp—"

"He told me you were down on him."

"Oh, he did, did he? And why am I supposed to be down on him? Never mind; don't tell me what he said. Look here, Dee, I know it's useless to point out the questionable morality of inviting men to your room, especially when it's yours only by courtesy. But surely you must see how stupid it is to entertain your boyfriends practically under your father's nose."

"He told me to let him in."

"Good God, you sound like a Victorian maid-servant. So why didn't you tell him no dice?"

"He's kind of persuasive."

"I'll bet. He's also kind of treacherous."

"You keep saying that." She moved restlessly, scratching at the edge of her cast. "Do you really mean it, or are you just being catty? About not trusting him, I mean."

"I am being catty, but I also . . ." A sudden wild suspicion took root and sprang into full growth, like a monstrous man-eating plant. "Wait a minute. Wait just a minute. What has Hassan been telling you?"

In my excitement I grabbed her by the shoulders, so that she had to look at me. I knew then that Hassan's hold on her was not the simple biological urge I had imagined it to be. There is one emotion that is unmistakable on a person's face. Fear.

If I had been clever enough, I might have convinced her to talk to me. I'll never know. I didn't get the chance. While I hesitated, groping for the right words, I heard footsteps approaching the door, and Bloch's voice.

"Tommy? Is Dee with you?"

Dee made a vicious face and hobbled out to reassure her doting daddy. I stood staring at the blank panel of the door and listening to their

voices—Dee's sharp and brusque, Bloch's ad-
monitory, soft, affectionate. All sorts of odd
thoughts were swimming around in my mind;
among them was the memory of Dee's seemingly casual questions about the tomb and its
value. Was it possible that Hassan . . .

John didn't think so, but John had only been
guessing. He would have called it "theorizing,"
but that's only a fancy word for guessing. Yes, it
definitely was possible that Hassan had vital information, and it would be just like him to use it
as a bait, a golden, glittering bait for a susceptible girl. But the girl seemed susceptible to other
suggestions at the moment. Definitely I must
talk with her, as soon as possible—for her sake as
much as for my own.

At supper she seemed just the same, if slightly
more sullen than usual. She avoided me then,
and when I tapped on her door later, she didn't
answer. Maybe she was asleep. But, knowing
what I know now, I doubt it. I didn't expect to see
her at breakfast, and I didn't. She seldom came
down for that meal, and her semi-crippled state
made it reasonable that she should not. So it
wasn't till afternoon that we realized Dee was
missing.

When Bloch came looking for her, as he had
the previous day, I feared she had sneaked out

with Hassan and that this time she was going to get caught in the act. But it soon became apparent that she was nowhere to be found. With her cast and crutches she couldn't get far, and yet she was nowhere in the vicinity of the Institute.

By that time the Institute was alerted, and buzzing like a beehive. I was maneuvering nervously in the lower hall, trying to catch John alone for a minute, when Bloch made my tact unnecessary. Tight-lipped and frozen, his face was fairly calm, but his voice snapped like a whip when he spoke to John.

"Have you checked on that kid Hassan?"

John gave him a long, measuring look and decided to tell the truth.

"Yes. He's gone too. No one has seen him since last night."

Bloch's face didn't alter, but all at once he raised one arm and brought his fist down on a little table with a crash that knocked it, and the vase of flowers it supported, to the floor.

"I'm sorry as hell, Sam," John said. "But that's what it looks like. I should have seen it coming."

"No, I saw it, but I didn't want to believe it. It's my fault."

"They can't have gone far. We'll catch up with them."

But they didn't. The absconding pair had had

a good start, all night and most of the day. Inquiries around Luxor produced evidence—too much evidence. Hassan had been seen: (1) boarding the morning plane for Cairo; (2) catching the night train for Aswan; (3) heading into the desert on donkeyback. At least, three men answering his description had done these things. The first two travelers had been accompanied by women in western garb; the third had been followed—on foot, naturally—by a humble figure in dusty black which covered her from nose to toes. None of the women had had a cast on her leg.

Bloch, now gray and haggard, shrugged at this last.

"She could have taken the cast off. She'd have had to."

"But that would be dangerous." I calculated, roughly and rapidly. "It's been less than a month, hasn't it?"

"She wouldn't think of that. She's only a kid."

He went off, leaving me aching for him, to check on his calls to Cairo. The authorities there had been alerted, and ports and airports were under surveillance. This precaution paid no dividends. The day wore on into night, and most of the next day passed, with no news. Attempts to identify the travelers by train, plane, and donkey failed. Apparently Dee and Hassan had simply vanished into the blue.

I was sitting on my favorite bench in the courtyard next afternoon when the gates opened and Bloch came in. His steps dragged, and his shoulders had lost their jaunty swing. When he recognized me, and gave me a ghost of his former grin, I could have cried.

"Sit down," I said. "You look exhausted."

"I am pretty tired. Been out half the night."

"I suppose John has talked to Hassan's friends in Gurnah?"

"I gather the boy doesn't have any friends." Bloch looked as if he wanted to spit.

"No one who would hide him?"

Bloch looked at me.

"Do you know anything, Tommy?"

"I'd tell you if I did. You've been so kind to me."

"You're a nice girl."

He patted my hand. I wished desperately that I could think of something which would relieve the exhaustion in his face.

"You know," I said, "Dee talked to me the day before she left. It probably doesn't mean anything, and I haven't mentioned it to anyone else . . ."

"What?"

"I don't want to get your hopes up. It was just that I had a funny feeling that she knew something about the tomb—or rather, that Hassan did, and that he had spoken to her."

He made me repeat every word she had said. Any well in a desert, I thought, and did my best to remember.

"Was that all?" he asked, when I finished.

"I think so," I said, sounding more doubtful than I felt, because I hated to crush this last feeble hope.

"Well." He was silent for a long time, staring down at the ground.

"Mr. Bloch, go in and lie down. You must be worn out. If I think of anything else I'll tell you. I promise."

He looked up at me, and his eyes were dead as stones.

"She was the only one," he said simply. "And her mother dead all these years . . ."

I made an inarticulate sound of sympathy; there was no comment that seemed appropriate. He patted my hand again.

"Guess I'm too restless to lie down. I'll take a walk. Get tired enough to sleep."

He took a few steps and then turned. His smile was pathetic.

"Care to come along?" he asked diffidently.

If he had asked me to stand on my head and sing "Yankee Doodle," I would have done it—anything that he thought would help.

"Sure," I said.

The sun was dropping westward and the light had a mellow glow that made all colors richer and turned the rocks a smooth shining gold. We ambled along, in a silence that gradually grew easier, until we reached Deir el Bahri. My undirected walks often ended there. I never tire of looking at it, and the change of light on the stones gave it a thousand different aspects. Now it was pale amber, oddly Greek in its colonnaded beauty.

We climbed the first ramp. There was no one around; the crews working on the temple repairs had gone home for the day, and the tourists were back at their hotels, soaking themselves in liquid internally and externally. We had the place to ourselves.

We sat down at the foot of a pillar and talked about the temple and its unusual builder, the queen who had taken a king's titles and position. Bloch seemed to prefer impersonal subjects, and he was knowledgeable about Queen Hatshepsut—as he was about all matters archaeological.

"I've always been fascinated by her architect

boyfriend," I said, and then stopped as I realized the subject might have painful connotations.

"Me, too," Bloch said placidly. "I admire his gall. Have you seen the little drawings of himself he put in her sacred temple?"

"Yes, I love them. But I'm sure she let him put them there."

"Maybe she did, but I'll bet the snooty court was scandalized. You know, I've read about those little figures a dozen times, but I don't think I ever took a look at them."

"Why, they're right over there. Want to see them now?"

He was agreeable, but when we reached the entrance to the back part of the temple, roofed and pitch-black inside, he hesitated.

"I don't think I've got the energy after all, child."

"Another time, then."

"You go ahead." Suddenly he looked as if his strength had completely given out. He dropped heavily onto the ground, and I realized that he wanted to be alone.

Luckily I had plenty of matches in my purse, because the corridor was dark as pitch. The guides usually light little candles when they take the tourists in. I found the right room without any difficulty, and knelt down to find the well-remembered figures. Senmut, the queen's architect, had always appealed to me. I felt sure he must have had a lot of sex appeal. Somehow he impressed me as a cocky, dashing sort of man. Maybe it was the air of panache about the hasty little drawings he had scratched, prudently, behind the doors so that they would be hidden from anyone entering the room.

The doors were gone now, but I had to squat in order to hold my match near the small incised sketches of a kneeling man. When the match went out it was very dark. But not as dark as the utter blackness that swallowed me when something hard hit me square on the back of my bent head.

Sometimes it's hard to define the point at which an ordinary dream slips over the edge into nightmare. Often the events are prosaic; in the retelling they may even sound amusing. It's not the plot of a dream that makes it dreadful, but the atmosphere, the emotional climate.

In my dream I was standing, as I had so often stood, in the doorway of the Director's study at the Institute. I recognized the familiar, harmless furnishings: the institutional buff walls,

the big scarred desk, the bookshelves piled
with magazines, pamphlets, photographs, broken pottery, and even a few books. A man sat at
the desk, his back toward me. I knew he must
be one of two people—my father, or John. I
couldn't tell which.

That was when the dream turned to nightmare, when my dream self began to twist its immaterial hands together in an agony of terror
and doubt. I knew, with the illogical certainty of
dreaming, that one of two men occupied the Director's chair. And I couldn't tell which.

The doubt was nightmarish, for even in rear
view there could be no mistaking one man for
the other—John's bright silver head for Jake's
cap of smooth black hair, John's broader shoulders for Jake's lounging elegance.

Then the swivel chair began to revolve, and
my dream image went sick with inexplicable terror. In a moment I would see the face of the man
who was slowly turning toward me. I would
know—and I couldn't bear to know.

The chair turned, and turned, and turned . . .
and stopped. I saw the figure clearly now, as I
saw the faces. Not face—faces. The figure was
neither one man nor the other, it was both. Two
pairs of eyes saw me. Two pairs of lips parted,

and two voices chanted syllable by matched syllable, articulating with the precision of a Greek chorus,

"There is no tomb. There is no tomb. There is no—"

My dream shape began to scream. It screamed and screamed, trying to drown out the voices which rose above it like a diapason. My image's feet tried to run, but they were rooted to the floor. . . .

I screamed myself awake. The echo of the sound was still ringing in my ears when I recovered consciousness, and the absurdly sickening fear of the vision still permeated my shaking flesh. The darkness was thick, absolute blackness without a spark of light. I had to raise one hand and feel my own eyelashes, pointing upward, before I could be sure my eyes were open. A drop of some liquid rolled down my nose and dropped onto my upper lip. Blood? No—the less melodramatic but equally saline solution. Perspiration. It was hot in the lost, dark place, hot, close, musty. The first deep breath I took brought an odd smell strongly into my nostrils. A compound of dust and dead air, of lifeless stone, and fainter, suggestive ghosts of other scents. I had not smelled that scent often, or recently, but it is unforgettable.

The denial of my dream was false. There was a tomb, all right. And I was in it—prone and imprisoned, like its other, sightless, silent occupant.

Chapter 7

"Death shall come on swift wings to him who shall violate this tomb."

I have had occasion to bless my memory; but I wished, in that breath-snatching moment of revelation, that my memory hadn't come up with that particular sentence. It was the famous Pharaoh's Curse, but the words had not been written by the Pharaoh's contemporaries. Some enterprising publicity hound had composed them, after the death of Lord Carnarvon had all the nitwits of the world gasping about Egyptian curses. I knew the Egyptians had only cursed violators and destroyers of tombs, not innocent victims of kidnappers like myself. Anyhow, I didn't believe in curses.

Try telling yourself that, though, when you wake with a splitting headache and a bone-dry throat, in absolute darkness, in an ancient Egyptian tomb. People may believe one thing in broad daylight, but it's not what they believe when they walk through a cemetery at midnight.

For an endless space of time I lay as rigid as the mummified form which, somewhere in the darkness, shared the room with me. I even tried not to breathe loudly. Into my mind, unbidden and unwelcome, came the fear that I might hear something else breathing.

Perhaps it wasn't quite so bad for me as it would have been for an average tourist with no background in archaeology; but past a certain point, degrees of terror are meaningless. I think the only thing that saved my reason was the flashlight.

It was lying on my chest, like a lily on a corpse. (I didn't think of that simile at the time, which is just as well.) I felt its cold hard shape as soon as I calmed down enough to feel anything. It gave me a horrid shock for a moment, but as soon as my snatching fingers touched it I knew what it was; and the yellow beam of light was the most exquisite sight my eyes had ever beheld.

I sat up clutching the torch in both hands and admiring the light—just the light, not what it showed. Then the beam caught a flash of color and a shape; and I was on my feet, moving the flashlight wildly and gasping.

The room was rectangular, perhaps twenty feet long by fifteen feet wide. Walls, floor, and ceiling were of stone—the living rock of the cliffs out of which the tomb had been cut. Most of the rock surface was concealed by a thin coating of plaster almost entirely covered by painted scenes. The ceiling was blue, with a pattern of tidy yellow stars. I turned the light on the wall nearest me; and a sudden sharp surmise stabbed my brain and swept away the last wisps of superstitious terror.

The colors of the paint—green, red-orange, cobalt, white—were as fresh as if they had been applied the previous day. But the scenes were not of the conventional rows of mortuary deities weaving a web of ritual protection around the sleeper in the tomb. Instead, an enormous yellow-painted sun orb filled the entire left upper section of the wall. From it stretched down rays of light, ending, rather endearingly, in little divine hands which extended the signs of life and health to the two human forms bathed in the pictured sunlight. The lower part of the wall was hidden from my sight by a heap of objects—boxes, jars, chests, baskets. The funerary equipment—untouched, undisturbed except by three thousand years of time—of a queen of ancient Egypt.

Queen?

The same strange surmise made me turn my light next toward the object in the center of the room, which filled most of the floor space and concealed the remaining walls from my sight. It was a giant stone box which stood almost as high as my dusty head. The lid had been removed; it lay on the floor beside the sarcophagus. Lid and box were oddly plain, lacking carved scenes and inscriptions except for a single line of hieroglyphic signs which ran around the side of the sarcophagus.

I didn't need to move closer to see the signs, nor to recognize them for what they were. The titles were not those of a queen. The tomb was not a queen's tomb, though Nefertiti's frail, slender bones might lie in another chamber of this place. Here, saved not only from thieves but from the virulent hatred of his contemporary enemies who cursed him as a heretic, was the mummy of the sole Eighteenth Dynasty king whose tomb had not been found in the Valley of Thebes. The mummy of Akhenaton, the most controversial, romantic figure who had ever occupied the seat of Pharaoh.

The wooden box next to the sarcophagus had split, perhaps from the effect of the dry air; out of the opening spilled a fragment of cloth that caught the light in a fabulous glitter. When I bent to examine it more closely, the end of the shaking torch brushed it, and a section of spangle-sewn linen dissolved in a shower of gray dust. The spangles dropped to the floor with a child-ghost of musical jingles. I stood up with a gasp, and with a horrible feeling of sacrilege.

There was a gilded chest with carved lotus flowers on its sides, a cabinet of rough wood, closed and sealed, a box of ebony with ivory inlays containing a matched set of round translucent alabaster pots . . . And in the far corner—I steadied the light with both hands—yes, it was. A box of what could only be papyrus scrolls, dozens of them.

The tomb of Tutankhamen? It had been a bagatelle, a trifle, an empty hole, compared to this tomb. The fact that it existed at all, in Thebes, would overthrow all the accepted scholarly theories. No wonder no one had ever searched for Akhenaton's tomb. Everyone assumed he had been buried in his private city of Amarna, far north of Thebes. Probably he had died there, for this, surely, was a reburial. The boy-king Tutankhamen had decided, perhaps at the death of

Nefertiti, to move his father's body from the abandoned city of the heresy back to the safe, guarded cemeteries of Thebes. But by that time the old religion had been restored and the iconoclastic king was anathema to the furious priests of the gods he had tried to destroy. The reburial had to be secret, quick, careful, not only to guard against the usual tomb robbers, but to protect the king's body from the priests who hated him. Its location must have been lost from the beginning. Probably it had never even been recorded on the cemetery lists, for these were under the supervision of the very priests who might have threatened it.

The flashlight beam darted like a drunken firefly, for my hands were shaking—not with fear, but with pure excitement. For a brief but exalted time I felt the full force of the passion that moved John. I knew exactly how Mr. Bloch had felt the day he jumped up and down and yelled "Wow!" I would have yelled myself if I hadn't known that a hearty shout would shake the fragile treasures that heaped the floor.

"Wow," I said softly, and grinned, a little sheepishly, as the attack ebbed. It was almost like being in love. Forcing my hands to steadiness I let the light move slowly around the part of the room that was visible to me, and a frown furrowed my forehead as I saw the evidence of the thieves' activities.

A pile of objects wrapped in paper, stacked to one side, were ready to be removed. The lids of many chests and boxes had been taken off. Nothing had been deliberately broken, but some of the objects wouldn't endure even the brush of a fingertip. It had taken Carter ten years to clear the tomb of Tutankhamen. This clearance would have to be completed in the same number of days, or less. Half the contents of the tomb would be lost through such rough handling, including the incredible heap of papyri in the corner, which might be far and away the most valuable single thing in the tomb. John would give ten years of his life to locate the tomb, and he would cheerfully sacrifice his right arm to keep those papyri intact.

If I could warn the authorities before the thieves returned, most of the treasure could be saved. But I will admit that my chief concern was for the survival of a less ancient object. Me.

Someone had gone to a lot of trouble to put me in the tomb, so I assumed that murder was not his intention. Obviously he no longer needed my help to locate the tomb. I couldn't think of any other reason for preserving an inconvenient and antagonistic witness; and I wanted out before someone came and told me what the reason was.

I was under no illusions about the chances of escape. If there were an easy way out, I wouldn't have been brought here. Which meant that I had better stop playing archaeologist, and start looking.

I knew, generally, what I was looking for. The sarcophagus chamber is usually the last room of a tomb complex, preceded by other rooms containing shrines and funerary equipment, and by a long corridor which leads to the outer exit in the face of the cliff. So, in one of the painted walls of this room, there must be a door.

The wall behind me, and the one on my right, had no openings. I tiptoed gingerly around the sarcophagus, groaning as another segment of spangled robe dissolved into dust at the mere vibration of my footsteps—and there, on the left, was the opening.

It was a square, roughly cut hole, just high enough to crawl through. When I got down on my knees and poked my flashlight through the aperture, the light slammed back at me in a dazzle so bright I was momentarily blinded.

Professional archaeologists may sneer at gold, but it does have a certain glamour. I went on through the hole, even though I knew now that it probably was not the exit I sought. I found myself in a second burial chamber, smaller than the outer one and almost entirely filled by a strange structure that looked nothing at all like the sarcophagus in the other room. I knew the great stone box was inside the structure I saw—an enormous wooden shrine, completely covered with gold leaf in intricate patterns and concealed beneath a pall of fine linen so thickly sewn with sequins that it looked like gold lamé, and which reflected light like a polished mirror.

I edged cautiously around the glittering object and found my theory confirmed. This was the end, the final chamber of the tomb. If it was not, the exit was still concealed, for I could see no break in the gorgeously painted walls.

I backed out of the room on my knees, as if I had been in the presence of royalty—and nearly dropped the flashlight as I realized that the casual figure of speech was literally true. Nefertiti slept there; I was as sure of it as if I had seen her face, that gracious fine-boned face poised on a lily-slender throat, that was so familiar from her famous bust. Only her face wouldn't look like that now. It would be withered and dried, the lips drawn away from the teeth, the delicate nose shriveled . . . Suddenly I wanted, very badly indeed, to get out of that tomb.

Still, I paused for a moment in the outer sarcophagus chamber as a mild resurgence of archaeological fervor hit me. Nefertiti's burial was obviously undisturbed, as her controversial husband's was not; the lid of his sarcophagus had been lifted from its place, surely by Jake and Abdelal, for the heart scarab must have been taken from the king's mummy. It carried his name as well as hers, and we had assumed it belonged to her because of our identification of the statue. Was it only a coincidence that the two objects taken from the tomb suggested Nefertiti instead of Akhenaton?

I shook off question and lack of answer with an impatient twitch of my shoulders. There was no time for speculation now. The first door led only to another burial chamber, so there must be a second door, which would take me to the corridor and the exit. Walking as if on eggshells, I moved around to examine the one wall I had not yet seen. The door was there. Unlike the hole in the first wall, which must have been hacked out by the thieves, this one was original—man-high and wide, a regular rectangular doorway. My heart gave a leap of joy, and then a second, convulsive bound of terror. The doorway did not frame the blackness of long-closed corridors. It shone faintly yellow with light—a light that grew slowly, steadily stronger.

Before long it was a steady yellow glow that dimmed my flashlight beam. An arm appeared, carrying an electric lantern. The arm was followed by a body and by a face. I had had ample time to speculate about the identity of the man who was approaching. A number of names had flashed through my mind. Of them all, this was the most expected, and the one I least desired to see. Hassan.

The flat brown mask of his face was set in an odd half-smile, and his eyes were empty as holes in a piece of wood. His head was bare. He wore native dress.

He stood in the doorway, swaying gently; and then I realized why his eyes looked so empty. The pupils were almost invisible, shrunken to dots.

My inconvenient memory presented me with an old adage, advice to a woman who is about to be raped: "Relax and enjoy it." Once I had thought that mildly witty. Now I felt sure that some man had composed it. The reality, of which I had already had a preview, wasn't funny at all. And really, I thought, stepping care-

fully back before Hassan's slow advance, you
couldn't expect a man to realize ... The only
reason why they include it in their law codes
and lists of sins is because it's a form of property
violation. Like stealing a horse. Nobody asks the
horse how it feels about being stolen. Presum-
ably it doesn't care.

Hassan put the lantern carefully down on a
pile of boxes. His hands were beautiful under
the light, long-fingered and graceful. I knew,
with a sick certainty that defied masculine max-
ims, that if those hands touched me again I
would start screaming my head off.

I turned the flashlight off; there was no sense
in wasting the light. It would go out anyhow
when I hit Hassan with it. If I got the chance to
hit him ... The flashlight made a lousy weapon.
It was aluminum, too light to be dangerous.

Keeping my eyes fixed on Hassan's handsome,
dreamy face, I crouched and set my fingers scrab-
bling among the objects that littered the floor. He
had stopped moving. He was utterly relaxed and
smiling. He had all the time in the world.

My fingers closed on something solid. I never
knew what it was. It might have been a chunk of
rock, or a priceless gold statue. All it meant to me
was a missile.

Fear had cleared my brain, but it hadn't given

any supernatural skill to my throwing arm. I missed Hassan. The object smacked into the pile of boxes, which wobbled and swayed and then collapsed, carrying the lamp with it.

If it had been an oil lamp the whole place would have gone up in flames; the ancient wood and fabric were dry as tinder. Instead the lamp hit the floor with a smash and tinkle of broken glass, and darkness swooped down.

I took three running steps to the left. On the third step I kicked over a basket, and a small shower of objects rolled on to the floor. The sound was drowned in the louder crash of Hassan's body hitting the sarcophagus. The shock must have shaken his drugged peace; he gave out with a string of sibilant Arabic curses, and under cover of his profanity I moved again, slithering around the corner of the sarcophagus.

My heart was pounding like a kettledrum; it seemed to me that Hassan must hear it. One hand braced on the hard stone side of the sarcophagus, I tried desperately to plan. Even if I found the exit doorway, in the dark and without interference, I wouldn't be any better off. He knew the way out and I did not.

Then Hassan spoke. It was the first human voice I had heard for hours, and the shock of it nearly sent me sprawling.

"Where are you? Why do you run away?
There is no way out. Come . . ."

The whispered syllables echoed and dissi-
pated, unlocalized. In my panic I made a mistake. I moved. The sole of my shoe scraped the
floor and then I felt movement. A hand brushed
my face. I let out an involuntary yell and backed
up, stepping heavily on some object that splin-
tered and squashed. Luckily he was no better at
locating sounds than I was. He passed me so
closely that the breeze of his flapping robe sent
goose-pimples leaping up on my arms.

I stood perfectly still, with one foot in a ruined
box and splinters stabbing my ankle. I didn't
even breathe.

I knew that there was only one chance of escaping him for good. There were objects in the
litter which might serve as weapons. I remembered particularly a group of round stone pots
which had once held cosmetics. If I could get my
hands on one such heavy object, and then let him
catch me, I might be able to knock him out.

It might work—if I could find a weapon, if he
didn't strike it out of my hand, if he didn't have
the elementary sense to pin my arms first of all. It
was a terrible plan. It would fail, if for no other
reason than that I would never be able to bring

myself, in cold blood, to let the little swine touch me.

Yet I knew that I had to do something and do it fast. My ankle was streaming blood from a dozen splinters, and I was beginning to shake uncontrollably with terror and the strain of standing in absolute stillness.

Bending from the waist, keeping my knees stiff, I willed eyes into my fingertips and brushed them lightly across the floor. I bit back a gasp of relief when they felt, almost at once, the shape of one of the heavy stone pots. Not only did I have a weapon, but I knew approximately where I was. The pots were in a corner near the box of papyri.

Then I heard him, and the quickened blood in my veins froze. He too had been making plans. My senses, sharpened by the loss of sight, interpreted his intent. No more wild dashes for Hassan. He was doing what he should have done from the beginning—slowly moving along the narrow corridor between the wall and the sarcophagus. His outstretched arms would almost span the space; there wasn't a chance of slipping past him. All I could do was retreat; and sooner or later he would corner me—in a literal corner or, if I got out into the corridor, in a blind alley.

He was making no attempt to be silent; he had no need to be. But the soft noises of his inexorable approach gave me the chance I needed. I raised one foot and stretched it out. My toe touched the object I expected to find—the box of papyri.

He was so close by then that I marveled he did not sense my presence, as I sensed his. I had only seconds in which to act; but the act would take less than a second. One brisk movement of my foot, and the contents of the box would spill out onto the floor, three feet from where I stood. Surely Hassan wouldn't pass up a lure like that one, so close as to be unmistakable. When, and if, he dived at the sound, I would hit him with my handy alabaster pot. I pulled my foot back a few inches, to give the movement impetus.

I couldn't do it.

I find it hard to believe myself. I had been brought up in the business, of course, and had absorbed its ideals through my very pores. Not fifteen minutes earlier I had been so infected by the sheer joy of discovery that I had temporarily forgotten my own danger. But if anyone had proposed, even at that great moment, that I risk myself for some damned antique, my laughter would have been decidedly rude.

But I couldn't kick that box. Not that box, not

even with Hassan practically breathing down the back of my neck. Of all the things in the tomb, those papyri were the most provocative. They might contain anything—love songs, poems, the lost ritual of man's first vision of One God, historical records . . . Well, it sounds insane, even to me. But when I went down, with Hassan's beautiful strangling hands wrapped around my throat and Hassan's beautiful heavy body mashing me, I managed to twist my own body so that our combined weights hit something other than that infernal, betraying box of papyrus scrolls.

I never did get a chance to use my alabaster pot. It was under me when I hit the floor, and it nearly dented my spine. I got Hassan's hands off my throat by clawing at his eyes, and then I screamed till my throat ached—pure reflex, because there was no one to hear me. . . .

When I saw the light, over Hassan's shoulder, I was sure my brain had given way. There was no physical source from which light could come; my flashlight was buried somewhere across the room and Hassan's lantern was broken. Yet the light persisted and grew stronger. I saw the open door, saw the space behind it turn from black to gray to yellow.

Hassan was too absorbed in his own activities

to notice the light or the man who came into the room—a man who carried a lantern in one hand and a big black pistol in the other. The lantern lifted and the newcomer took a long leisurely look at the view. Then the gun lifted. It centered right in the middle of Hassan's back. I let out a loud, startled shout. I didn't care if the nasty little devil got filled with as many holes as a Swiss cheese, but any bullet that hit him would probably hit me as well. Perhaps the newcomer realized this too. The anger faded out of his face. With a deft movement he reversed the gun and brought it down in a smashing blow on the back of the boy's head.

Hassan went limp, knocking the last scrap of breath out of my lungs. The newcomer rolled him off me with a contemptuous foot, and extended a hand to help me up.

I stayed on my feet for about three seconds. Then I dropped with a thud at the base of the sarcophagus and huddled there like an embryo, covering my face with my hands.

I felt I was entitled to a first-class case of hysterics; but I couldn't enjoy them yet. Not with Mr. Bloch and his big black gun looming over me. Somehow it never occurred to me that he had come rushing to my rescue. The rescue was only incidental, possibly temporary. How he had found the tomb when all the experts had failed, I could not imagine, but his motives, and his identity, were only too clear. Now I knew who had banged me on the head at Deir el Bahri—and why.

"Tsk, tsk," said Mr. Bloch. He put his lamp on the floor and returned the gun to his jacket pocket.

I watched him through my fingers. His face was pink and scrubbed; he had surely shaved within the past hour. He still looked tired—and no wonder, he had probably been up all night for several nights, looting the tomb. What a consummate actor the man was! I gritted my teeth in silent rage as I remembered the pensive figure drooping on the doorsill as I went back into the black recesses of the temple where he had carefully steered me after discovering that Dee had talked to me before her disappearance. And I had been so reluctant to destroy the man's "last hope" by admitting that she had told me absolutely nothing! "And her mother dead all these years . . ."

"Rrrr," I said, low in my throat like a dog, and wondered if there were any chance of getting the gun away from him. I decided the chance was fairly slim. He was twice my age, but he was also twice my size. Yet I think I would have tried, if I hadn't seen something else. There was more light, in the next room, and the sound of voices. Bloch had brought his porters with him.

"Thanks," I said, dropping my hands and giving him a crafty smile.

He waved one neatly manicured hand.

"Why, don't mention it. The boy has been getting a bit above himself lately. Excuse me just a minute."

He disappeared through the door and returned almost at once with an armload of goodies—several bottles, a folded blanket, and a white cardboard box. The box almost brought on the fit of hysterical laughter I was fighting to control. It was one of the picnic lunches packed by the hotel.

Mr. Bloch handed it to me with a courtly bow.

"The condemned man ate a hearty meal," I said.

"Now don't talk that way," Mr. Bloch said reproachfully. He looked around for something to sit on, and finally, wrinkling his nose, he joined me on the floor. "I wouldn't hurt a nice girl like you."

"Except for a little tap on the head."

"Sorry about that," said Mr. Bloch solemnly. "But you know I can't take any chances. You won't have to stay here long, Tommy. And I'll do

my best to see you're comfortable. Have a sandwich," said Mr. Bloch, offering me the lunch box.

"I'd rather have a drink, if you don't mind."

"Gracious, I didn't think. Of course you must
be terribly thirsty."

I watched intently as he opened one of the bottles. He used a pocket knife with a dozen attach-
ments; and thirsty as I was, my eyes ignored the
bottle in favor of the knife. Heavens, the man
was a walking arsenal; if I could get my hands on
one of those weapons, gun or knife . . .

The lemon pop was repulsive stuff—luke-
warm, bubbly, and sickeningly sweet. But it was
wet. The sheer sensual pleasure of the liquid in
my dusty throat almost distracted me; but I noticed into which of Mr. Bloch's pockets the knife
went.

"Now," he said, as I wiped fuzz off my chin,
"let me just put your mind at rest. I can't take
much more time over this business. It's a pity, because some of these nice things are going to get
busted up, but your friend is giving me a hard
time. I've got to get this stuff out tomorrow
night—tonight, in fact, because it's almost morning now. After I've finished, I'll let you go."

"You can't do that," I argued idiotically. "If I
go to the police—"

"Well, now, I don't like to underrate you,

child, but I think it'll be a case of your word against mine. And I've got two good witnesses to swear I was haunting the telegraph office all night long."

I took another swig of the nasty lemon drink and cogitated. Maybe he was telling the truth. Maybe he wasn't. Well, I'd find out soon enough. And maybe I wouldn't like the answer.

I shivered. Mr. Bloch patted my hand. He was a very accomplished hand-patter.

"Don't you worry, Tommy. I wouldn't hurt a nice American girl like you."

"Prove it," I said. "Convince me. I'd love to believe you."

Mr. Bloch grinned.

"You're quite a girl. See here—pick out something."

"Huh?"

"A little souvenir. Compensation for that tap on the head." He picked up a casket made of ivory and ebony, with four squat legs. It was secured by a piece of rotting twine wound around two ivory knobs, one on the side of the box and one on its lid. Bloch snapped the twine with a twist of his fat fingers and raised the lid. The interior swam with color—turquoise, coral, lapis-blue, gold. Bloch's hand dipped into the casket and lifted out a necklace. It had pendants of pierced stars inlaid with carnelian and minute, granulated gold balls; they hung from a delicate gold chain.

"Pretty," he said, dangling it. "Here, take it."

I doubt if there was a woman alive who could have kept her hands away from it. It lay across my fingers like a web spun by magic golden spiders.

"What . . . what am I supposed to do with this?"

"Why, keep it." Bloch's eyes were narrowed, contradicting his casual tone. He hadn't missed a nuance—my quick intake of breath, the caress and clasp of my fingers. "I'm not trying to bribe you. I don't have to. Just a memento, you might say."

I was speechless. With an amused quirk of his lips, Bloch took the ornament and draped it around my neck, above the collar of my torn, filthy tailored blouse. The ancient clasp still functioned. I sat in a paralysis of bewilderment, with the metal of a dead queen's jewels cold on my throat.

"Looks nice on you," Bloch said pleasantly. He glanced at his watch. "Time's running on. Afraid I've got to run too. Now, honey, you just take it easy. Get some sleep."

"Oh, please . . . please!" I clutched at his arm,

and not all my panic was assumed. "I'm afraid to stay here in the dark."

"What are you afraid of? Hassan? That young man won't bother you anymore."

He twisted one hand in the front of Hassan's robe and hauled him up. The boy's head hung obscenely limp on one shoulder. He looked dead. Bloch, displaying a strength I had only suspected before, dragged the lax body out through the door and returned, dusting his hands.

"Is he . . . is he dead?"

"Not yet. No, not just yet. You see, I need him for a while longer. For a particular job."

"Hassan the Assassin," I said, with a nervous giggle. "That's his job, isn't it?"

"Some people," said Bloch didactically, "don't particularly relish killing, but they don't mind it, either. It's just a way of earning a living. Others get a real kick out of hurting people. Like our boy Hassan. In my business I prefer the first type. They're more dependable. But I have to use what's available."

"And reward them suitably. Am I part of Hassan's pay envelope?"

He was almost at the door; but when my words reached him he spun around, very lightly for a man of his bulk. His face was mottled with anger.

"Hell, no! You think I'd let one of these dirty Arabs mess around with a decent American girl? Darn it, Tommy, you owe me an apology!"

I was silent, seeing, with my inner eye, a succession of brown faces—Abdelal, Achmed, Mr. Fakhry of the American Express, all the familiar, friendly faces of the men who had worked for my father. There wasn't one of them whose boots Bloch was fit to polish—if they had owned boots. My panic vanished in a rush of cold anger. I said deliberately,

"I misjudged you."

"You sure did!" He took a few steps toward me. Incredibly, his reputation meant something to him; he was willing to spend time defending it, never knowing that he represented something so alien to me that he might have been a buggy-eyed monster from another planet.

"Tommy, think of me as a businessman. That's all I am. I don't resort to violence—except when I have to, naturally. My gosh, you talk as if I liked killing people!"

"Oh, I'm sure you don't particularly like killing people."

"Course not. And I'm going to take good care

of you, don't you worry. See here, I'm going to leave you a blanket. By gosh, I'll even leave another flashlight; I see yours got broken. Now eat your nice lunch and take a little nap, and I'll come back tonight and let you out. Okay?"

He gave me a broad, toothy grin which was meant to be reassuring. I couldn't help thinking of the unfortunate young lady from Riga. Before he left, he fussily picked up the bits of broken glass from Hassan's lamp; but when he turned for his final word, he was no longer smiling.

"Don't waste time trying to get out of here, Tommy. The outer door is granite; it takes three men to move it. I've also arranged a little trap near the entrance. I meant it for unwelcome visitors, but it'll do just as well to keep people in as to keep them out. If you run into it, you'll be here permanently. Just don't move out of this room and you'll be all right."

The movements and voices in the next room went on for some time. Finally they began to fade, and the light faded with them, as if the men were retreating down a long corridor. Then light and voices vanished; and I was again alone in the dark.

Alone, but no longer afraid. Fumblingly I located the lunch box and opened it. I didn't need a light to identify the contents. They were always the same: cold chicken slices, a ham sandwich, an orange and a tangerine, a hard-boiled egg, a tomato, and a slab of dry cake. I wasn't hungry. But I knew I was going to need all the wit and strength I could get, and that dry ham sandwich might provide the one extra burst of energy that would save a life.

John's, or Mike's. Or maybe both. That was the job Bloch needed Hassan for.

Bloch was correct. The police wouldn't pay any attention to a hysterical girl. They didn't even dream that a tomb existed. If I started babbling about Nefertiti, they would shrug, shake their heads sadly, and write me off as some kind of pyramidiot.

But if my wild tale were backed up by two responsible, respected professionals, Bloch would be in real trouble. He was already in trouble; because, if I knew John and Mike, they would be taking Luxor apart rock by rock looking for me. Probably all exits from the country were being watched. If Bloch hoped to get away with his loot, safely, he would have to get rid of both archaeologists.

I smacked my egg viciously against the sarcophagus, with only a fleeting awareness of the incongruity of the gesture, and started to peel off the shell. I wished my watch hadn't stopped.

Bloch had said that it was almost morning, but I couldn't take his word even for something as minor as the time of day. He was as crooked as a pretzel. But if he was telling the truth, then I had a little time. The attack could not be made during the day, especially by Hassan, whose courage was of the rodent variety. The danger period would begin at sunset—when the tourists had deserted the west bank, the villagers had gone to bed with the chickens, and the darkness was unbroken by street lights or shop windows.

I peeled my orange and sucked it slowly. Bloch had tidily removed the empty pop bottles, so the fruit was the only liquid I had. I was going to be very thirsty before nightfall, for the air in the long-closed place was as dry as a mummy. But thirst was the least of my worries.

I wondered whether my fatigue and distress were not making me overly fearful about Bloch's intentions. If he did mean to kill both men, he had a problem, because he didn't dare risk any suspicions of murder. It would be hard to rig up a convincing accident which would dispose of two strong, healthy men. The duality alone ruled out most of the good old reliable household accidents, from electrocution to overdoses of sleeping medicine. How about falls—off cliffs, for instance? Again, with two people to dispose of, that method would not appear very plausible. Drowning? It would be nearly impossible. Both men were strong swimmers.

I spat the orange seeds into my hand; there was nobody around to report me to Emily Post. I couldn't seem to think of any more accidents. Food poisoning? Possibly, but with the risk of a postmortem . . .

Then I almost choked on the dry slab of cake. If Bloch wanted to get me out of his hair without offending his sensitive nature, the simplest course would be to slip something in my food. By the time he returned I would be neatly laid out and getting cold—no nice American girls weltering in their blood or turning blue in the face.

It took some willpower to sink my teeth into the cake; but I forced myself to do it. If I began yielding to wild fantasies, I would never get out. Common sense told me that if the man had meant to poison me, he wouldn't have put anything in the cake, which was not even iced. No, if he had planned for me to eat something nasty, it was already inside me, so there was no need to worry. And, against all reason, I was inclined to believe Bloch when he said he meant me no harm. It was peculiar to find a soft spot in a man so totally without scruples, and yet it is just such incongruities that make up a human being. I finished the food to the last crumb.

The poisoning idea had distracted me. I sat in the darkness, chin propped on two very dirty fists, my back up against the sarcophagus, and went on thinking. Bloch was obviously quite ready to sacrifice Hassan. How about having Hassan kill the two men openly, and then get shot escaping from the scene of the crime? Bloch could shoot the boy himself, and he would probably do a very neat job of it.

Suddenly the heavy food seemed to weigh nauseatingly on my stomach. It was working out only too well. A murder wouldn't interfere with Bloch's plans so long as the murderer was caught right away, and so long as his motive had no relation to missing tombs or smuggled antiquities. Hassan's part in Dee's flight was an open secret, and I was willing to bet that the whole village of Gurnah knew he had attacked me and tried to kill his own brother . . .

Yes, Achmed knew Hassan was guilty; that knowledge explained the former boy's strange behavior. Like his father, he had been torn between two emotions—the village tradition of solidarity against authority, and a healthy hatred of his treacherous brother. Hassan was mad and bad and sick; no one would be surprised if he ran amok and slaughtered two more people, and everyone would be quietly relieved if he was eliminated.

I was shivering so violently that my head banged on the stone of the sarcophagus. My imagination is too good. I could see the whole thing as vividly as reality. The crouching, feral figure of Hassan, quite unaware of his employer's real plans; the sudden leap, the bright flash of the knife . . . Hassan might need help; he couldn't handle both men alone. But he could do the actual killing, finishing off a bound and helpless prisoner. Hassan would like that. He would do it slowly, smiling; first a prick, then a probe, before the blade sank home, in heart or throat . . .

I surged to my feet, clutching the flashlight like a club. Assume it was about seven o'clock . . . Then I had some twelve hours. Not too long, if I had to chip a passage through solid rock. Not long enough. But if there was no other way, Bloch would find me stretched out on the floor, still chipping, when he came back.

Chapter 8

For the first time I walked through the doorway and into the outer chambers of the tomb.

They and their contents were fabulous, fantastic, incredible—but by that time I was running out of superlatives and my sense of wonder was smothered under a heavy layer of terror. I noted almost absently the curve of a gilded throne seat, the winking sparks of gold and crimson and blue reflected by the rounded sides of glass bottles nested in a painted chest. Bloch and his men had been busy; there were vacant spaces on the floor, and some of the rougher boxes were empty.

One object roused me a little—a big gilded shrine with a curved top, whose interior gaped emptily. On the golden floor of the shrine two sets of uncanny miniature footprints still remained. One of the golden statues which had made those prints was now in John's safe at the Institute. The other, surely a statue of Nefertiti's husband, must have been taken by Bloch. I wondered how much he would sell it for. Ten thousand? Twenty-five? And that was one item from the whole collection.

As I shuffled cautiously through the close-packed treasures, the plan of the tomb became clear. The main sarcophagus chamber and its smaller auxiliary lay at the far end of the tomb from the entrance. Next—from my point of view—came two storerooms and a good-sized hall with four square pillars. At one side of the hall was the tiny chamber containing the empty shrine. And on the far side of the hall, directly opposite the door through which I had entered, was another doorway—an impressive structure with sloping sides and a squared-off lintel. This opened on to the corridor which led to the outer world.

The beam of my flashlight died in the distance of that long passage cut through solid rock. It was over two hundred feet long, and it sloped steadily upward. Twice I climbed roughhewn stairs, once scrambled on bruised hands and knees up a steep ramp strewn with gravelly rock. There were footprints on the dust of the stairs; and on the last of the two flights I stopped, gripped by an eerie notion. The marks I saw in the thin dust had been made by Bloch and his crew, but beneath them were the half-obliterated traces of my father's feet. He, in turn, had scuffed unheeding over the prints of sandaled soles left three thousand years ago by the retreating funeral party.

Footprints in the dust, unmarred by wind or rain—ephemeral mementos of mortality that had survived the flesh that made them. It was strange to think that there still might be, in some remote angle of a stair, a physical fragment of Jake.

Jake's footprint in the dust. It was a neatly ironic symbol of his role in the whole affair. The fact that I was the one to be trapped in the tangled jungle of deceit whose seeds he had innocently planted only made the irony more complete; for Jake would never have countenanced these latest developments. Guilty he might be, in the legal sense, but he was innocent of intent to harm a living soul. Probably he had thought of the whole business as a gigantic joke, and of himself as an archaeological Robin Hood, robbing, not just the rich, but the rich of another time and place, whose withered flesh had no more need of gold. Yes, odd as it might sound, innocent was just the word for Jake. He always had a quality of childlike selfishness about the consequences of his actions. In our relationship I had been playmate and nursemaid as well as daughter.

Standing there on the dusty stairs, with the air of dead centuries clogging my throat, I realized that I owed Mr. Bloch something after all. He had given me back my father—considerably tarnished, but established, now and forever, in his proper place in my memories, and forgivable, if only by comparison. Compared to Bloch, Jake hadn't been so bad.

I went on up the stairs. I had to keep the flashlight trained on my feet to avoid stumbling, but was dimly aware that the corridor walls blazed with color, with painted scenes and inscriptions in hieroglyphic writing. My legs ached from climbing. Surely I must be nearing the entrance . . .

"Near the entrance." That was where Bloch had set his trap.

I swayed to a stop at the top of the stairs, the flashlight slippery in sweating hands. Bloch was capable, I felt sure, of setting a particularly gruesome trap. I wished he had given me some clue as to its nature; it could be anything from a block of stone propped up to fall and mash my skull, to a nest of scorpions in a corner of a stair.

I shone the light straight ahead, squinting to see through the dust-laden air. The tunnel stretched on; but at the very end of my vision, where the narrow beam was overcome by darkness, I thought I saw another set of stairs.

I covered the next section of corridor like a snail, like a tortoise, testing every foothold before I put my weight on it, flashing the light over every inch of wall, ceiling, and floor. Once I stopped, my heart blocking my throat, as a deep rectangle of shadow took shape on the low ceiling. It was only a rough overhang of rock which the workers had not smoothed. By the time I reached the stairs, I was gasping.

There were eight steps. I stood at the foot and counted them. Eight steps and, at the top, the end, the exit, the door to the outside world. Only the door was closed. The opening was blocked by a monolithic chunk of stone that glowed palely red, speckled with tiny flecks of black, its color distinct against the pale buff rock of walls and floors. Walls and floor had been shaped from the Theban cliffs, a soft limestone. The slab was Aswan granite, carried all the way from the southern border of Egypt to bar irreverent hands from the slumbering dead.

The ancient Egyptians cut limestone with copper tools. It is still something of a mystery as to how they cut the much harder granite. And I didn't even have copper tools.

I sagged against the wall, forgetting for a moment the possibility of a trap. Then I remembered and leaped back into the middle of the corridor. From that spot I stared in frustrated despair at the stairs. They were such lovely things to booby-trap, those steps. I could think of six ways of doing it, and Bloch's experience was bound to be broader than mine.

The slab was a beautiful piece of stone, smoothly finished, about four feet high and three feet wide. I didn't have to see its other dimensions to know that it was, to all intents and purposes, immovable. I knew all about stones like this one. They were called portcullis stones by archaeologists, and they were often used, in the passageways of tombs and pyramids, to block the way so that thieves couldn't pass. They were made of the hardest stones obtainable, weighing in the thousands of pounds. They were not hinged or balanced, because they were not doors. They were barricades.

My head felt like a balloon stuffed with cotton,

and my ears buzzed. The air was very bad and I was dizzy with tension and despair. I wished I could sit down, but I was afraid I might sit on Bloch's trap. I wished I had a cigarette, but Bloch had taken my purse. I damned Bloch. And caught myself, on the third syllable of a four-syllable expletive, as a new idea blossomed in my tired brain.

Why had the gentlemanly Mr. Bloch, who had supplied me with lunch boxes and flashlights, deprived me of an object which is almost as vital to a woman as her clothes? My purse was certainly not in the tomb; I would have seen it. He couldn't be afraid of anything it contained, because I carried nothing more lethal than a nail file. Could it be because an object as flimsy as a nail file might conceivably be useful to me in my present situation? A nail file—or a piece of sharp glass, like the glass in Hassan's lamp, or an empty pop bottle?

It was a preposterous idea. Again I seemed to hear Bloch saying, "It takes three men to move the door . . . I've laid a little trap near the entrance . . ."

Did it? Had he? Or were those remarks only bluffs, to frighten me and frustrate me so that I wouldn't try to get out? Once again I turned my light on the granite slab. Three men? It would take a charge of dynamite to move that stone. No one could move it. No one *had* moved it. There was another way out—and I knew what it was.

In my surge of excitement I nearly leaped up the stairs. But I wasn't quite ready to dismiss Bloch's second statement as the bluff which the first statement surely must be. I could hear Jake now, lecturing on the history of tomb robbing. It had been, now that I thought about it, one of his favorite subjects.

Almost all the royal tombs had been robbed in antiquity, despite the complex methods of protection the Pharaohs had employed. The location of the rooms was no secret to the workers who had carved them; and granite portcullis stones had one limitation. They were finite in size. Intelligent thieves didn't bother trying to move them or cut through them. The thieves simply went around them, tunneling through the softer sand- or limestone of the surrounding rocks.

My thoughts of Jake were fairly kindly just then. He had gotten me into this, but maybe, just maybe, he was going to get me out. Somewhere along the wall there was another exit. It would be blocked, but not by anything as massive as granite. Jake and Abdelal had come in and out,

Hassan had come alone. Anything Hassan could move, I could move.

My memories of Jake's lectures, reinforced by simple common sense, gave me another vital piece of information. The secondary, thieves' exit must be very near the original granite slab. Limestone is softer than granite, but it isn't cheese, and no one cuts any more of it than he has to. The original thieves had probably cut right alongside the granite, and reentered the corridor as soon as that obstruction was passed.

So I had to climb those stairs . . .

My foot was on the lowest step when I heard it. It was not a loud sound, but the very fact of noise, in that place where nothing but I myself had a right to be moving, paralyzed me with an icy shock of terror. The paralysis didn't last long. I was off down the long corridor as soon as my sluggish senses identified the quality of the noise. A dry rustling noise—just the sort of noise that might have been made by grisly, desiccated mummy wrappings in a horror story. Or by the scales on a sliding, footless body.

I stopped at the bottom of the next flight of stairs, not because I had regained my nerve, but because I had lost my breath. Shaking like a bowl of custard, I managed to focus the flashlight back

along the way I had come. There was nothing to
be seen. The creature had not pursued me. I
hadn't expected that it would. It was waiting,
near the last stairs. Near the exit.

It was hopeless. Without a weapon, without
even boots to protect my legs against enven-
omed fangs, it would be suicide to try to pass the
watcher at the doorway. With a weapon—well, it
wouldn't have been easy, but I might have done
it. Snakes are sluggish and lazy unless provoked,
and a pistol . . .

I laughed out loud, and the hoarse chuckle
was the most gruesome sound I had heard all
night. So all I needed was a pistol. Just the thing
to find lying around an ancient Egyptian tomb.
There were a lot of heavy objects, certainly; but
anything heavy enough to immobilize, let's say,
a cobra, was too heavy for me to throw accurately. A king's tomb would probably contain
weapons—things like spears and boomerangs
and bows. Their wooden shafts would be de-
cayed, their copper points green and rotted . . .

Then came the eeriest experience of that whole
eerie episode. I was standing, hand braced
against the wall, staring blankly at the painted
figure of a god which decorated this section of
the tunnel. He was a stiff white shape seated on a
throne, his black face framed by the bizarrely

shaped White Crown. Osiris, Lord of the Westerners, judging the dead. An odd sight to find
here, in the tomb of the king who had cursed the
old gods and abandoned them. Had Nefertiti returned to the old faith after her husband died, or
had his successor, young Tutankhamen, placed
the hallowed figures on the outer walls to de-
ceive any suspicious priestly visitor? I wondered, staring . . . And as I stared, the form of
Osiris faded from my sight. Again I remembered
a moment from the vanished past, but this time
memory was so vivid that I could have sworn I
saw a dead face, and heard a voice that had been
silent for ten long years.

Jake looked young and handsome that day;
his dark eyes sparkled, his hair was a little un-
ruly. We were standing in the Jewel Room of the
Cairo Museum, and in the case before us were
the golden ornaments of a king, the fabulous
treasure of Tutankhamen. Under the thick glass
two daggers lay displayed. One was gold, with a
handle of exquisite beauty, carved and bur-
nished. The haft of the other knife was set with
tiny balls of beaded gold in elegant patterns inlaid with colored glass. It ended in a knob of
pure rock crystal. But the blade was not gold; it
shone with a wicked gray gleam. And Jake had
said, "Iron. One of the earliest examples. It's in

remarkably good condition, isn't it? When it was taken from the king's mummy it was bright as steel, barely touched with rust."

The memory scene vanished as abruptly as it had come. Again I stood swaying in a dark, stone-cut corridor, my eyes fixed on a painted god. Osiris judging the soul. The judgment of the dead . . . and Anubis, jackal-headed, leading the dead man; Thoth, god of wisdom, by the balanced scales, pen raised to record the verdict.

If there was any justice in the universe, there should be something for me in that tomb which would mean salvation instead of death. I was almost running as I went back along the corridor toward the sarcophagus chamber.

Hours later, that curious vision seemed the most ironic joke of all. I had searched three rooms, dozens of boxes, and at least a hundred baskets. In the process I had done a lot of damage, despite my efforts to be careful. Some of the fabrics were gone for good. It didn't matter. If I didn't get out of the tomb in time to warn John and Mike, the more delicate objects were doomed in any case. And, without ever voicing it aloud, I had made my own last judgment. All the objects in the tomb put together were worth less than a human life.

I had found incredible things: jewelry enough

to stock a small shop, all so beautiful that under other circumstances I might have contemplated a little tomb robbing on my own account; small triangular loaves of fine bread, aged into stony petrification; sandals of leather, and gold, and straw, set with semiprecious stones; jars of wine and jars of milk, still retaining a scummed sediment; lamps and vases of porphyry and alabaster; a writing palette of ivory with the owner's name and titles incised in delicate hieroglyphs. But though the loot included a golden dagger, it was only a ceremonial weapon, too dull and soft to scratch my finger.

I had worked my way back to the sarcophagus chamber. Only two objects in the room remained unexplored. One was the box of papyri in the corner. I had a phobia about those scrolls, and it was unlikely that a weapon would have been tossed in among them.

The other unsearched object was the mummy of the king.

I sat back on my heels and turned my flashlight onto the stone sarcophagus. It was a beautiful quartzite which picked up the light in myriads of tiny sparkles.

In the past twenty-four hours I had done a number of things I would rather not have done, and my plans for the coming hours included several more improbabilities. Yet this one act seemed to me not just improbable, but utterly beyond my capabilities.

Of course I had known, all along, that the mummy was the most logical place on which to find the knife—if there was a knife. Tutankhamen's iron dagger had been on his body; iron was precious stuff in those days, rarer and more useful than gold. Ordinarily it would have been impossible to get at the mummy, through three coffins and a heavy stone sarcophagus lid, but someone had thoughtfully done the heavy work for me. The heart scarab had come from this burial, not from the queen's, which was clearly undisturbed. I would surely find, not only that the coffin lids had been removed, but that the bandages of the mummy had been slit or stripped away.

I sat in the hot, shadowed gloom and tried to stop shivering. My cowardly impulses produced frantic arguments: the boy king's dagger was unique; there was no reason to expect another such weapon here. I had already wasted hours on a fruitless search, prompted not by logic but by a meaningless memory. Why waste more time on a job that was not only distasteful, but almost surely useless?

The more sensible part of my brain came back

with the counterarguments. Tut's dagger had
been a sport, but so was his unrobbed tomb.
There was only one other royal unrobbed tomb—
the one I was presently inhabiting. If I had
wasted three or four hours on the less likely possibilities, it was worth spending fifteen minutes
more to investigate the most likely place.

The sarcophagus was about four feet high. I
could just rest my chin on its rim. I didn't; the
idea gave me the shivers. Holding the flashlight
at arm's length, I shone it down into the well of
blackness inside the stone rectangle.

Then, for a full minute, I stood motionless,
with my eyes fixed on the wall of the chamber in
a pained stare that saw nothing of its muraled
beauty. I did not want to look down into that sarcophagus. My guess that the coffin lids had been
removed had been confirmed by one hasty
glance at black emptiness; the topmost lid of a
nest of coffins would have been visible just below the rim of the sarcophagus. The coffin lids
were gone, and when I looked down, I would see
the mummy itself.

In that hushed darkness even the sight of a
shrouded form would be unnerving, but I had
good reason to suspect that I would see more
than that. Had Jake unveiled the face? He must
have been tempted to do so; a mixture of scien-

tific interest, ghoulish curiosity, and romantic
fascination would have prompted most people
to look on the features of the most controversial
of all the Pharaohs, the very flesh that had
walked the soil of Egypt over three thousand
years ago. I devoutly hoped Jake had resisted his
impulses. I too would like to see the face of
Akhenaton. But not right here and now.

I had thought that an unwrapped mummy
was the worst thing I could see. I was wrong.

The light seemed dimmer, dustier, as it
streamed down into that ultimate repository of
the past. It shone on the rims of the golden
coffins I had expected to see, and on one of the
lids, tilted awkwardly back against the inner
side of the sarcophagus. The other lids were
missing; possibly Bloch had already removed
them. The mummy had not been unwrapped,
not entirely. The bandages of the head were still
in place, covered by a thin veil of sheerest linen. I
didn't notice that. I didn't even see the other details I have mentioned, not then. I saw only one
object, which filled all of my consciousness.

On top of the ancient mummy, laid out with
hands crossed on the breast in ghastly parody of
the mummy shape, was the body of a woman.
She looked like one of the painted statues the
Egyptians placed in their tombs. Often the eyes

of such statues were inlaid with crystal. Her eyes, open and staring up, had the same dull shine.

I sat in a huddled heap at the foot of the sarcophagus, my arms wrapped around my body. I had been sitting there for a long time, maybe for hours. Part of the lost time was hidden in a hazy fog of memory, possibly a faint, possibly sleep; God knows I was tired enough. My search was over. I had been prepared to desecrate the frail body of the king, but I could not touch the more recent dead. And I couldn't examine the mummy without removing that which covered it.

Anyway, I thought dimly, what difference did it make? I could never get out by myself; I had been silly to think I could. My eventual fate depended not on my actions but on Bloch's; and his decision would rest on motives which were as undecipherable to me as the painted hieroglyphs which covered the walls of the tomb chamber. More so; I could read a little Egyptian. I would never understand a mind like Bloch's.

The flashlight wavered and shook, clutched in my quaking hands. Its beam glanced off a painted gold-trimmed box, sent sparks dancing from the gold collar of a cat carved out of green schist, which perched atop an oil jar. Maybe the cat was a memento of the king's mother, who had been fond of pets; there was one painting of her with her furry striped tabby waiting for scraps under her chair as she dined. The flashlight beam seemed dimmer, dustier; little motes swam in its paling light.

The flashlight was dimming and my mind was wandering . . . neither of them were good omens. If I encountered one more unexpected horror, Bloch wouldn't have to worry about disposing of me. When he came back, he would find me sitting at the foot of the sarcophagus staring into the shrouding darkness, my mind as empty as Dee's, and maybe just as permanently.

With my last shred of sense, I switched off the flashlight. Whatever else happened, I had to save that light for action. I didn't need it while I sat thinking—if you could call what passed through my mind thinking. The darkness leaped at me black-winged, like a bat. But after the first moment I found it rather restful.

Maybe it was high time I did some thinking. I had been rushing around like an animal in a cage, dashing myself insensately against the walls. Maybe there was a means of escape I hadn't seen, not because it was physically hidden, but because I was too preoccupied to recognize it. Maybe there was some hope for me in the tangled web of other people's actions which I had never understood.

Bloch? He would do whatever he considered necessary for self-preservation. But did that really include slaughtering everyone who got in his way? Surely an excess number of deaths would be as dangerous to him as a hostile witness. Dee's disappearance had already concentrated official attention on the town, an attention which must have intensified since I vanished into limbo. If John and Mike were found dead, the affair would take on proportions of a war. Achmed knew about the tomb, and by now, I suspected most of the adult population of Gurnah was also on the trail. It would take a full-scale massacre to make Bloch safe from suspicion. Not that he would mind a massacre, but I imagined he would find one hard to arrange. Bloch must know that. He must realize that flight was his best hope. And if he fled, he didn't have to kill anybody, including me.

I gave an audible sigh of relief, convinced for the moment by my wishful thinking, and leaned back against the side of the sarcophagus. Was it only my imagination, or did the stone feel colder than it had before? Yes, it was only my imagination. Still . . . I slumped forward, elbows on my knees, so that my back didn't touch the unyielding material with its unholy contents.

I didn't like to think about Dee. Poor little wretch; I was haunted by the feeling that I had failed her somehow, that if she had had confidence enough in me, she might have told me enough to save her life. Her death certainly suggested that Bloch was doing himself more than justice when he claimed to be reluctant to murder young American girls. His own daughter . . .

"You damned fool!"

I said the words out loud, straightening so suddenly that the stone at my back grated uncomfortably on the bones of my spine. Well, but . . . I'd never formulated that notion before, never given it conscious thought. Once it was expressed, its absurdity was immediately apparent.

Dee was no more Bloch's daughter than I was. Anyone but a donkey would have realized that long ago, from a dozen tiny but significant hints. And I, of all people, should have recognized Dee's type; it floated in and out of my own profession, never staying long because it lacked the grim determination and the talent necessary for success. "Models." The category included a lot of young girls who did a lot of things besides showing off clothes.

Bloch had hired Dee for a specific job—as a carrot with which to entrap a singularly stupid rabbit: me.

Once that fact was accepted, a lot of the pieces of the jigsaw puzzle slid into place. Bloch was the man to whom Jake had gone ten years before—not to buy the statue, but to furnish the men and the money for a systematic rape of the newly found tomb. Jake's unexpected death had ended the partnership and the project; for Jake would have had wits enough to keep the tomb's location to himself as a guarantee of fair play. Probably he hadn't even told Bloch about Abdelal. So, for ten years, Bloch had watched—again, me. He must have been watching, for he had known when Abdelal wrote to me, and he realized at once what the letter must signify. So he had hired Dee and inserted the mysterious advertisement, through one of his assistants, who had arranged to put the newspaper right under my oblivious nose. Meanwhile, back in Egypt, Bloch had corrupted Hassan, who was ready and willing to be corrupted. Perhaps he had tried to question Abdelal. No, that was impossible because the letter hadn't reached me until after the old man . . .

Once while I was walking in an adolescent daydream along the plateau above the Valley, I almost stumbled into a cleft that seemed to open up right at my feet. I remember the shock of surprise. In the musty darkness of the sarcophagus chamber the same unseen hand snatched savagely at my insides. The gap that had suddenly opened up was a flaw in my reasoning—a flaw so wide, so deep, that it tore the whole neat puzzle to pieces.

How had Bloch known about Abdelal's letter?

He had watched me, that was my superficial explanation. For ten years? So closely, so continually, that he even knew what mail I received? In novels the master criminals do things like that, but in real life master criminals don't have the manpower to waste on such nebulous possibilities. Bloch must have checked, after Jake's death, to make sure he had left no memoranda about the tomb, and my very inaction must have convinced him that I was unwitting. Jake hadn't expected to die, and he wasn't the sort of man who anticipated disasters. He hadn't even made a will.

Bloch would have had no reason whatsoever to watch me. Then how had he known about the letter? And how did he know that it had bearing on a quest he had abandoned ten years earlier?

By that time I was leaning forward with my hands clenched in my tousled hair, as if tugging could clarify my thoughts. For now, of all times, I had to think correctly.

Take the second question first. It was easy. The mere fact of the letter would have alerted anyone who knew the Arabic character and the history of Jake's discovery. Abdelal had loved me, after his fashion, but elderly Egyptian gentlemen do not wax sentimental about looking once more on the faces of old friends. He would not write unless he had a serious purpose. And if Abdelal had something important to tell me about Jake—as he had stated—that something could only be related to the one unusual, extraordinary episode in Jake's career. And if Abdelal knew the truth about that episode, he must know about the tomb. And if he knew about the tomb, he could only know because he had been concerned in its discovery. And if he had been concerned—then he knew where the tomb was.

The sound of my breathing, harsh and fast in the smothering dark, hurt my ears. It was working out, as neatly as a puzzle once the key piece is in place. I could dimly make out the shape of the final solution. That solution was the thing that quickened my breathing.

The reasoning which led from Abdelal's uncharacteristic involvement with the international mails to the conclusion that the location of the lost tomb was still accessible, in the mind of a living man, was one any interested party might have figured out. But he would have to know about the letter. The knowledge could not have come from the receiving end, from me, except by a set of coincidences which I could neither visualize nor admit. It could only come from the sending end. Who in Luxor could have known that the letter had been sent?

The post office? Possibly a clerk, a local boy, had noticed the letter and talked about it. But a lot of mail goes out of Luxor during the tourist season. It was unlikely that a busy, bored clerk would be struck by a particular letter. It had not even had a return address on the envelope.

Abdelal's family? Hassan leaped to mind as the obvious villain. But again it was unlikely that the old man would have confided in his unpleasant offspring, or been careless enough to betray his secret.

The air pumped in and out of my lungs with a force that made them ache. The conclusion I had been trying to avoid was forced upon me. Two people in Luxor had known that Abdelal intended to write me. About other sources I might conjecture; about those two, I knew. One of them had told me.

The conclusion was doubly valid because it

was confirmed by independent evidence. Bloch had found the tomb, interpreting data that not even I, for whom it had been meant, could interpret. By himself Bloch couldn't have located the tomb. He lacked not only an archaeologist's intimate knowledge of the terrain, but an intimate knowledge of me and my past activities, dreams, and hobbies. He had to have help, expert help.

Now I knew why he was not worried about my evidence. He wouldn't have to arrange a clumsy accident to rid himself of two damaging witnesses at once. Accidents that kill one person aren't difficult to arrange, particularly when the victim does not suspect that the man closest to him may be his betrayer. Hassan wasn't the only inhabitant of Luxor whom Bloch had corrupted. He had another ally—an archaeologist. There were a dozen archaeologists working in and around Luxor, but only two of them had known that old Abdelal had wanted the address of his former friend's daughter.

John McIntire and Michael Cassata.

Chapter 9

Osiris still sat in judgment on the painted wall, but now his white robe looked duller. The flashlight batteries were definitely failing. Knowing Mr. Bloch, I had a feeling that he had meant them to fail.

I held the flashlight in my left hand. In my right was an object for which any archaeologist in Luxor would have abandoned wife and children. A dagger with a gold hilt, the gold covered with minute beads of gold set in spiraling patterns whose coils were filled with a mosaic of tiny gems—rock crystal, turquoise, garnet, lapis lazuli. The blade wasn't so pretty; but it shone like steel, with hardly a touch of rust.

On the floor of the burial chamber Dee's body

lay next to the sarcophagus. She didn't weigh much, but it had been awkward lifting her out from the bottom of the sarcophagus, like dragging something out of a well. Bloch must have had her killed soon after she disappeared, for she had been dead some time. Rigor mortis had come and gone; the body was limp, which made things easier for me.

I had had another piece of luck. The dagger lay on the mummy's breast, not far from the slit chest bandages. That was a real break, because it would have taken me a long time to rip off the rest of the bandages. Some of them were rotted with age, but the top layer was stuck together in a hardened mass as if by glue. The substance wasn't glue, but a kind of resin; nobody knows why this sticky stuff, which hardens into a black, stiff mass, was poured over the wrapped mummy, but it often was. So I was very fortunate to see the gleam of gold on the mummy's left side, over the ribs. I wondered why Jake hadn't seen it when he slit the bandages and removed the heart scarab. I would like to have believed that he had a premonition of my need; just then I'd have relished a few reassuring omens.

These last lines sound absurdly calm and collected for a person who had performed the actions I have described. Yet they convey my state of mind with a fair degree of accuracy. Under the thrust of my latest theory I had passed through and beyond normal fears into a state of frozen calm. If I couldn't get out of that place in time to warn the man who sat unsuspecting in his room at Luxor Institute, I didn't care whether I ever got out. If I couldn't get past the snake, it was welcome to bite me. If it did, I could always use the knife to cut my wrists. According to the tales I had heard, bleeding to death is comparatively pleasant—compared to dying from snakebite.

There are a lot of snakes in Egypt, and a good many of them are poisonous. Usually they avoid houses, but at least twice during my stay poisonous reptiles had found their way into the courtyard at the Institute. Jake had killed one of them, blowing its head off with his pistol. Abdul the gateman had disposed of the other, pinning it to the ground with a knife.

Abdul was a good teacher, but it had been ten years since I tried to throw a knife. It was very unlikely that I could put this one in the right place. But I meant to try.

So I went marching on, enveloped in abnormal calm, and the gods of ancient Egypt marched with me in solemn processional, along the walls to right and left. Anubis, Osiris, Maat, slim goddess of truth with her jaunty feather

crown, Isis, wife and mother, Re, Hathor, who
symbolized love and beauty. Stiff and remote,
frozen in formal hieratic poses, the deities of another land and time. . . . I should have felt small
between their sacred ranks, but as I plodded forward I began to feel as if I were part of that procession—as if the arms that were raised in
blessing and in protection over the dead cast the
same ritual safety over my disheveled modern
head. To put it in practical terms: Maybe my
imagination had created the rustling noise.
Maybe there was no snake.

Which just goes to show that omens are no
good. There was a snake.

This time I both heard and saw it. The dry,
scaly rustle drew my eyes to the spot by the foot
of the stairs where a flat, pointed head raised itself on springy coils. I had one brief view; and
then the flashlight flickered and went out.

A few hours earlier I would have run screaming back down the dark corridor, and likely as
not dashed my brains out against the wall. Now
I didn't even bother to swear.

It did occur to me to say a small prayer. But if
there ever was a case of the Lord's helping those
who help themselves, this was it. I could hardly
expect Him to furnish me with another flashlight. Anyhow, I was somewhat confused as to

where to direct an appeal for divine aid. Outside in the village they prayed to Allah, who is, to be ecumenical, just another name for God. But down here in the dark the old gods were still alive. They had not vanished when the light went out; indeed, they seemed to be crowding closer. Ibis-headed, hawk-headed, jackal-headed, impossible composites of man and beast . . . All I can say is that just then they seemed—at least—possible. Maybe a prayer to ibis-headed Thoth, who presided over writing and all works of wisdom, might be appropriate.

Then I remembered the other flashlight.

There is some excuse for my not remembering it before. Bloch had forgotten it, or had assumed that the fragments of Hassan's torch came from the first one he had left me. After I put it down, Hassan and I had danced heavily around the room knocking things galleywest. I had assumed that the flashlight had been smashed, and I was probably right. But the part of a flashlight that breaks is the bulb. The batteries might still be good.

My progress back down the long corridor in the absolute blackness would have been nightmarish if I had not been still in the grasp of my odd mental detachment. As it was, I simply regretted the loss of time. I had to move slowly because I didn't know how far I was from the stairs. For a while I got down on hands and knees and crawled, but the floor was littered with tiny pebbles and gravel, and my hands were already scraped raw.

After miles of scuffling, one foot went off into space. I had found the stairs. I had forgotten how many steps there were, and I almost dropped the flashlight at the bottom when my toes, prepared for another step down, contacted rock ten inches above where I had expected it to be. The impact jarred my teeth together so hard I saw stars.

Perspiration popped out on my forehead as I went on more slowly. If I dropped this flashlight, I would be finished. There would be no recourse but to feel my way back, ignoring the snake and hoping that it was either not poisonous or not easily aggravated; and then to fumble over the entire wall surface near the granite slab in the forlorn hope of locating the plugged-up exit by feel. There were too many weak spots in that plan.

One thing happened during my gropings across the littered floor of the sarcophagus chamber. It almost broke my icy shell of self-possession, and I still dream about it sometimes—the moment when my questing hand, spurning jars and boxes and scattered gold, touched Dee's cold cheek.

Well, I found the flashlight and got the end unscrewed and put the batteries into the other torch. I was careful to point the repaired light toward the ceiling before I turned it on, and when the blessed beam of yellow appeared, I went quickly out of the room without a backward look.

The light was good, and that is the understatement of the year. It was also clear and strong, but that was not so important. Whatever I did had to be done quickly.

The snake was still there. I turned the light full on it and it responded; the flattened head swung silkily toward me, and two eyes, like glittering bits of obsidian, stared, not at me, but into the source of the light.

The snake was a racer. Common, big—and nonpoisonous.

I said, "Excuse me," as I walked past it, and heard it slither nervously away on down the corridor.

It wasn't until I got to the top of the flight of stairs that the reaction hit me, when my eyes fell on the gold hilt of the dagger clutched in my sweating hand. I laughed for a long time, and possibly I shed a few tears, and I know I called Mr. Bloch a few names. He thought he was pretty smart—and, by gosh, he was. Poisonous snakes aren't that easy to find in a hurry, and they are annoyingly undiscriminatory about whom they bite; but he had been sure that if I summoned up nerve enough to test his warning, the mere sight and sound of a reptile, any reptile, would send me scuttling. And he had been so right! He had only miscalculated in one thing, and I couldn't blame him for that, since I had not known the truth myself until I realized that one man's life was more important to me than tombs, treasures, or fifty cobras all spitting venom.

I put the dagger down on the top step—and then I picked it up and stuck it in the pocket of my skirt. You never can tell when a dagger will come in handy. I turned my flashlight toward the right-hand wall.

At first I saw nothing significant. After I had scanned every inch of the surface, I still saw nothing significant. The wall painting farther back along the corridor petered out at this end, being reduced to red line sketches at the foot of the stairs. Here, at the top of the stairs, there was nothing except a coating of plaster covering the crumbly stone from which the tomb had been cut—the first step in preparing a rough surface for painting. The plaster was cracked, but not in a regular pattern, and all the cracks seemed superficial. I turned to the left wall.

If it had been a snake, it would have bit me.

The aperture was about three feet by two and

roughly rectangular. The substance that filled it looked, at a casual glance and in shadow, like the same plaster that covered the rest of the wall, but this had been a hasty job; the color wasn't quite the same, and the plug didn't even fit the contours of the opening very accurately. I knew better than to push on it, though. It hadn't been put there to keep people in, but to mask the opening from the outside. I put my forefinger, with its dirty, torn nail, into the widest of the cracks, and gave a hearty tug.

And found myself lying on my back, feet in the air. Clutched to my bosom I held a piece of flimsy wood, which had popped out of the hole with an ease that sent me sprawling.

I thought up a few more picturesque names for Mr. Bloch. If he had not been a master at plucking at people's nerves, I could have walked down the corridor, and out, hours ago. I added a few epithets for myself and thrust my head impatiently into the black, gaping aperture in the wall. It was another stupid move, on a par with most of the moves I had made that day; my forehead banged into a hard, unyielding surface, so hard that once again I saw stars.

I shook my head blearily till the stars went away—all but one. That single bright point of diamond light continued to blazon the darkness. I shook my head till my hair flew, but the star didn't go away. Funny, I thought dizzily . . . I must have given myself a real bang on the head. I must be having hallucina—

It *was* a star. A real star, or maybe a planet; I was in no state to be scientific. Star, planet, or flying saucer driven by little green men, it was the most beautiful sight I had ever seen; for the glittering cold-white dot hung in the blue-black sky over Thebes. I was out.

Or nearly out. As my ringing head testified, there was still something between me and freedom. If I had stopped to think, I might have known that the hole did not open directly onto the cliff face, for the granite slab this side tunnel circumvented had to be two or three feet thick, and it must be masked on the outside by additional thicknesses of the local limestone. Otherwise the brilliant polished granite would have stood out like a stoplight, signaling potential thieves.

The side tunnel also had to be concealed from the outside. Apparently it had been casually filled with loose stones, so that anyone peering into the hole would see only debris which concealed the rough wooden panel. Most of the stones had been removed, to facilitate Bloch's comings and goings. The one largish boulder I had banged my head on was the major obstacle.

Then, belatedly, I realized the grimmer significance of the star. Night had fallen, and during the night Bloch would be back. He might be on his way now. He might have sent Hassan off on his last job. He might—my pronouns were getting mixed, but no more so than my frenzied thoughts—he might be dead by this time.

There were a lot of loose stones in the tunnel. I clawed at them, careless of my bleeding hands, and of the noise they made bouncing down the stair behind me. The big boulder was hard to move; I lost part of a nail in the process, but I paid no attention. As soon as the boulder was out of the way, I went in. The tunnel was short. By the time my heels were into it, my head was poking through the outer opening. And the sight that met my eyes was so astonishing that for a few seconds I forgot the need for haste.

I, and the lost tomb, were in the Valley of the Kings—the one place in Thebes which had been so thoroughly explored that no one thought of looking there.

I wasn't in the main Valley, but in the less popular West Branch. Even so, it was fantastic to think that this tomb had escaped discovery. Across the way was the tomb of Akhenaton's father; nearby, the tomb of the later Pharaoh who was one of his favorite officials. We should have thought of this. Perhaps we would have thought of it, except for Jake's sly precaution in taking only ornaments which would be identified as belonging to Nefertiti. No one would expect to find her tomb in the Valley of the Kings. But her husband . . . heavens, hadn't someone once said that he was the only king of that period whose tomb had not been found in the Valley? So much for premonitions; some stab of insight should have struck me when I heard that remark.

Yet all this was ex post facto reasoning, easy to see after the event. We had all been fooled, not only by Jake, but by another dead man—the young king Tutankhamen, who had reburied his father smack under the noses of the vengeful priests, in the sacred Valley which they controlled, perhaps in the very tomb which he had planned for himself. He died at eighteen; poor boy, he probably thought he had plenty of time in which to build himself another tomb. Instead he had ended up in the cramped rooms in the outer Valley, whose unroyal dimensions had been noted by many archaeologists.

Hamlet saw no reason why he should weep for Hecuba, but I shed a few tears for Tutankhamen. Maybe they were caused by the pain of my scraped knees, or by relief, or fatigue; but I doubt it, and I don't feel like apologizing for sentimentality, not even now.

I mopped my wet face with my skirt, blending dust and salt water into a horrible mask, and turned my mind to more practical considerations.

My goal was Luxor Institute, and my aim was speed, as much speed as possible. The quickest route from the Valley was via the well-known footpath over the hills to Deir el Bahri. But that path started in the main Valley, half a mile or so from my present location. Half a mile doesn't sound like a great distance; it is only about four city blocks. But this half mile was not smooth-paved sidewalk, it was convoluted rock, split by crevices and clefts, lacking street signs, street lights, and other conveniences. Some of the ravines could be circumnavigated. Others, like the road the poor old chicken had to cross, were too long to go around, and climbing down into them and back up out of them could be dangerous as well as time-consuming. My sense of direction has never been good; and if I got lost trying to go around ravines, and started off in the wrong direction, there was nothing but desert for hundreds of miles.

There was another path, one on which no one but an idiot could lose his way. This branch of the Valley of the Kings connected with the east branch; all I needed to do was follow the path at the bottom of the wadi, proceed along the path of the main Valley, and pick up the footpath near the tomb of Tutankhamen. The trouble was, this route would take a lot more time. Then, too, there was the small matter of getting up, or down, the cliff face in which my hole was situated. From my view of the opposite cliff, I knew I must be fairly high above the valley floor, nearer the top than the bottom. I didn't know what sort of climbing conditions I might encounter up above, or even whether a climb was possible. Down below, the slope was hidden in shadow, as was the Valley floor, but I always assume, as a general principle, that it is easier to go down than to go up.

I squatted there debating, and rocking dizzily with fatigue, for longer than I should have; and while I did, an eerie thing happened. Slowly the valley floor brightened, like a stage illuminated by waxing footlights. Rocks seem to spring up, shadow-limned, out of the dark shadow sea of the floor. The cliff face opposite paled till it glowed like a gray ghost. So receptive was my mood to wonder that it took me several long, shaken breaths to realize that the area really was getting lighter. The moon had risen.

I was in favor of light, the more light the better, but it had its good and bad points. I would be able to see my way better, but so would others better be able to see me. I slithered forward to the very edge of the hole, but my dazzled eyes still clung to the magic of the sight before them—moonrise over the Valley of the Kings, a landscape in silver and black, arched over by the vast luminous canopy of star-spangled sky; the moonwashed rock pale as milk . . .

I nearly fell out of the hole straight onto my head. Now, when it was too late to be of any use, I understood at last what Abdelal had been trying to tell me.

The Arabic name for the Valley of the Kings is the Biban el Melek. When I was thirteen, a particularly ghastly age for girls, my rudimentary sense of humor had found the resemblance between "melek" and "milk" worth noting, and I had decided to give a name to the one site in Thebes whose ancient name was unknown. I could even remember the occasion on which I had discussed the problem—good heavens, of course it had been Abdelal with whom I had discussed it, and our talk took place in this very Valley on a moonlit night when the silver light turned the stones to creamy white. I had gone on many walks with Abdelal, but that was the first, last, and only time I had seen this part of the valley under the full moon.

And that, I thought wearily, was probably the most useless inspiration I had had in a week of dumb ideas. I had wasted enough time already, and if I didn't get moving soon, a deadly combination of exhaustion, nervous reaction, and dread would weaken me to the point where I couldn't move at all.

I poked my head out of the hole and stared straight down. The first ten feet below my perch were discouraging, a sheer drop of unbroken rock, or so it appeared. Below that was a long slope of weathered stone and pebbles, a scree, I think mountaineers call it. Getting down that wouldn't be difficult, but it would be noisy as a drum solo once the rocks started to roll with me. I turned on my back and looked up. As I had suspected, the rim of the cliff was only about thirty feet above. A long, narrow crevice ran almost straight down and ended a few feet to my right, just about at the point where the original opening of the tomb ought to be. There wasn't the slightest trace of red granite showing, but that wasn't surprising; Bloch would make sure that dead giveaway remained concealed.

I turned around. If that sounds easy, let me point out that the tunnel wasn't much wider than I was. Finally my head was pointing back toward the tomb and my feet were sticking out the hole. Lowering myself onto my stomach, I squirmed backward, over loose stones that scratched my skin, and groped for the first toe-hold.

I was pretty sure I would find one, because Bloch's portly form had been up and down that cliff several times. But he knew where to put his feet, and I didn't, and I was just about ready to go back into my hole and take my shoes off when my rubber-tipped toe slipped into a crack.

I let my weight sag, taking some of the drag off my arms; but still I wondered whether I ought not get rid of my shoes, at least while I was descending. That pause for thought, which couldn't have lasted over ten seconds, became probably the most important ten seconds of my life.

In shifting weight, my hand dislodged one of the small stones which I hadn't bothered to take out of the tunnel. It fell straight down onto the loose stones of the slope. I leaned over to follow its progress, swearing under my breath; and so I was staring directly at the spot when Hassan's face rose slowly and solemnly into view, like the Nome King coming out to take the air.

Below the ten-foot drop, off to my right, there must have been an overhang, a little hollow in the cliff, just above the start of the slope. I hadn't seen it from above. Bloch had not missed a single bet; and I ought to have expected this. Naturally he had to watch the entrance, not only as a check on me, but to make sure no other searchers found the tomb.

Hanging there like a fly on a windowpane, I stared down at Hassan, and Hassan's big brown eyes, flat as poster paint, stared back at me. He was deep in his drugged trance, so deep that nothing less emphatic than the last stone, striking inches from his nose, could have aroused him. The sort of effort to which he had been aroused was only too clear from his expression. I don't know whether Bloch had given him a lecture, or whether different stages of the drug affected different glands; but I could tell just from the way he looked at me that my dubious virtue was no longer in any danger. Something else was, though.

I went up the cliff. There wasn't any other way to go. Considerably later, I realized that I could have popped back into my hole and held Hassan off indefinitely by dropping rocks down on him. I didn't think of it at the time, which was just as well, because it wasn't a very positive sort of plan.

I must have made use of the handy crevice in ascending, but I don't remember how; that part of my recollection is blurred. I went over the top of the cliff as if I had been shot from a cannon, and my feet were running when they hit the ground. The view was absolutely spectacular— thick-strewn stars and an enormous ivory moon stuck on a velvet sky, cold light turning the tumbled rock to melted, hardened silver. I wasn't interested in aesthetics, but I was very, very interested in finding a star to steer by. Here I was doing the very thing I had almost decided not to do, and I damned well needed to know where I was going.

I could hear Hassan, still on the cliff face. His bare fingers and toes made no noise, but there was a constant rattle of pebbles from the crumbly rock.

As my eyes scanned the jewel-hung heavens, trying to pick out some star conspicuous enough to guide me, I saw something that made stars unnecessary. Soaring high above even the height of the plateau rose the slopes of the pyramid-shaped mountain called the Qurn, the landmark of western Thebes. With that huge shape beside me, I couldn't go far wrong.

The light was bright, but deceptive in its tendency to warp shadows, and the ground was horribly uneven. Running was unsafe. I ran, though. At first I seemed to skim like a stone skipping across water, barely touching rock with my toes. After the hours of cramped anxiety, it was wonderful to stretch my legs and feel cool, pure air in my lungs—and best of all, to progress, to cover ground.

The first exuberance of movement wore off only too soon. My breath held out better than I had expected, and I was lucky enough not to twist my ankle. But the flesh between my shoulder blades began to crawl. I didn't dare look back. I didn't dare take my eyes off the treacherous broken ground even for a second; but I thought I was going to die of suspense unless I saw how far behind my pursuer was.

It was almost a relief when the first bullet whined past my head and spanged into a boulder ten feet to the right.

The shot gave wings to my heels, not so much with fright as with reassurance; if he was so far behind that he risked shooting, he must not be too sure of catching me. I doubted that he could hit me, not in the deceptive moonlight, at the rate I was going. He didn't have a rifle; I would have seen it. And Jake had told me once about the limited accuracy of hand weapons. Good old Jake— one way or another, he had managed to drum quite a few useful facts into my youthful head.

The second shot confirmed Jake's accuracy, if not Hassan's. It went far wide and high. I didn't even see where it hit.

I went bounding on, exuberant as a goat, drunk with speed and suspense, for another hundred yards or so. Then two things hit me without warning, and simultaneously—the first stab of pain in my side, a warning of failing breath, and the realization that Hassan had stopped shooting.

Whirling around like a top, I tried to look in eight directions at once. All around me, east, west, north, and south, the abandoned rock stretched away, milky white under the moon, gashed by angry black shadows. The bulk of the Qurn soared up, obscuring the stars; but there was no living creature in sight.

Clutching my side, where every breath jabbed like pleurisy, I strained my eyes to find my pursuer. Seeing Hassan had been a shock, but not seeing him was worse. The thin clear air had gone to my head like champagne, producing theories which had the spurious inexorability of wine-fed logic. Hassan knew where I was going; there was no other sensible place to go to. The mountain gave me a general direction, but I lacked close landmarks, and I might be moving in a wide arc instead of taking the shortest route. All Hassan had to do was get to the main Valley first, and wait for me.

I thought that maybe I would just lie down, under a handy rock, and wait too—wait for morning and for people, lots and lots of friendly people. Hassan might be anywhere, behind any of the million rocks that lay between me and the path. He could pick me off at his leisure. I didn't have a chance.

While I thought this, I was walking, plodding along like a worn-out mechanical doll, one foot up, one foot down, one foot up . . . I hadn't taken a dozen steps before I tripped over a rock no bigger than a baseball and fell flat on my front, with a tinkle of breaking glass.

I took the wreckage of the flashlight out of my pocket and looked at it blearily. This was not my night for flashlights. There was something else in my pocket, and by this time I was in such a state that I had actually forgotten what it was. The feel of the dagger's hilt, cold and knobbly in my fingers, reminded me. It also got me to my feet, and moving. The weapon had brought another mental picture back into my mind—the picture of Hassan using his knife, but not on me.

It was just a guess, that dreadful vision, but if there was a ghost of a chance that my complex reasoning was correct, then I didn't dare delay. Finding Hassan outside the tomb had reassured me for a while; if he was there, he couldn't be at the Institute committing a murder. Now I saw the flaw in that argument. The Judas at the Institute would be too fastidious to get blood on his own hands. His part would be to deliver the victim to Hassan, and with the victim trusting him completely, he could pick his own spot. The Valley was a nice isolated spot—and convenient for a ready-made grave. That idea was worthy of Bloch's twisted efficiency, and so was the idea of bringing the victim to the murderer instead of vice-versa. By guarding the beginning of the path, Hassan could kill two birds with one stone—and that statement had never been more literally true.

I started running, aching sides and lacerated knees forgotten. The killing wouldn't take place till after dark. It wasn't very late; Bloch had not yet come to the tomb. The next hour, the next ten minutes, might be the crucial time.

Tumbled rock and broken stone, and the spangled illimitable sky—they seemed to go on forever. I was running in a nightmare, through a landscape as alien as anything in my worst dreams. When I recognized the first landmark, I didn't believe it. Then the whole terrain shimmered like an image mirrored in water; the view was the same, but the meaning had changed. I knew now where I was. Ahead and to the right my blurred eyes caught a streak of brighter white on the moon-bleached ground—one loop of the distant path.

I slowed to a walk, rubbing my forehead with gritty, damp palms. Pretty soon I would have to get down on my hands and knees. Try to sneak up on Hassan before he saw me. If Hassan was there. Then . . . then I would . . .

Would what? Now that I had almost reached my first goal, what on earth was I going to do?

I sank down on the ground with a whimper, kneading my aching eyes. So vivid was my imaginary picture that I had half expected to see Hassan, lurking, and to see dark figures coming along the path. And even if I saw precisely that, there was absolutely nothing I could do to prevent disaster. The warning I must convey was too unbelievable to be communicated in a series of shrieks, which was all I could transmit at a distance. Hassan could shoot me while I was waving my arms and yelling, and the other murderee would be fair game for his unsuspected companion.

I pounded my fists on my knees in a fury of frustration, and stopped with a quickly swallowed yelp as hands and knees responded with jabs of pain. This was the culminating folly of all my stupidities. I had been so proud of myself for getting out of the tomb and across the cliffs; and yet all I had really accomplished was to lose precious hours whining over nonexistent dangers, and responding to every one of Bloch's tricks like a rat in a maze. A really intelligent person would have been out of the tomb hours ago, in broad daylight, when help was at hand. Now I was about to pay for those lost hours. I had accomplished several things which I would have believed to be beyond my powers; but there were things I simply could not do. And one of the things I could not do was sneak up on Hassan and take his gun away from him. I could die trying; but it would be an incredibly stupid way to die, just as futile as many of my other recent activities. Just once, couldn't I think of a smart way to do things?

One thing I could do; and I began to crawl,

painfully. I could keep on trying to reach the Institute. My theories were just theories after all, as immaterial as moonlight, and maybe just as deceptive.

Then I heard the voices.

In the still desert night they carried a long way. I recognized them—both of them.

I leaped to my feet, forgetting that in the moonlight I was as visible as if on a stage. My eyes were no longer blurred; cleared by terror and the confirmation of my worst fears, they seemed to see as through a telescope.

To the left, about thirty yards away, was the yawning gulf of the main Valley of the Kings. To my right the path over the plateau began, chalk on white paper. On the path two forms—only dark silhouettes at that distance—moved and spoke.

The expected shot came before I had a chance to start screaming. One of the rock chips smacked into my calf and stung like a hornet. I was aware of a smug, ridiculous sense of triumph. My reasoning had been correct. Hassan, as well as the other two, was definitely in the neighborhood.

I was doing just what I had decided it would be foolish to do—jumping up and down, waving my arms, screaming sentences whose meaning, if any, was lost after ten feet. I paid no attention to Hassan and his gun; my every sense was concentrated on the two shadowy figures on the path, too far away . . .

One of the figures turned on the other, in a movement whose general menace was plain, even if the details were lost. Then one shadow was down on the ground and the other was running, not toward me, but toward the spot where the path dropped down over the rim into the Valley. Hassan was there, and he kept on firing—not at me, but at the man who was racing toward him.

I don't like to remember the figure of folly I made as I bounded over the rocks with my tattered skirts flying and my tangled hair standing straight up. I was yelling like a banshee, and—this is the part that makes me blush—waving my gold-hilted dagger wildly in the air.

I might have used it. But by the time I arrived, it was over. Hassan sprawled on the ground amid the billows of his full skirts. His eyes were closed, so I knew he wasn't dead. The moonlight whitened his face and gave it an inhuman beauty and a wholly deceptive purity.

I looked at the man who stood over him, panting like a hot dog.

"Didn't he shoot you?" I inquired idiotically.

"Well, he did, now that you mention it," said John. He added, with an apprehensive eye on my raised arm, "So you don't have to finish me off with that dagger."

The dark patch on his right side wasn't shadow. My arm dropped like a dead log, and John leaped back as the knife skimmed his shoulder.

"Goddamnit!" he began; and the familiar roar, the sight of his black brows drawing together in the beautiful, well-known scowl, finished me. I fell heavily against him and wound both arms around his waist. He let out a loud, unheroic bellow.

"You're supposed to grit your teeth," I said. "You can't be much hurt, or you wouldn't be able to yell like that."

"You're squeezing me right over my bullet hole," John said coldly. His tone was so nearly normal that it wasn't till I tried to pull away from him that I realized he was holding me in a grip that hurt, and shaking like a man with a chill.

"Where the hell have you been?" he asked, in the same rigidly controlled voice.

"In the tomb," I said; and regretted the answer, for his grip slackened and the eyes that met mine were narrowed with speculation. I had forgotten that nothing short of decapitation will distract an archaeologist from archaeologizing.

"You found it?"

"I didn't find it; it found me. Bloch found it. He put me in it; I've been there for days and days and days, trying to get out ..."

"You look terrible," he said, scanning my face interestedly.

"Thanks a lot. I half killed myself trying to get out, and worried myself sick ... And it's all your fault; I thought Hassan was going to kill you."

"And I thought Hassan had killed you." He looked like a stranger; the expression in his eyes was one I had never seen before. "I've aged ten years in the past day. When I saw you just now jumping up and down like a jack-in-the-box, I thought my brain had cracked at last. If I hadn't seen you, I'd have broken Hassan's neck; that's the only thing that kept me going, the hope of getting my hands on that young swine ... Tommy, Tommy ..."

His kiss wasn't a work of art, like Mike's. It hurt. It didn't leave me limp and flaccid. I kissed him back with a violence that nearly strangled him. I don't think he noticed. I was the first to give in; when I pulled my mouth away, it was because I needed it for breathing. I could feel my face turning blue.

For several long seconds we stared at each other in silence, mutually bemused. Then he grinned feebly.

"I don't believe it," he said.

"It'll grow on you," I assured him. "I think I've got my breath back now, so if—"

"That's enough for now." The grin broadened. "First I'd better check on our friend back there. I was in a hurry the first time I hit him."

"Too much of a hurry," said Mike's voice.

John's left arm swung me around and held me close to his side. I was glad to have something solid to lean on. This was the culminating stupidity of the evening—probably my last stupidity. Mike had a gun. It must have been his own, because Hassan's pistol lay where it had fallen. I could see it out of the corner of my eye, a glint of dark light on the ground.

"I've been up and around for some time," Mike went on conversationally. He raised one hand to wipe away a trickle of blood from the corner of his mouth. "Didn't want to interrupt you. It took you two long enough to find out what everybody else has known for weeks."

He beamed at us benevolently. Standing there, all six feet four inches of him, slouched, slim and relaxed, he looked so normal that I had a moment of reviving hope. But the gun in his hand wasn't normal, especially the view I had of it—a round black hole pointed straight at my midriff.

"What did you do, bite your lip?" John asked.

"Yep. You caught me off guard. I didn't think you had the slightest suspicion."

"I've known for days."

"You have?" I twisted my neck to stare up at him. "And I thought . . . I screamed myself hoarse trying to warn you . . ."

"Was that what you were doing?" His eyes twinkled, and I had a vision of the banshee figure I had made with my screams and my brandished dagger.

"What did I do wrong?" Mike wasn't unduly concerned; he was simply expressing a scholar's curiosity about his own errors.

"I suspected ten years ago that if Jake had taken anyone into his confidence, it would have been you—his favorite disciple, as you said. He would have needed help to get into a place as inaccessible as these tombs usually are. Then, when Abdelal came around looking for Tommy's address, I realized that he was the most likely person to have found the tomb.

"For a while there you looked innocent. But too many things happened as a result of information only you could have known. To give just one example, only the three of us—you and I and Tommy—knew that Achmed was meeting us that morning. And of the three, only you and I knew where the meeting was to take place. You couldn't have attacked the boy yourself, nor contacted a local crook; you were with me that whole afternoon and evening. But you could easily have picked up the telephone and notified a second party, someone who had access to a phone.

"That led me to Bloch, and I've had my suspicions of him all along too. He was no more fooled by the statue than I was, and once I was convinced that Jake had found himself a tomb, Bloch's role was obvious. When he turned up this season, friendly as a pup and making suggestive remarks about contributions to excavation, my suspicions were confirmed. Tommy's appearance with Bloch's lady friend was the last straw. Something had alerted Bloch, and it must have been the same thing that alerted me—Abdelal's letter. But you and I, Mike, were the only ones who knew about the letter."

Mike flushed.

"So I made a few mistakes," he said belligerently. "Think you're so goddamned smart, don't you? Good old Mike, the stooge . . . Well, the stooge found what you couldn't find."

"Thanks to me and my big mouth," I said bitterly. "The Valley of the Kings by moonlight . . . That was all you needed, the general location. And of course you never did pass on to John what was in Abdelal's letter."

"Why should I? I've taken a lot of crap from John all these years. Mike, do this, Mike, do that . . . Well, I'm through. Turn around, both of you."

"Oh, no." John shook his head. "If you want to kill me, you'll have to do it face to face. Why the hell should I make it easier for you?"

Mike's face, which had been taut with anger, went slack. With his mouth open and a lock of fair hair dangling over one eye, he looked like a young student.

"Kill . . ." he stuttered. "I'm not going to kill anybody! I just want to tie you up. When Hassan wakes up, we'll carry you down to the tomb, and—"

"I've heard of reluctant heroes," I said, "but you're the most reluctant villain I ever met. Mike, you jackass, what do you think Hassan was doing with that gun, practicing? Do you really believe Bloch can afford to leave John alive?"

"He knows." John's voice was cool, but every

muscle in his body was tight as a stretched rubber band. "Don't let the boyish charm fool you, Tommy. Bloch is willing to commit murder to keep his loot, and Mike—"

"Nobody is going to murder anybody!"

"Bloch murdered Dee," I said. "She found out what he was up to and tried to blackmail him."

"Nonsense. Dee ran off with Hassan . . ."

His eyes rolled wildly toward the peacefully snoring form of Hassan, who was not looking like the most ideal candidate for the role of young Lochinvar.

"With Hassan," Mike repeated weakly. "Hell's bells, Bloch wouldn't hurt his own daughter."

"She wasn't his daughter."

Mike shot a startled glance toward John, who nodded.

"I wondered," Mike admitted. For a moment he looked doubtful; then his chin jutted out. "Even so . . ."

"Oh, stop it," I shouted, my stretched nerves giving way. "She's dead; the girl is dead, dead, dead! I saw her. I felt her, for God's sake! She was cold, cold and dead! Am I penetrating that thick shell of studied stupidity, or shall I say it again?"

Mike's face turned a funny color. By day it would have been a delicate green. The effect by moonlight was indescribable.

"Not in the tomb," he said.

"Not only in the tomb, in the sarcophagus. Why not? It's just the place for a body. But doesn't it strike you as a ghoulish touch?"

Mike's hand was shaking so badly that the gun wobbled. One more smack in the self-esteem, I thought, and he'll crack . . .

"Haven't you seen the tomb?" John asked conversationally. "You, the brilliant finder himself?"

Mike didn't answer—but his hand stopped shaking. John's question had broken the mounting stress, and restored his control.

"He hasn't seen it," I said, giving John a furious glare. "He didn't find it. He was speaking generally, weren't you, Mike? All he did was give Bloch the vital clue—the particular valley, the one stretch of cliff, as somebody once expressed it. Mike hasn't had time to search on his own. But Bloch has been out looking for his dear lost daughter. And he has a crew of jolly little crooks, some of the less desirable citizens of Gurnah, who could help him search—once he knew the general location."

"I haven't seen it yet, no," Mike admitted. "But I know all about it. They found it right where I said it would be. And Bloch says it's sensational, better than Tutankhamen's."

"Tommy just came from there," John went on, his placid voice belying his tightening muscles. "Is there anything left, Tommy, now that Bloch's men have slammed things around?"

Watching Mike's expressive face, I began to see what John was after. I didn't think it would work, but the least I could do was help.

"I'm afraid I did some damage myself," I said guilelessly. "When Hassan and I were rolling around . . . Oh, Lord. I didn't mean it to sound like that."

"It conveys quite a graphic picture," said John, in a voice that was not so well-controlled. "Just as a matter of curiosity—how did you come out of it this time?"

"Same as last time. John, I'm sorry."

"*You* are sorry?" said John, with a savage glance at the sprawled figure of Hassan. "Well. To return to the original subject . . . Knowing Hassan, and," added my beloved, "knowing you, I suspect that your rolling around, as you so happily phrase it, left very little intact?"

"Now you just look here—"

"I'm not blaming you," John said magnanimously. "I'm just curious. What did you bust?"

"Some pots," I admitted. "A couple of the ceremonial robes. I was sick about that . . . John, remember the robe of Tut's that was all sewn with sequins and spangles? She had one like that, only the linen was as sheer as chiffon—"

"Had?" Mike sounded like a bronchial frog. The news of Dee's death had distressed him, but this was real tragedy. I got ready to administer the *coup de grâce*, adjusting my weight so that John could move without my interference; and then, like the innocent I was, I outfoxed myself.

"There may be other robes," I said smoothly. "And I think the papyri are all right."

I still insist that nobody but an archaeologist could have predicted the effect of that statement. I had calculated part of the effect, with an insight which did me credit. What I had unfortunately forgotten was that there were two archaeologists present.

"Papyri?" said two croaking voices in unison.

Mike had forgotten his gun. It dangled loosely from fingers which had dropped to his side. Someone could have walked right up to him and gently removed the weapon from his grasp. But that someone, obviously, was not going to be John McIntire.

"Papyri?" he repeated. "Texts?" He let go of my waist, grabbed me by the shoulders, and spun me around. "How many?"

"A whole big fat boxful," I said between clenched teeth; and raising one foot, I brought it down as hard as I could on his toes. "I almost did that to your precious scrolls, in my efforts to preserve that jewel which is . . . Oh, damn you, you stupid . . . you . . . Egyptologist! I wish I had stamped on the lot of them!"

John's eyes came back into focus; for a minute he had looked as doped as Hassan. By that time Mike had already recovered himself.

"Okay," he said, pointing the gun roughly in my direction. "Okay. So there are papyri. We'll get everything out. I'm going down there myself. I'll go right away. As soon as Hassan . . ."

"For God's sake, Mike," I said desperately, "give us a chance! Hassan will kill John, and not in a neat nice way, either; he won't be feeling very kindly after that punch in the face . . . Mike, think of the tomb; you ought to care about that if you don't care about us. Bloch hasn't got time to be careful; he's going to smash half the objects. Both the mummies will get mangled. His mummy, Mike, think of it, his . . ."

So there it was, the operative word—not a noun, as I had thought, but a simple little pronoun. My voice trailed away into silence that was broken only by the pounding of my heart.

At my side John was rigid and still, held by the same shock that had paralyzed Mike. Then Mike's frozen lips moved, articulating the word with painful precision.

"His . . . mummy."

Bloch had been so right not to let the poor young boob into the tomb. That pink-faced rascal was, among other things, a superb judge of character. Mike had his conflicts too, more complex than the ones that had vexed Abdelal. The right pressure, rightly applied, would bring to the surface that one motive which was, despite all else, the dominating one of his life. The actual sight of the tomb and its marvels might have done it. The news I had to tell would do it too. I felt tired and a little sick, but no longer afraid as I spoke, almost negligently, the words which would save us.

"His mummy. It's Akhenaton's tomb, Mike. She's there, with him, but it's his tomb. The walls are covered with paintings and inscriptions; there are four rooms crammed with objects— and two mummies, both intact. Ten years' work, Mike, just to get it out. Another half century to assess and study it. The most important single discovery that's ever been made in Egypt."

Mike sat down, section by section. He put the

gun on the ground beside him and covered his
face with his hands. His bent elbows, stuck out at
right angles to his head, and his raised knees,
made him look like a big, sad, sand-colored
grasshopper.

For two long breaths we stood still, staring.
Then John let the second breath out in a long
sigh; he stepped forward and scooped up the
gun. Mike didn't move.

"We'd better take a look at Hassan," John said.
"This back-and-forth routine can get monoto-
nous."

With an uneasy glance at Mike, all right angles
on the ground, I followed John. Hassan was still
out, but his breathing seemed quicker.

"What did you do, fracture his skull?" I asked.

"Hope so." John handed me the gun. "Try not to
hit me, will you, if you have to shoot anybody?"

He tied the boy's wrists and ankles roughly
but effectively with strips torn from his robe. I
supplied the dagger with which he cut the cloth;
and it was the only time that night that the
weapon, which had cost me so much in time and
nervous energy, did anything useful.

I thought for a minute, when John got a good
look at the dagger, that I would have to tie Hassan up myself. But he got a grip on his higher in-

stincts and did the job. The rough handling—a littler rougher than it needed to be, I think—restored Hassan to his senses, and when John rolled him over, he began a long speech dealing with John's ancestry and my habits, which John interrupted by jamming another piece of the robe into his mouth.

Then we turned our attention to Mike.

He was still sitting on the ground, in the same position; he looked as if he had turned to stone and would never move again. I'm not sure about John, but I know my own feelings oddly resembled those of an embarrassed hostess who sees one of her guests break down during a party.

"What are you going to do with him?" I whispered, jerking my head toward that annoyingly pathetic figure.

John shrugged.

"He didn't really do anything," I argued. "John, he really didn't know. You saw his face . . ."

"He didn't know the same way the citizens of Dachau didn't know what was going on up the street."

"Well, but that's—that's people. Unfortunately. Isn't even the refusal to actively commit evil something, in this world?"

"Oh, God, maybe so." John passed one hand across his eyes; he looked, briefly, old and haggard. "But it's a sad commentary, on the world and on your experience of it, that you can say that. If that's the best you can do with regard to Jake—"

"This hasn't anything to do with Jake!"

"Good God, it has everything to do with him! The same pattern, the same degree of guilt—the result, even, of his careless tampering with other peoples' lives. Tommy, once and for all you must see Jake for what he was—not a saint, not a demon, just a man driven by an overmastering compulsion. I've been less than fair to him, myself, because—because of several unworthy motives. But I can understand *his* motives."

"So can I. He wanted money."

"Jake never gave a damn about money. Not until those last years, when you began to change from a gawky child to a terrifyingly accurate image of your mother—a very lovely woman, by the way. You know how she died?"

"In childbirth. Don't try to make something—"

"In childbirth, in a Cairo hospital. We had the best doctor in Egypt for her; but Jake always believed he wasn't good enough. If she had been in New York or London . . . That was the thought that haunted him. I could see it in his face, that last year, every time he looked at you—the fear that there was nothing better in store for you; only marriage to another poor, struggling scholar stuck for life in a backwater job and, at the end, a repetition of her fate. Yes, I know, it was illogical and unreasoning; but the terrors that drive human beings to extremes usually are irrational. He was desperate to get you out of here, into a world where you would be courted and admired and cherished. That was why he wanted money."

The silence seemed to last forever.

"So," I said finally, "that makes me the cause of it all."

"In one sense of the word—yes."

"Why did you tell me this?"

"Because I'm a stupid fool." His shoulders sagged, but his eyes, brilliant with a bitter honesty, never left my face. "I'm naïve enough to believe in justice—which I had failed to render to Jake—and the exercise of which will probably cause me to lose the thing I want most. All I can offer you is the same world Jake sold his soul to get you out of—a world which has not been particularly kind to you in the past."

He stood there poised, waiting for me to speak—and I couldn't think of anything to say.

The right words—and they had to be right—
wouldn't come. His words had affected me
deeply, but not in the way they would have done
some days ago. The subject of Jake now seemed
oddly irrelevant. There were more important
things to talk about.

"Well, that's all right," I said incoherently.
"But what are we going to do about Mike?"

Incredibly, they were the right words. John's old
incandescent smile lightened his face.

"If you ask me to go easy on the young idiot
for your sake . . ."

"For your sake," I said.

The look he gave me made my knees go weak;
but when he spoke, it was not to me.

"Mike."

Mike took his hands away and looked up.

"Okay," he said vaguely. "Police? Okay. I don't
know what I . . . Coming."

He sounded drunk, and he looked drunk as he
angled his way up to his feet. When John made
no move nor sound, he produced a ghost of his
old grin, and started to amble off toward the
river, along the path.

"Mike."

Mike stopped. His head sank down lower, between his shoulders.

"I'll give you half an hour," John said. "By tomorrow some smart cop will start asking questions, and I can't promise to keep you out of it, even if Bloch does. But if you've left the country, I don't think they'll bother chasing you."

For a long moment Mike stood stock-still. Then he just—went on walking. I knew why he didn't turn around or try to talk. It took a long time for the tall, drooping figure to disappear.

"That was nice," I said inadequately.

"Not so nice. He's finished professionally. I don't know what he's going to do. Maybe he'd be better off in jail, or dead."

"I've always thought," I said carefully, respecting the bitterness in his voice, "that the people who make those smug decisions are overstepping their right. If he wants to be dead, he can be. But you've let him decide."

"I suspect something, too," he said, after a moment. "I suspect you're going to be nice to have around. That is—if you want to be around."

"That's not the most graceful proposal I've ever received," I said. "If it is a proposal."

"It's not my field," said John, and grinned. He put his arms out and I went into them, unhesitatingly. "Tommy, don't commit yourself. This is a hard place, and God knows I'm no prize . . ."

"This is my place. It's in my blood and I'd die if I ever had to leave it."

"I think that assessment is correct. But—"

"I'd die if I ever had to leave you," I said extravagantly, meaning every syllable.

"I've been in love with you since you were fifteen. That's a hell of a thing to admit, isn't it?"

"Makes you some kind of sex maniac, I'm afraid."

"I'd rather be a sex maniac than a father symbol," said John, with no humor at all in his voice.

"But that's . . . You're crazy. I *love* you," I said, with the air of someone voicing a new, unarguable theory.

"Tommy, when you came roaring down that path a while ago, where were you going in such a hurry?"

"Why—back to the Institute," I said, bewildered. "To warn you."

"About what?"

"About Mike, of course. I figured out, while I was crawling around that abominable tomb, that either you or Mike had to be involved with Bloch. The letter—"

"I understand that part. I went through the same kind of reasoning myself, remember? Only I knew Mike had to be the guilty party because I wasn't. How did you know? Or did you?"

"Of course I knew! I just told you, I knew it was Mike because . . ." My mouth fell open in honest surprise. "I don't know. I mean, I did know, but I don't know how I knew."

"Fine," John said contentedly. "That's the kind of triumphant illogic I like. It wasn't because I . . . remind you of Jake?"

"You aren't a bit like Jake. John, darling, I'm not looking for my father any longer. I've buried Jake, decently, in the tomb he found. What could be more appropriate?"

"The tomb!" John let me go, so suddenly that I staggered. "Good God, I'm standing here wasting time while that son-of-a-bitch Bloch is wrecking my tomb. Look, Tommy, you—"

" 'Wasting time.' Oh, well," I said, with a shrug, "I might as well get used to it . . . Let's go. I'll show you where the tomb is. You take that gun, I'll take this gun. I guess I can walk a few more miles and shoot a few people. After all, I—"

"You talk incessantly, and to no purpose. Tell me where the tomb is. Don't show me, tell me."

I looked at him. Then I told him where the tomb was. It wasn't hard to pinpoint the location, though the news staggered John momentarily, just as it had amazed me.

"Of all the places," he muttered, chewing his moustache. "Okay, I can find it. When you get back to the Institute, send Mark and Al and Achmed, and Feisal Reis; tell them to hurry. I'll

contact Cairo myself in the morning; I don't
want any intermediaries in this deal. You'd better go straight to bed. Don't wait up for me. But
wash your face first, you look like a sandstone
statue."

"Father image my foot," I said bitterly. "Jake
never bossed me like that."

"And that is what is wrong with you today.
Pull in your lower lip and get moving."

"You are not going back to the tomb alone.
Bloch and his men have probably arrived by
now."

"My God, how insulting can you be? Don't
you think I can handle one overweight, middle-
aged crook all by myself?"

"One," I repeated, choking. "Bloch's got half a
dozen men with him, you arrogant jerk."

"Local boys." John dismissed them with a flip
of his hand. "They won't be any problem."

"You point your finger and go 'bang,' and they
drop dead? John, you can't. You're hurt . . ."

"Hurt? Oh that, that isn't anything. Look, darling, I know you're tired; but there isn't any easier way back. I won't be long."

I considered weeping, but I was fairly sure
that wouldn't work. None of my reasonable arguments would move him in the slightest. Besides, he was paying me an unusual but immense

compliment by treating me as a partner, engaged in a job that was as meaningful to me as it was to him. In that seemingly casual assumption I could dimly see the seeds of something too important to risk.

"Okay," I said.

He gave me an approving smile and a quick kiss—a piece of candy for a good child? I didn't care; every corpuscle in my body stood straight up when he touched me. I watched him striding off, shoulders confident, taking without hesitation the straightest path to the spot he was seeking. He didn't look back. And all at once I knew that things would work out just as he expected. By the time Mark and Al arrived, panting with zeal, everything would be under control. John would probably be sitting on Bloch's stomach lecturing a group of Gurnah men, who would be smoking his cigarettes and trying to look as if they had just wandered in by accident. In the name of God, the Merciful, the Compassionate.

I started back along the path I knew so well, at the end of which lay safety, lights, companionship—and, when he had taken care of his more important business, my love. All the things I had been searching for so long, without knowing it.

Not least among them, at the moment, was a hot bath. There was sand in my shoes, my

pocket, my hair, my fingernails—probably my
ears. I could feel it gritting inside my clothes
with every step. The dagger, now back in my
pocket, banged against my thigh. Something
hard and scratchy tickled my neck.

I reached into my blouse and pulled it out. I
had forgotten the necklace—not surprising, under the circumstances. The ancient clasp had
held firm through all my wild activities.

It lay across my spread fingers, holding an en-
chantment that surpassed even its beauty. Nefertiti's necklace. I squinted down at it cross-eyed,
and I wondered. Bloch was the only person who
knew I had it, and he would be too busy trying to
deny the undeniable to remember this little detail. It was only fair that I should have some souvenir, after my terrible experiences . . .

I grinned to myself, a little sheepishly, as I
went on, and I left the necklace lying outside my
blouse. Mark's horn-rimmed glasses would
jump right off his nose when he saw it.

"Good-bye, Jake," I said softly. "In the name of
God the Merciful, the Compassionate."

And besides, maybe the Director of Antiquities would agree that, after all my trouble, I was
entitled to a little memento.

*Turn the page for a look inside
the wonderful world of
Elizabeth Peters. . . .*

The Camelot Caper

For Jessica Tregarth, an unexpected invitation to visit her grandfather in England is a wonderful surprise—an opportunity to open doors to a family past that have always been closed to her. But sinister acts greet her arrival. A stranger tries to steal her luggage and later accosts her in Salisbury Cathedral. Mysterious villains pursue her through Cornwall, their motive and intentions unknown. Jessica's only clue is an antique heirloom she possesses, an ancient ring that bears the Tregarth family crest. And her only ally is handsome gothic novelist David Randall—her self-proclaimed protector—who appears from seemingly out of nowhere to help her in her desperate attempt to solve a five-hundred-year-old puzzle. For something from out of the cloudy mists of Arthurian lore has come back to plague a frightened American abroad. And a remarkable truth about a fabled king and a medieval treasure could make Jessica Tregarth very rich . . . or very dead.

> "Gothica in the irreverent trappings
> I like best."
> *New York Times Book Review*

Summer of the Dragon

A good salary and an all-expenses-paid summer spent on a sprawling Arizona ranch is too good a deal for fledgling anthropologist D. J. Abbott to turn down. What does it matter that her rich new employer/benefactor, Hank Hunnicutt, is a certified oddball who is presently funding all manner of offbeat projects, from alien conspiracy studies to a hunt for dragon bones? There's even talk of treasure buried in the nearby mountains, but D. J. isn't going to allow loose speculation—or the considerable charms of handsome professional treasure hunter Jesse Franklin—to sidetrack her. Until Hunnicutt suffers a mysterious accident and then vanishes, leaving the weirdos gathered at his spread to eye each other with frightened suspicion. But on a high desert search for the missing millionaire, D. J. is learning things that may not be healthy for her to know. For the game someone is playing here goes far beyond the rational universe—and it could leave D. J. legitimately dead.

"No one is better at juggling torches while dancing on a high wire than Elizabeth Peters."
Chicago Tribune

320

The Love Talker

Laurie has finally returned to Idlewood, the beloved family home deep in the Maryland woods where she found comfort and peace as a lonely young girl. But things are very different now. There is no peace in Idlewood. The haunting sound of distant piping breaks the stillness of a snowy winter's evening. Seemingly random events have begun to take on a sinister shape. And dotty old Great Aunt Lizzie is convinced that there are fairies about—and she has photographs to prove it. For Laurie, one fact is becoming disturbingly clear: there is definitely *something* out there in the woods—something fiendishly, cunningly, malevolently human—and the lives of her aging loved ones, as well as Laurie's own, are suddenly at risk.

"[Peters] keeps the reader coming back for more."
San Francisco Chronicle

321

The Dead Sea Cipher

Opera singer Dinah van der Lyn is trying to soak up a little history between singing engagements on her tour of the Middle East. But when she hears cries for help through her hotel room wall—cries uttered in English despite the fact that there are few Americans at the Beirut hotel where she is staying—she knows that something sinister is afoot. The police are at first dubious of her suspicions of foul play. After all, as the granddaughter of a rabbi and the daughter of a minister, her politics may be questionable. But as she travels through the fabled cities of Sidon, Tyre, Damascus, and Jerusalem pursued by a handsome government agent and a mysterious Biblical scholar, she begins to fear that she may not be safe in this most holy of places—instead, she may be heading straight into a deadly trap.

"Danger and romance. Excellent."
San Francisco Chronicle

Devil May Care

It is the beginning of the best of times for Ellie—she is young, happy, rich, and soon to be married. Ready to spend two weeks house-sitting her eccentric Aunt Kate's Virginia mansion, she is looking forward to a quiet vacation in the secluded, cat-filled home. But when a mysterious apparition pays a visit late one night, she knows her peaceful time away will be anything but. For Ellie fears that a book she found in an antiquarian shop—a book she intended to be a special gift for her aunt—has revealed some long-buried secrets of the town's upper class. And as mysterious visitors begin to pay visits to the home, Ellie starts to worry whether the town aristocracy wants to keep these secrets hidden . . .

"Elizabeth Peters is wickedly clever . . . [Her] women are smart, strong, bold, cunning, and highly educated, just like herself."
San Diego Reader

The Copenhagen Connection

Elizabeth Jones never expected to spot her idol, Nobel Prize-winning historian Margaret Rosenberg, at the Copenhagen Airport. And after the esteemed scholar's secretary is injured, Elizabeth is even more shocked to learn that Rosenberg wants to enlist her as her new assistant. Thrust into a foreign world of glamour and intrigue, Elizabeth rushes from Tivoli to the Little Mermaid in the eccentric historian's wake. But when kidnappers take Rosenberg, leaving only a mysterious ransom note, it's up to Elizabeth and her employer's rude and surly—yet devastatingly handsome—son to locate her. Through restaurants, down dark alleys, and deep into the cave-ridden countryside, the duo are caught in a deadly game of chase . . . and they may be the kidnappers' next targets.

"Elizabeth Peters' many fans can count on her for romantic mysteries, full of action and suspense, and *The Copenhagen Connection* is no exception."
Publishers Weekly

324

The Jackal's Head

Althea "Tommy" Tomlinson claimed she came to Egypt as just another tourist, traveling around the country in the company of her spoiled seventeen-year-old charge. But what really drove her was a burning desire to discover the truth behind her father's disgrace and subsequent death ten years before. She had known something was terribly wrong—but what? Finding out might clear her father's name, but it could also prove to be perilous. For the secrets buried deep in the sands of the desert were as old as the treasure of Nefertiti . . . and unearthing them could result in one of the greatest archaeological discoveries ever . . . or lead to her own death.

"Elizabeth Peters is truly great."
San Francisco Chronicle

Legend in Green Velvet

From kilts to bagpipes to the windswept hills, archaeology student Susan loves all things Scottish. So when she is offered the opportunity to go to a dig in the Scottish Highlands for the summer, there is no question in her mind that it's a dream come true. But after a strange and sinister soap box orator slips her a cryptic message in Edinburgh, and when her room is looted immediately afterward, Susan suspects that she holds a secret that someone would stop at nothing to get their hands on. But who has set their sights on her? And when she and the handsome young laird Jamie Erskine are pursued by the police, who want to speak with them about a mysterious murder, it's up to the fledgling archaeologist to get to the bottom of the crime. Here's another kick-up-your-heels tale of mystery and suspense from one of the world's most beloved writers.

"This is Peters at the top of her form."
Austin American-Statesman

The Night of Four Hundred Rabbits

Christmas is supposed to be a time of family, presents under the tree, and fond memories. But for college student Carol Farley, her most surprising gift is contained in an envelope waiting in her room, an anonymously sent piece of mail containing a newspaper clipping. Blurred, but recognizable, it's a picture of her missing father, and for the first time in years, Carol senses that he may still be alive. And when several other anonymous letters provide clues that he may be living in Mexico, Carol decides that someone wants her to fly south to find him. As the pyramids of Mexico's Avenue of the Dead tower above and around her, their beauty is shrouded in the terror they suddenly hold for the young American. For the person who sent her to look for her father may not be her only enemy . . .

"A thriller."
Fresno Bee

(((((Listen to)))))